CW00833541

The Gentleman Banker

Amadeo Peter Giannini, 1870–1949

The Gentleman Banker

Amadeo Peter Giannini:
A Biographical Novel

By GIORGIO A. CHIARVA

Translated by Martina Benedetti Marshall
and Danielle Guida
Edited by Donatella Melucci

with a contribution of The Italian Cultural Society
of Washington D.C.

THESPRING

Washington, DC

Copyright © 2019 by Francesco Brioschi Editore s.r.l.

New Academia Publishing, 2022

Originally published in Italian by Francesco Brioschi Editore s.r.l. in 2019, with the title, *Il banchiere galantuomo*.

Translation into English by Martina Benedetti Marshall and Danielle Guida. Edited by Donatella Melucci.

All rights reserved. No part of this book may be reproduced or transmitted in any form or by any means, electronic or mechanical, including photocopying, recording, or by any information storage and retrieval system, without permission in writing from the copyright owner

Printed in the United States of America

Library of Congress Control Number: 2021951806
ISBN 979-8-9852214-0-4 (alk. paper)

 THESPRING is an imprint of New Academia Publishing

New Academia Publishing
4401-A Connecticut Ave. NW #236, Washington DC 20008
info@newacademia.com - www.newacademia.com

Contents

Foreword

In San Francisco, the memory of Amadeo Peter Giannini is still very much alive today. On a recent trip, I was lucky enough to meet several people who told me, with emotion and enthusiasm, family stories linked to this extraordinary character.

This story begins in 1869, when the phenomenon of emigration from Italy was quite substantial. From the Fontanabuona Valley, in the province of Genoa, where Favale di Malvaro is located, tens of thousands of people left for the USA, many of whom made their fortune leaving indelible marks on the American economy and culture.

Giannini's story begins like this, when his parents emigrated to move to San José, California, where Amadeo Peter, also known as AP, was born. From then until his death in 1949, there was a succession of events so unique that, at times, it is difficult to believe that those things really happened.

Giannini was a unique case in the financial landscape of his time: he was an innovator, a bright visionary, a friend and supporter of the people. His behavior has always been marked by sobriety and determination, ethics and risk; he was a champion of the Italian emigrant minority and a staunch opponent of all speculation. His figure dominated the American banking landscape for half a century: a long time advisor to presidents, Giannini stood up to the likes of J.P. Morgan, Rockefeller, and Rothschild, a lone giant opposing the interests of other bankers who were allies amongst themselves, not always in line with his ethical criteria.

To write this novel I drew heavily on my imagination, while still following the historical trail that I got from many sources. All the main events, almost all the secondary ones and a good part of Amadeo's thoughts are not of my own invention, but are well documented in books and university research. It is not uncommon to find interpretations that are also somewhat conflicting on certain facts, even regarding the composition of the families that I mention, but I have received multiple confirmations of the main events. Even many events which, at first glance, may seem secondary, or concepts or behaviors he supported, which seem to be the fruit of my imagination, are instead authentic and reported by numerous testimonies. Historians will forgive me for some of the liberties I have taken and some facts that I have omitted, but I felt that a good novel must pleasantly accompany history and not just be a cold list of events.

PART I

1

The darkness of the night was almost stifling and the silence of the countryside was broken only by the rare chirping of birds that sensed the arrival of a new day. On the cart that was taking him home, Luigi was deep in thought, lying down on the trunk and leaning against his fabric suitcase, typical of an emigrant. He was looking around without seeing and without curiosity, with his hands sunk into the pockets of his pants. By now, he had finished the cigar they had given him at the port and was turning it, extinguished, between his teeth. After almost three years away from his homeland, he couldn't contain his impatience. But he had it all planned out and didn't want to give up the dream he nurtured for so long. How could he forget the harsh words with which Virginia's father had dismissed him? That man considered himself a "rich man" just because, on his land that was large but in the mountains, he collected twice or three times as many chestnuts as the others. Why did he not consider the love Luigi expressed to Virginia and the fact that he had always proven himself to be a good, honest, hardworking young man? Of course he understood that Virginia was still little more than a child, but in those valleys there were many girls getting married at that age. The rejection was surely not because of that, he was convinced. Now, however, her father couldn't say no to him. After three years of hard work in America, he would show him that he was not like the others, that he could do it and that he would support his family.

His love for that girl, whom he had left as a child with a promise of marriage, along with his pride and stubbornness, which were his main characteristics, had created a formidable mixture that allowed him to earn not only a lot of money but also respect in the community of Italian emigrants.

He set out to be a farmer and, in fact, he had done so. But he had also speculated on the sale of small plots of land that he would buy, prepare to be cultivated, and then resell at very good margins. And he lived on very little, the bare minimum; he saved every single coin, and reinvested whatever he could by putting it to good use. He was used to risk, hard work and a life of sacrifice. The land where he was born did not give anything to anyone, you always had to earn your bread. His parents taught him from an early age that nothing was owed, and Luigi had learned that lesson very well.

When Virginia's father said those harsh words to him three years earlier, Luigi stood silently, turning his hat in his hands. He understood very well what the man wanted to tell him. Underneath the unpleasant, authoritarian, almost offensive words, you could feel the anxiety of the loving parent: - I don't want my daughter to also have the life of hardship that we did.

But those words hit him like fists. He looked speechlessly at Virginia's father, pushing back the tears and the knot in his throat, and made the decision he had been pondering for some time, but that his love for Virginia had made him put off. Without thinking about it too much, he told his future father-in-law: - I'm going away, but I'll be back soon and I'll marry Virginia.

After a few days, he disappeared from home without saying goodbye to his friends and without even seeing Virginia, with whom he had actually only spent a few short Sunday afternoons and always under his mother's surveillance. For Luigi, the separation was heartbreaking and only the certainty that he would return soon gave him the strength to leave.

Luigi was overcome with fatigue on the cart that now carried him home, but every time he laid his head down to sleep, excitement and memories brought the speeches he prepared and the answers he expected back to his mind. He imagined his hopes fulfilled and Virginia's happiness. The dreams were so real that they didn't allow him to fall asleep.

The cart jerked on the rocks of the road. They were halfway through the Fontanabuona Valley and approaching Favale. How many tears he cried on that same street three years earlier when he left! He was ashamed of it now and smiled at the thought of how much pain he had suffered and how many sleepless nights he had spent. He played with the hole in his pocket with one finger. His appearance was that of a poor man returning defeated from a bad adventure in distant lands. This thought still made him smile. His appearance did not at all reveal what he had conquered in these last years: the possibility, but he thought the certainty, of finally having Virginia all to himself.

In that alert half-sleep, Luigi noticed the faint glow from the east that began to sketch out the mountains around him, a glow that just barely separated the black outlines of the mountains from the clear sky. This is how he realized that they had already left the valley and were turning north, heading back up towards the village. He recognized the Caucasus Mountain looming high on the left. In front of him, with his heart in his throat, he saw Monte Pagliaro standing like an insurmountable barrier overlooking that narrow valley. But he did not have to pass it, at the foot of that mountain was his other half. Sunrise was approaching, just as he wanted, just as he had dreamed: to arrive before Virginia's father went to work and to present himself at their door by surprise, unexpected.

The cart that he had rented was driven by a poor man who was used to shuttling between the ships at the port and the warehouses. Luigi had to show him the route at every turn and now he too, after almost eight hours of travel, was tired and hungry. He had chosen him because his was the only cart with rubber wheels, a novelty at the port of Genoa: maybe the ride would have been more comfortable. He had promised him that he would pay him double what he earned in a week if he travelled by night, and despite that promise he had a hard time convincing him. Now Luigi saw his head bob and noticed the movements he made to keep himself awake. Bacicin was his name, he was a good man. At the beginning he had even tried to make conversation, just to understand why that strange client had refused to leave in the morning, seeing that the boat had docked at dawn, but Luigi was not in the mood. How could he explain three years of waiting, the tensions, the hopes, the fear of failure, the fear that in the meantime Virginia would have forgotten about him, that her father had changed his mind? In three years, he had only written a few cards, with his messy handwriting, but he had never received anything in return, only a couple updates from the Favalesi whom he had met. He asked to quicken the pace, but even the horse was exhausted and, after trotting a few yards, he returned to his regular pace.

Here, Favale was growing closer. There, on the left, the small cemetery with a few flickering candles that signaled its presence. Luigi had a sudden doubt: "What if my folks were in the cemetery instead of at home?" he thought. No, it was not possible. He would have known, in some way he would have known. But the fear stayed in his thoughts.

Here were the first houses. Now he had sat upright, excited and moved as he looked at them. The first house was where bearded Ninin lived, so old, he thought. Who knew if he was still alive, but maybe he was, because the sound of his agitated cows in the barn was clearly audible.

Here was the bakery, already at work. The scent of bread mixed with the smell of manure entered directly into his heart, welcoming him. From the half-open door, a thin and faint line of light just barely illuminated the fountain and the stream of water that trickled from the tube and fell into the stone basin, emitting the only sound in the silence of the night other than the rattling of his horse's hooves on the hard dirt path. But the other houses were not yet lit, maybe everybody else was still asleep. A strong wave of emotion overtook him and he had to dry his eyes. Yes, he had returned, and these were his sounds, his smells, his aromas. He would have wanted to get out and call out to everybody: "I'm back! I'm back!"

He felt the desire to yell, but he had a plan in mind and did not have time to waste. There were still a few houses to pass before reaching the village of Monleone, not far away. The rubber wheels also helped make less noise. They finally arrived at the intersection, then the slight incline to his home.

Luigi was emotional, his parents were not expecting him, nobody was expecting him. He had to stop for a minute. He dried his eyes with the sleeve of his jacket, cleared his throat, and picked up the two suitcases and the accordion. He had never played accordion in his life, but he had bought an old one complete with a case to hide his money in, the gold coins that he would show his future father-in-law. They were closed in multiple little cloth pouches to avoid making noise when he moved his bag. Wisdom of an emigrant...

The house, the crumbling stone walls, the door at the top of the two steps and that lone window that looked out onto the street. It was still the house that he remembered, gray stones and old wooden boards. He knocked softly, he didn't want to attract the curiosity of the neighbors. He knocked again. Finally he saw the darkness open and the light of a candle on the floor above. A head looked out. Father. He had aged, one could see that even in the dark. He emitted a guttural sound, almost choked. The window closed and agitated voices were immediately heard from inside. His folks. Luigi had his heart in his throat. After three years, they were still alive. He had thought of them often, around the fire, in silence, alone without their only son! Even from them he had only had vague news. But the noisy footsteps down the stairs, the clogs dragging on the floor, took him away from these thoughts and finally the door opened.

- Luigi, Luigi, you're back, Luigi! - his father exclaimed in his thick Genoese dialect.

Every child from Favale emigrated as soon as they turned eighteen, but the youngest always stayed to look after the parents. But the Giannini's had that only child that had decided to leave them on their own. His father had never been an affectionate man, nobody from those mountains was, but the memory of many half-spoken words with his wife in front of the fire at night, the memories of his young son and the feelings broken by that departure that should have never happened, erased his innate reservation and he now threw himself crying in the arms of his Luigi. The mother, a little late, joined the hug and now the three of them cried on each other's shoulders.

- Luigi, why did you not tell us that you were coming back? We were so worried about you.

- Dad, Mom, how are you? It's such a pleasure to see you again.

- My son, you've changed, you've become a man, and you've also lost weight, what strong arms you have.

In the house nothing had changed from when he had left, the same poverty, the minimal decor, no commodities. Luigi affectionately observed those few things. But he could not waste time, it was almost sunrise.

2

Seated around the table with the steaming coffee in hand, mother and father looked at their son, trying to get him to tell them everything about the last three years. But Luigi was impatient, he responded with monosyllables, or nearly, while he was busy taking apart the accordion.

- Excuse me, but I have to go to Virginia before her father leaves. Could you give me two empty baskets, please?

- What do you need them for? - asked his father.
- I have to prepare a surprise, a beautiful, beautiful surprise.

He had such excitement in his voice and in his eyes that his parents did not dare ask anything more.

Luigi took the two cases, the wicker baskets that were used during the chestnut harvest, put the gold coins in them, covered them with a layer of chestnuts, and then lifted one on his shoulders and tucked the other under his arm. They were heavy, but Luigi set off running towards the De Martini's house.

He arrived out of breath, and without waiting for his heart to stop racing, he knocked loudly. Only the father was already awake and he was getting dressed. He went to open the door just as he was, in pants and shirtless, worried to receive bad news. He was stunned when he recognised Luigi in the dim light, out of breath, with two wicker baskets under his arms.

- Good morning Pietro, forgive me for coming so early, but I wanted to show you my baskets of chestnuts, if they are sufficient for the promise I made.
- Luigi... when did you return?.... I haven't seen you around these days... I almost didn't recognize you.

He looked in awe at the man that had left three years ago as a child and had now returned as an adult, strong, determined.

- No, in fact, I arrived last night and I was anxious to have your consent before you left for work.
- Come, come in, don't stand there at the door.

At that moment, like a whirlwind, Virginia arrived, and without any shame she threw herself to embrace Luigi. Immediately behind her, her mother was shouting at her to get dressed.

Luigi, with the baskets in hand and Virginia clinging to his neck, entered the house with difficulty and looked for where to place the two baskets. Pietro, embarrassed, tried to cover himself and called loudly for his wife to quickly bring him a shirt while also shouting at Virginia who was jumping happily around them. There was quite a stir in the house.

- Here, Pietro, these are my crops. I am very proud of them, and I would like you to look at them closely before giving your opinion.

His eyes sparkled.

Pietro looked at the chestnuts. He usually gathered ten, twenty, fifty times as many. What was there to be so proud of? But Luigi placed the baskets on the table, first one and then the other, which, bending slightly, let the top layer of chestnuts slide away to reveal the coins. A wealth that Pietro had never seen.

- Luigi, where did you get these coins? - he asked suspiciously.

- Do not worry, Pietro, they are the fruits of three years of hard labor in America. I did it for Virginia, to show you that I am capable of supporting a family, well and honestly. Believe me.

Virginia and her mother stared open-mouthed, finding difficulty in believing that it wasn't all a dream. Even the father struggled to understand. They were all speechless and exchanged glances as if to ask each other tacitly for advice.

- What do you think? Do you think that we can pick up the conversation where we left off? Do you think that I kept my word?

The mother went off to get a jug of milk and put the coffee on to boil. She took the opportunity to secretly wipe her eyes, which were full of emotion. Pietro, perhaps to buy time, went to the cupboard to get a piece of bread that he sliced into pieces.

- Come Luigi, sit down, eat something. I am confused. You left three years ago, almost secretly and now you show up like this… at dawn… with no one expecting you… I don't know what to say… here, let us toast to your return… welcome back, welcome back.

Pietro really was confused. By now he had almost forgotten about that promise three years ago. Had it not been for his daughter who never missed an opportunity to remind him, he would have already found another husband for her. But now it was different, perhaps this stubborn young man truly was a good match.

In the meantime, Virginia had been sent back to her room and was listening with baited breath from behind the half-open door. From upstairs she could not see the kitchen and the words that reached her were almost incomprehensible. She was incredibly excited and could not sit still while her brothers, now awake, caused so much confusion that they prevented her from listening.

Then, Virginia understood that they were saying goodbye and that Luigi was leaving. She ran to her father and questioned him with her eyes. On the table there were only chestnuts. What had happened?

-    Go back to your room, immediately.

Her father was being gruff, but his face showed that he was happy. With those coins, his daughter would finally have a future worth living.

The news that Luigi had returned spread around town in a flash, but that initial astonishment had not yet subsided when the additional news was added, that he had returned to marry Virginia and that her father had approved. The news of the coins, on the other hand, remained secret for some time, but then began being retold like a fairy tale, passing from person to person. It was not news to divulge, but Virginia's mother had to tell the town wives something to justify the consent to the marriage. And so the news spread quickly, spiced up with the most imaginative comments. In the village, therefore, there was only talk of Luigi's skill and abilities and everybody commented on his return from so far away just to marry Virginia. The villagers knew from the stories of their emigrant relatives, whose few joys and many failures they had known, how difficult it was to make a fortune in a foreign country.

3

Dawn was still far away. The almost total darkness was broken by a dim, flickering light that barely illuminated the three steps of the entrance from the wide open door of the house. Bursts of faint sobs could be heard from within. Dignified sobs, a woman's. From the second story window, a head observed the street and retreated immediately. An old woman was hurrying down the road, drying her eyes. She climbed the steps wearily and entered without knocking and without saying hello. She had a letter in her hand for her children who had also emigrated: she would have given it to Luigi and Virginia, who would maybe meet them.

Luigi's house was a stone structure, solid but small, the stable below, two rooms above, and even higher the chestnut drying room that his parents had partially adapted many years earlier to accommodate their only child. Now he was leaving again, going to 'Merica on the ship from Genoa and the cart took many hours to arrive at the port.

Luigi and Virginia had married three months earlier, with a countryside party where a composed cheerfulness had tried in vain to drive away the sorrow. Even Pinin's accordion, which always accompanied weddings and which made even the elderly dance, had not succeeded, but this time it was different. Everybody in town knew that was the curse of poverty: their land could not keep their best children. They had to emigrate to survive.

In church, the women were in the front and the men in the back, hat in hand, all dressed up to watch those two kids who would soon be leaving them. Then, in the churchyard, their parents offered everyone a glass of wine. It was Virginia who had wanted such a simple ceremony; she had insisted on the fact that they had to save up to go to 'Merica. She wanted it that way even though Luigi could not be considered "poor." In fact, at that moment he was probably the richest of all the guests. Even more so than her father who was nicknamed Pietro of the Rich.

Virginia wore a traditional wedding dress that someone had lent her. The parish priest had asked around until a magnificent dress with bobbin lace from Portofino and red velvet from Chiavari was found. It was a bit loose because Virginia was thin and petite, but her father had brought a real seamstress from the city who altered the dress and made her look truly beautiful.

They had fallen in love at first sight. One day, Luigi had seen that little girl that he had always known as a beautiful, stunning young lady with great character and a strong spirit. She was little more than a child, but she already behaved like a woman working in her family like an adult, if not better. When she came home from school she immediately rushed to help around the house and she always worked hard. Her parents were in the fields working and she took care of her siblings and the house without needing anyone to tell her anything. When she realized that Luigi, soft-spoken and polite, was looking at her and greeting her timidly, she fell in love with him immediately, even though he was quite a bit older than her. The few times she had been able to be with him and talk to him briefly, her mother was always watching them closely.

Then, one evening, her father spoke with her mother in private and she understood that the conversation was about her and a marriage request from that handsome boy. But she did not understand her father's reply. Then Luigi suddenly disappeared and she took it very poorly. She closed herself in, no longer spoke to anyone, answered in monosyllables, refused to eat, and always had red eyes. Her mother had to break the silence and revealed that Luigi had made her a promise of marriage and that he had gone to 'Merica to make money. From that moment on, her days passed between euphoria and misery, between joy and despair at the thought of how many days were yet to pass before Luigi's return. Rich - because she was sure that he would return a rich man.

Until that extraordinary morning when they heard a knock on the door and everyone thought of a misfortune. Instead, she recognized the voice of her Luigi and, without caring about the presence of her parents, how she was dressed, or what they thought, she rushed down the stairs and ran to hug him.

But now Luigi and Virginia were leaving the house and all their loved ones, relatives, and few friends. The mountains were their home, a part of their life, but it was too hard to live and they had other expectations, and Luigi had shown that he knew what he was doing.

Virginia had moved to Luigi's house since the wedding day and now, in silence, with a heavy heart, she had collected her few belongings in a canvas suitcase that they had given her. She had made the bed, neat as usual, and washed herself in the basin with the cold water from the pitcher as she watched Luigi out of the corner of her eye. She was calm, sad but calm. Instead, Luigi was agitated. He tossed and turned in bed all night. They had even made love as if to seal the farewell to that bed, that room, and that house. They would never see it again. And they would certainly never see their parents again, nor would she ever see her brothers. They all had been crying constantly for two days. For her, it was almost a liberation to be able to leave and no longer see all the sadness for which she felt responsible. But in the sadness of the farewell, she also felt excitement for the adventure.

Luigi was more nervous, maybe even a little scared. The fact that he had made that decision weighed heavily on him. He had not slept for several nights, wondering if facing that long, treacherous journey towards an unknown land was the right choice. He certainly had more experience now, but alone it was a different story. Virginia was still a child, what right did he have to make her take such a risk? Yet, it was she who spurred him on when he was in doubt.

4

From the window, the sound of the cart wheels on the rough stones of the road and the thud of the horse's hooves could be heard. Luigi looked out the window to make sure that it was their cart. It would have brought them straight to the port of Genoa, going back on the road he knew well by now.

In front of the door, the horse, waiting still, shook its head and struck a hoof on the beaten earth.

From the open door of their room, they could hear the hiccups of the mother, who was waiting for them at the bottom of the stairs. They heard the footsteps of the father who was climbing the stairs to come and call them.

- Come now, Bacci's here. - he said softly, in dialect.

He kept his eyes low and moved slowly.

Luigi came closer and hugged him. Always in silence, there was no need for words.

They went downstairs, Luigi in front with the two suitcases, a few things crammed away, and the case for the accordion once again padded with coins, with Virginia directly behind him. The father waited a few minutes at the top of the stars to give his wife time to hug the kids, then he came down too, cautiously, almost as if he was scared to make noise. How beautiful those two lunatics were, and how brave. He wiped his eyes surreptitiously with the wrinkled handkerchief that made his pocket swell. At the foot of the stairs, he first hugged Luigi and then Virginia. She was so petite and his son so large, a real man. His wife kept crying, almost in silence, so he put his arm around her shoulders and together they watched the two kids move away. Virginia's parents and brothers had also come, along with a few friends, all in silence like a funeral procession.

- Thanks for coming, Bacci. - Luigi said in Genoese.

Luigi always had kind words for everyone, even in times of difficulty. He helped Virginia up and sat down by her side. Then they turned around and waved briefly as the horse began to move. Luigi stayed a few moments looking at his parents, in-laws, friends, the house, the road. A new life was beginning.

5

Genoa
1869

There were many on the ship, many more than there had been the time before. Luigi and Virginia stood on the stern and watched the dim lights of the distant city.

All around them there were many men, a few women accompanying their husbands, some families with children hugged closely to their parents, some standing and some seated, gathered in small groups all huddled together, trying to preserve their identity in that sea of strangers as they looked towards the land.

They were poorly dressed and came from pretty much all the regions of Northern Italy. Many from Piedmont and Liguria, many also from Tuscany, fewer from Lombardy and near France, and very few Southerners. Few were speaking.

Luigi had paid for two tickets in a cabin for six, the nicest that they could allow themselves. The cheaper dormitories were too crowded and he wanted to spare Virginia from a grueling crossing, like the one he had experienced on the previous trip. He still vividly remembered the various smells, the unpleasant noises, the vomiting and moans. At least in the cabin there were only six of them and the small window allowed them to let air circulate every once in a while. He had even managed to hide the accordion well and he had locked the door of the closet that had been assigned to him.

Even though the canteen was already open, many of the passengers were out on the deck offering salami and wine to try to mitigate the widespread sadness. It was a beautiful evening and the sea was particularly calm. It was not cold, on the contrary, the breeze provided relief after a hot September day, and it was a pleasure to enjoy the view of the coast that was slowly growing distant. The sound of the motors, the smoke, and the vibrations of the propellers were the background noise for the clear blue sky.

Many of the passengers looked towards the upper deck, slightly behind theirs. The gentlemen who had been able to afford a nice, comfortable cabin were starting to appear, served by waiters with white gloves in restaurants with fancy tablecloths and cutlery. Soon they would hear the music and the laughter emanating from the ballrooms. But those gentlemen were not emigrants.

The light of day had almost completely disappeared, and only a slight glow still lingered towards the mountains of Savona.

-    Over there, there is France - said Luigi, almost speaking to himself, in an effort to divert the sad thoughts from Virginia's mind.

Virginia was not yet sixteen, but she acted like a fully grown woman. From the moment they had boarded the ship, she had busied herself to make the cabin as comfortable as possible. She had immediately befriended their four travel companions, two Piedmontese couples, and had assigned the beds fairly, leaving the best bed to a couple much older than them. She had been firm and decisive so that everyone understood that order was needed for them to survive that trip in a decent manner.

Now, on the stern of that large white ship, after having prepared and organized everything, she had relaxed and was enjoying Luigi's arm that was wrapped around her shoulder. She looked around with curiosity. She had never seen a ship in real life before. She looked at the wooden masts that soared towards the sky and the shrouds that kept them straight and vibrated in the breeze, emitting a dull yet, in some way, musical sound. She also looked at the chimneys that erupted a dark pungent smoke and tried to compare them to the chimneys from her town. How often she had dreamed of this moment. The excitement of adventure was much stronger than the sadness for having left her family and the places she loved so much. Clinging to her Luigi, she watched the coast grow distant. She felt liberated. She knew that she was beginning a new life, her true life, and she was thrilled.

-    Listen, Luigi, my mom and I talked a bit.

Luigi pulled her close, still admiring the coast.

-    About what?

-    Girl talk. I've been thinking about it for a few days now, but I also thought it would be best to tell you today.

Luigi looked at her with concern.

-    What do you mean?

-    I think I'm expecting a child.

PART II

1
San José (California, USA)
1870

Luigi had spent three days going around looking for land to buy and cultivate. They were staying in a guesthouse on the road that connected San José and San Francisco, a small two-story building that had been partly redone to accommodate passerbys, almost all emigrants, who went to find their fortune. The other wing of the building was abandoned and in rough shape. They had bought a cart with a horse that they kept in the field behind the guesthouse and every day Luigi travelled on that cart looking to buy land to cultivate. That occupation had earned him lots of money in New Jersey where there was a lot to buy at a good price, but now things had changed

- I couldn't find anything to buy today either.

Luigi lay on the bed and spoke to his wife, discouraged.

- I was wrong to listen to those mediators who told me to come here because there was less demand and more advantageous prices. I cannot believe that in six months the prices have almost tripled. And yet… wherever I look… but who can afford such high sums? Ever since they arrived, the gold diggers have been buying anything at any price. With the money that we have, I could buy a small yard, but not a field to farm. I wouldn't want to spend everything, you never know. Today I even ran into a guy I met last time who had earned lots of money and moved here to find gold. He ruined himself. I have to admit that it scared me.

- Do you think we should go somewhere else?

Virginia looked at him anxiously: they had organized and had planned out their future, but now things had changed, and the guesthouse was eating up their savings.

- Did you not even find a job?

- No no… there are plenty of those… but I don't want to work under a boss… it's not for me… plus, the pay here is abysmal. We have enough money to start our own business, we have to have patience, we'll find something, you'll see. How about you? How did you spend the day?

- Good, good, I did the laundry… then I went to help Marie-Claire. Poor thing, ever since her daughter got married, the two of them were left to manage the guesthouse on their own. She can't take it anymore. Her husband is on the verge of a nervous breakdown, he doesn't feel alive without his daughter.

- That's strange, normally it's the women who are more upset.

- You know so little about women!

- I know them well enough that I married you, not a woman.

And with that he hugged Virginia tightly, pulling her onto the bed.

- And which animal would I be, then?

Virginia struggled to speak, squeezed between Luigi's arms, and she gently let herself fall onto his chest.

- You are not just any woman, you are my wife, and these things don't happen to you. How's the belly?

- Well, look, you can barely see it, and yet it's already been almost four months. Today I felt nauseous while I was downstairs, so Marie-Claire gave me an infusion that they use in Switzerland. Then I felt better. I was ironing her sheets, maybe that's why I got nauseous.

- What are we eating tonight?

- A nice vegetable soup.

- Again?

- Yesterday it was beans.

- Just think that I started craving chestnut pie. I emigrated to no longer eat chestnuts, after twenty years of eating only chestnuts, and now I crave them.

-   But then... you came to America for the chestnuts... not for me.

-   True, but I dealt with chestnuts for twenty years, while with you I've spent so little time that I don't feel nauseous yet. We'll see in twenty years, or thirty, or maybe forty. In any case, prepare yourself.

They often joked around. Their troubles did not dampen the joy and optimism and the great love that brought them together.

-   Today two new clients arrived. Many came, but then they saw the bleak environment, asked for the price, and left.

-   I feel sorry for Marie-Claire and her husband. If they go on this way, they will never become rich.

-   They're content, and seeing that Marie-Claire does everything, if there were more clients she wouldn't make it on her own.

-   What does Antoine do all day?

-   He goes around, comes back with a crate of vegetables that he gets as a gift, goes out in the field a bit, works a bit, never brings home any money but once in a while a bottle of wine. Marie-Claire tells me all this shaking her head and then says "we are old." She promised me that tomorrow she'll start teaching me French.

For Virginia, every novelty was a source of joy and enthusiasm. She had the great quality of looking at everything in a positive light, and even challenges were part of the adventure for her.

-   Good, but then how will I communicate with you? We'll have to speak to each other with gestures. I'll use Italian gestures and you'll use French gestures. Are we eating with them tonight?

2

A single lamp barely lit the dining room table. There were no other clients: the atmosphere was not particularly cheerful, and at night the workers from the nearby areas looked for noise, music, wine, and, precisely, cheerfulness.

-    Today I went to see a plot of land by the coast, on the road to San Francisco. A beautiful field, but too big for me.There would need to be four people to buy it. I couldn't do it alone. A piece of it is cultivable starting now, but the rest is waterlogged and needs a lot of work.

Luigi tried to start a conversation with Antoine, who spoke a mixed language.

-    Don't confiar in others. If you don't do it tout sol don't do it. Ici many bad people, don't confiar in anybody.

Antoine's Italian was almost incomprehensible. He spoke the same way in English and then slurred his words in a language that he called Spanish. Luigi spoke a little English but for him French was like Arabic: just a noise. Virginia only spoke Italian, or rather, the dialect of her home sprinkled with a few Italian words. The conversation was very difficult. But Antoine and Marie-Claire were good people and, even though they would have preferred having a house to themselves, Luigi and Virginia were welcome in that guesthouse. They felt safe and pampered.

-    I know what you mean, but the small fields are the ones that everybody wants and that makes the prices go up. The plot of land I saw only has one owner who has his employees that work the land, but he told me that one day he'll sell it because he wants to move to San Francisco and retire.

-    Moi aussi I want to retire. What are me and this old lady here doing? There is no longer anybody that obliges us to stay here. A small maison by the sea, near our daughter who may have enfants...

A week had gone by and not even the shadow of an attractive plot of land had passed. Luigi began to convince himself that he had made a mistake in his predictions. He was growing nervous, but he didn't want Virginia to worry.

- Still nothing today - he said throwing himself, exhausted, onto the bed. - By now I think I've visited every plot of land in a thirty mile radius. Maybe we should start thinking about moving.

Virginia looked at him worriedly. That they had made the wrong predictions was now clear, and with the money they had they would never be able to buy enough land to become rich. But the place was beautiful, the climate too, and the people overall were friendly. There were many Italians, some of them already came to visit them. To leave now would be disappointing for her. She lay on the bed by his side.

- This morning Marie-Claire told me again that she and her husband want to move, to leave the guesthouse.

- That's not new, she says it every night. I'm a bit tired of hearing her repeat it all the time.

- But this morning she told me, not him, and then she asked me "why don't you take it?"

- Are you crazy? Who has the money to buy this shack? And we don't have any experience, who will do the work? We are farmers, not hotel managers.

- I'm not crippled, I know how to cook, make beds, iron, and I also know how to smile at clients when they come in. And what do you think is different between taking care of a house and a guesthouse?

- But you're expecting a child, you can't overwork yourself!

- I'm perfectly well. I'd have fun, and I'm sure lots of people would come because we'll make it cheery, this place, and people would come, I'm sure of it.

- You're crazy, that's the only thing to be sure of.

That night, at dinner, Antoine started his usual lamenting again. Luigi had gone downstairs before dark and snooped

around to see if there was much work to be done. He had
walked around the house and had sneaked into places that he
had never peered into before. Even in the kitchen, under the
guise of asking what there was to eat. Then he had returned
upstairs to Virginia.

-    There is a lot of work to be done, also because half the
kitchen has to be redone. Lots of things need to be purchased
for the rooms and for the kitchen, and the whole main room
has to be redone to make it more welcoming. And the sign, it
has to be replaced with something that attracts the public.

-    Have you already spoken with Antoine?

-    No, no, of course not. It's better if Marie-Claire is there
too. We'll try tonight.

Now they were all seated at the table and Virginia looked
at Luigi apprehensively.

-    Antoine, if you both leave what will happen to the hotel?

-    I'm looking for somebody to take it and manage it
themselves. I come here once every month and I take the loy-
er, how to say… the rent.

There, that was the solution! Not to buy, to rent. Luigi and
Virginia made eye contact in excitement: that they could do,
the money would be enough. There was no need to spend too
much on the renovations, only four rooms would not have
been worth it, but Luigi had already calculated that in the
other section there could be additional rooms. If there were
enough customers.

3

-    Luigi… come, it's ready.

Virginia had cautiously looked out from one of the windows to call them for lunch. They had adapted a room that
now served as a kitchen, dining room, and bedroom as the
rest of the house was under construction.

Luigi and the three workers he had hired sat down at the table. Virginia had managed to find pasta made by Italians that was not bad and she had even paid quite a bit for it. With that, she had prepared a big pot of pasta and beans that emitted a delicious aroma.

-     If you make these dishes you can bet lots of people will come here to eat. It's excellent.

Tommaso, from the mountains above Savona, whom they had met on the ship and with whom they had also made the journey by train, spoke. They had lost sight of each other and by chance, just a couple days before, Luigi had run into him on his way to San José to make some purchases. He was a hard worker, taciturn and solitary, but he had accepted to work under Luigi with great enthusiasm and had even brought along two other workers he had met in the fields.

-     This morning I painted the sign. You should come see it, it came out really well. This time the people who pass by are sure to see it, holy crap! It's as big as the house.

Luigi was increasingly excited about the work that they were doing; he couldn't wait to open and he did not pay much attention to his friends' colorful language.

-     Why did you guys name it the Suisse Hotel? You aren't Swiss.

-     But the previous owners are, and we didn't buy it, we're just renting it. We couldn't change the name. Plus, it was already known by that name.

In the meantime, the other two were stuffing their faces with pasta as if they hadn't eaten for years.

-     Slow down, there's more left. No need to shove it down your throats.

Virginia watched them enjoy her meal with satisfaction. She had them at the guesthouse for a week and every day they showed great appreciation for her cooking.

-     Hey! Is anybody home? Anybody?

A voice was calling them from outside. Luigi poked his head out the window.

- I'm here, hello.
- Hello to you, I saw that you guys are fixing up the hotel, when do you open?
- What do you need?
- There are four of us and we work nearby. We don't know where to go eat.
- Come back on Sunday. We're celebrating the opening, and we'll offer you all a glass of wine.
- We'll be sure to be here, thanks.

Virginia looked at Luigi.

- I didn't know that Sunday was opening day…
- I didn't know either, I just decided now. So by Saturday we have to have finished. These are customers, we can't send them away. And we still have four days, you'll see, we'll make it.

Tommaso froze with his spoon halfway to his mouth.

- This Saturday?

4

- I can't take it anymore. I think you'll have to manage on your own tomorrow. Let's hope there won't be too many people.

Luigi threw himself on the bed. For four days he had woken up at five, eaten a bit of bread and cheese, when there was any, and come back to sleep at midnight. Now it was past two in the morning and Virginia was waiting for him. She had also been swept up in the work despite the fact that her belly was starting to show. She was tired too and had already fallen asleep on a chair while waiting for him. Tomorrow was the big day, the opening of their new hotel. Based on the amount of people that passed by and stopped to comment and congratulate them, tomorrow there would be a big crowd. Also because they had promised free drinks.

- Do you want something to eat?
- No, no, thanks. I'll sleep a couple hours, tomorrow I still...

And he fell asleep.

Virginia looked at him and began gingerly undressing him without waking him. The shoes, the pants, the shirt, then she turned him over under the blankets. She wanted to talk to him and tell him that she had thought of a name for the boy, or girl. She would have preferred a boy, a boy that resembled her Luigi, strong, decisive, how you have to be when you live near the border. Luigi had never told her what he preferred, maybe a son too. But now they were too busy to think of these things. And tomorrow there would be even more to do, but this time it would be fun.

When Virginia awoke, Luigi had already left.

It was barely dawn but the men downstairs were already hard at work. Virginia watched them secretively from the window. You could see that they were trying to work quietly. They spoke softly to avoid waking her and hadn't yet used a hammer. Virginia prepared the water for the coffee and sliced the bread. She had bought butter and two jars of marmalade from a neighbor she had befriended.

- Luigi, come, the coffee is ready.

Luigi glanced up at the window. "What an extraordinary girl," he thought, "she is sixteen, she's pregnant, she works like a man, and is always happy." His eyes watered. "With Virginia by my side, I could do anything."

- We're coming... come on boys, drop everything, let's go have coffee.

They planned out their day at the table.

- Now we have to clean the living room, get rid of everything in the front and clean outside as well. Gino, go with your cart to get the vases. You know where to go, and make sure they're nice plants. Virginia already chose them but double check to make sure they are the right ones. You need to get six and then put two downstairs in front of the stairs, two at the top and two on the side. That way, like Virginia says, the entryway is more refined. As soon as you're back, go get the bottles, be careful. When you arrive, call us and we'll help you unload. If you break one, we're all in trouble. We have to bring the tables and chairs inside. Virginia, the tablecloths. The cups are in the big box in the room next door. But that's the last thing. Then, Virginia, close these two doors. If somebody wants to see the rooms we'll only show them the two that are ready, so if you can, make sure they're organized. Come on, let's move!.

Virginia took him by the arm as he was leaving.

- You haven't said good morning to me yet.

Although the age gap between them was great and Virginia had not lost her childlike playfulness, the fact of having already shared so many adventures had brought them closer. Virginia had become more adult and Luigi more childish. Luigi hugged her tightly, lifting her and twirling her around.

- Today is the big day and you are wonderful.

At noon, Luigi had put on a nice black suit with a white waistcoat and immaculate dress shirt that she had given him, along with a black bow tie that signalled his authority. Virginia, incredibly elegant in a long white dress, was radiant. Standing next to each other in an effort to overcome their emotions, they stood in front of the entryway of their new hotel to welcome their guests. Above them hung the enormous sign. Antoine and Marie-Clare had already arrived and observed the final product with satisfaction. Strangely, Antoine was not complaining.

- Antoine, how are you? Are you well in the new home?

- I'm finally well. I take care of my daughter. She is also expecting un enfant, tu sais? I will be a nonno, bientôt. Nice job, here, bravo, my compliments. I told you that you did well to take this, you'll see what a great success.

- Thank you, let's hope. Look, the Sicilians are arriving... Hey! Welcome, it's a pleasure to see you. Come on in and have a drink. To our good health.

Virginia smiled, welcoming the guests. While they were offering drinks to the first arrivals, the sound of music from one, or two, no three accordions could be heard from outside. The fellow villagers from Favale had arrived. But how had they known?

Luigi and Virginia were touched, but they had to conquer their emotions because large numbers of people were starting to arrive and after an hour there were fifty people, music, wine, and lots of happiness. By nightfall, they already had the two rooms reserved for the entire week and seven people for lunch every day.

Hand in hand, they looked down from the bannister in the entryway to observe the crowd of friends celebrating. Somebody raised their glass, yelling loudly, "a toast to Virginia and Luigi!" Everyone turned around and raised their glasses, voicing their congratulations in various languages and dialects. And the accordions began playing again.

Before the sun set, a stranger arrived with a tripod and a wooden box on top of it, which he placed on the ground.

- Who is that? - asked Virginia.
- I don't know, I've never seen him before. I think he's a photographer, that looks like a camera.
- Is he going to take a picture of us?
- It looks like it, I didn't even know there was a photographer around here.
- Well let's strike a pose then. Come here, in front of the entrance.

That was the first photograph of Luigi and Virginia's American adventure.

5

The kitchen was well lit by a large window through which a light breeze only partly took away the heat of the stove. Virginia was cooking. She was a bit unkempt and red in the face due to the heat, and she struggled to move with her big belly. The new maid, a Mexican girl, moved around her to put away the dishes. And in the meantime she talked and talked, as always. But Virginia's thoughts were elsewhere, partly because she did not understand much Spanish and partly because what the maid was saying did not interest her. She was planning out her day in her head. She was so absorbed that when Luigi opened the door she jumped in fright and screamed.

Luigi lovingly embraced her and kissed her hair.

- Sorry, I didn't mean to frighten you.

- I was distracted. Nina doesn't stop talking… One of these days I'm going to cut off her tongue. What can she have to say…

- She probably talks about her lovers and you don't listen. One day she'll get offended, you'll see.

- Don't make fun of me and don't talk about inappropriate things. If she gets offended I'll deal with it. How is the work going?

- The vegetable garden is finished. I even finished planting everything.

- Two more people came to ask for a room this morning. How sad it was to have to tell them that our rooms are already full for the coming months. We have to do what we said, you know? Ever since we opened I've had to turn away so many people, it pains me.

- Antoine is coming on Friday to collect the rent. Let's try to talk to him about it then.

When they were finally alone, after having sent all their guests to bed, Luigi and Virginia lingered to regroup and schedule the following day. Then they stayed to talk about this and that, relaxing at the end of the day.

Luigi had gone to see the wing of the building that was attached to their hotel. It had been built to serve as a residence, but then, for some unknown reason, it had never been used. Now it was in poor condition and there was a lot of work to be done, both to reinforce the structure and to make it as cozy as the hotel. Luigi had dreamed of equipping all the rooms with a sink with running water, just like he had heard was the case in the hotels in the city, so he would also have to think about getting a water tank that was large enough, and how to fill it, especially because there could be up to fifteen rooms in that space . But neither Luigi nor Virginia were intimidated by this.

-    I'll talk to him about it, and I was also thinking that if he gives me a good price and fair conditions I could even buy. If he only knew how much the hotel is making now…

-    I don't know if we have enough money to buy it and have all that work done, though…

-    Eh, let's see what he says on Friday…

6

-    Antoine, try this wine. It's not French wine but it's starting to become a pretty decent wine. Some Italians made it not far from here.

-    Le vin… this is something we miss from since we have been here. I always remember our good house wine.

Antoine observed the wine with a critical eye, swirling it in the glass.

-    See these traces, this is la glycerine, how do you say? Glycerin? Oui? Glycerin. Here, red wine must have glycerin or else it's not good.

-    Listen, Antoine, now the hotel is full, but only today, and really few people pass by so I have a lot of free time. I was thinking of dedicating a bit of my time to fix up the space back there.

- The old place? To think that when we worked on that the people who were helping me slept there. It was in good shape then, but they told me they heard the sounds of the wood... how to say? Anyways, you understand.
- I was thinking of starting to work calmly, in my free time, to try to recover one or two rooms.
- I can't rent out a room, but if you're interested I'll rent out the whole thing,
- But if I rent the whole thing and then only manage to fix a single room, what will I do?
- Luis, I like you and I've seen that you use your time wisely... that's not always the case, here. I'll sell you everything and you do what you want with it.
- But I don't have a lot of money, and then to do all the work that needs to be done...
- Give me another glass of wine and I'll think of a good solution.
- Antoine is a true friend. I told him a bunch of white lies, I don't know if he believed them. But he offered me some conditions like a real friend. I was thinking that I should go bring him the money every month because if he comes here often and sees how we work, he'll get mad and then he'll say we tricked him.
- Which would be the truth...
- Oh please... we work like slaves and we earned all the people that come here... not them. Look at the difference from when we were living here, when they ran the place... we were the only clients... now we have to turn people away.

It had been just over a month since Luigi and Virginia had opened the hotel and they were already going to commit to a new costly and labor intensive expansion that, as always, seemed to be overly ambitious. Virginia, despite now being seven months pregnant, was not afraid of anything. The work did not seem to tire her, and the risk did not worry her, even the immanence of her delivery did not worry her in the slightest. Rest was not part of her plans. Luigi was never content with what he had; he always wanted more, always wanted better, and he had a great desire to become rich to show to others that he was the best. And he worked tirelessly for that.

But he still thought about that plot of land near San Francisco.

7

The opening of the new wing made up entirely of rooms took place quietly. They had spoken about it amongst themselves but thought that, at the end of the day, it was not a huge deal. It was simply an expansion, so there was no need to spend money to throw a party and provide drinks for strangers.

In almost four weeks, Luigi and his usual three helpers had done a good job. They had even bought a new sign which was much bigger and, most importantly, illuminated. There was nothing like it in San José. Two days after the opening, all twenty rooms were full and every evening the main room became one of the favorite venues in town. The big fireplace was not only a place of refuge, but also a main feature that attracted people to the guesthouse. It was quite enjoyable to sit at the tables and be enveloped in the warmth of the fire. It was cheery and comfortable. Luigi still had to add some finishing touches but it was practically ready, and by now his main concern was greeting guests and bookkeeping. Virginia was becoming larger every day.

Had it not been for the concern regarding childbirth, Luigi would have been bored: in the morning he went to buy food for the day from his friends, with whom he spent a bit more time than necessary. Then he went to the hotel counter, greeting the customers and exchanging a few words. He took advantage of these moments to improve, modify, expand.

He was never still, always impatient and thinking of what to do after Virginia gave birth. Everything was ready, all the necessary people had been warned, and Luigi was the most nervous. He even helped in the kitchen, mainly to lift heavy things, but ultimately he was bored. The wait made him uneasy.

At the hotel door he waved to a customer who was leaving.

- Be good, Luigg, I'll be back in three days.
- Bye, Carmelo, have a good trip. I'll keep your room ready for you.

Luigi came back inside. Virginia emerged from the kitchen, walking with difficulty.

- Virginia, I told you to rest in the room.
- I had to make the meatloaf, but now I'm really tired. I even feel some pains.

Luigi pulled up a chair and helped her sit down.

- Come here, I told you a thousand times that you're close. You shouldn't tire yourself out. Where does it hurt?
- Here, my back. And everything is spinning, here under my stomach. Oh oh oh, it's getting stronger. I think we're ready.

Luigi was agitated.

- Contractions, contractions… Lorenzo, get the horse! Go immediately to get Nina the midwife, hurry, now! Virginia, come, lean on me, let's go upstairs. Carmela… Carmela,… come quickly… bring the water upstairs… get clean sheets… come on, hurry!

He approached Virginia, helped her get up and together they walked towards the stairs. Virginia struggled greatly to climb the stars and Luigi was extremely agitated.

- Carmela, what are you doing? Help me to put her in bed.
- Luigi, calm down, nothing is happening… I'm just

about to have a child… many women have done it before…
I'm not the first you know?

Luigi looked at her. He smiled and kissed her hair.

It was May 6th, 1870 and Amadeo Peter Giannini was being
born, destined to become the greatest banker in the world.

PART III

1
San José
1876

The Santa Clara Valley was entirely cultivated; there were many farmers who had settled in that area for the climate and the fertility of the fields. The valley was the greatest supplier of fruits and vegetables for the nearby city of San Francisco. It was a pleasure seeing the colorful orchards which, in the springtime, were filled with flowers and emitted a marvelous aroma.

Luigi, just like every other day, was returning home after his rounds to check on the laborers who worked in the fields and, pulling the cart over to the side of the road, he stopped to look at the beautiful house that he had finally managed to build himself. His dream of becoming a farmer again, but this time of a big plot of land, had finally become a reality. The difficult but productive years at the Swiss Hotel had brought him a lot of money and now he could look serenely towards the future and towards his three sons who were giving him great satisfaction.

The cigar, handmade the Italian way, strong and smelly, hung from his lips partly extinguished. It was more of a habit than a true passion. In fact, for him, half was enough for the entire day, and when he threw it away it was more chewed than smoked.

He got off his cart while Bruno came towards him to take the horse and take him to the stables. He then waved to Virginia and, before heading to the office to balance the books, a quick hello to Amadeo who was studying in the boys' room.

- Amadeo, what are you doing? Come, go downstairs, Mom is waiting for you for snack time.

Amadeo turned around, looked at his father, and showed him his notebook.

- Look Dad, I drew an artichoke and the apple tree in the field.

Luigi was happy to have passed down his passion for the countryside to his oldest son, who often followed him through the fields and bombarded him with questions. He even befriended the workers, who all happily greeted him. It was they who had started calling him AP, after his initials for Amadeo Peter, and from then on he was known only by that nickname. Luigi tried to resist the American habit of shortening names, but he knew perfectly well that he would have to give in. He was the only one who called him Amadeo, even Virginia had been converted by then.

- You're so talented, but an artichoke is not as tall as a tree.
- No, but the artichoke is close and the tree is far away.

How could you blame him? That little boy was quicker than him and always managed to surprise him. Luigi looked at him lovingly. Amadeo reminded him of that trip from Italy and that evening on the boat when Virginia had announced that she was expecting.

- You're right, how did I not realize that sooner? Come now, Mom is waiting for us.

Amadeo ran down the stairs, sat at the large kitchen table, hurriedly drank his milk, then took a slice of bread, slathered it in generous amounts of the marmalade his mother had made, and ran towards the fields to watch a farmer hoeing the land. He watched as he ate his bread.

- Hi Gino, what are you doing?
- Hi AP, right now I'm hoeing, then I'll plant the new lettuce. What are you eating?
- Bread and jam. Do you want some?

And without waiting for a reply, he took off towards the house. The farmer stood watching him, smiling ,and then continued hoeing. After a couple of minutes, Amadeo returned with a piece of bread and jam.

- Thanks AP, but you shouldn't have. I can't stand here to chat and eat with you. Your father pays me to work, not to do nothing.
- And how long does the lettuce take to grow?
- It depends, this one will take at least three weeks. Do you know how much three weeks is?
- Yes I know, you have to go to mass three times. I'm not a baby! - Amadeo pouted.
- Good, you're right, now go play with the other kids. I have to continue.

Amadeo handed him the bread, turned around, and ran away. He went to watch the other farmers who were working a little ways away. The fields had become their home and without going far you could observe how different cultivations were going.

The sun, still high in the sky, was very hot and the farmers were sweating profusely. A cart with a tank full of water moved between the plots of land to provide some refreshment. For AP, it was a great joy watching the seasons change and the crop rotations, and he curiously questioned everyone to know what they were doing and why, or which season was best for one thing or another. He had friends among the farmers, almost all of them Italian but also some Mexicans and a few Chinese, with whom it was more difficult to communicate.

2

At sunset, the whole family gathered at home for dinner. The house was a large colonial house with a large window that overlooked the fields and, in the distance, the sea of the San Francisco Bay. Just like every night, Luigi, Virginia, and the three sons sat around the table.

- Yesterday three laborers came to work. I should stop

hiring foreigners, but now there are few Italians who want to be farmhands. They told me that those three were piss drunk at the saloon yesterday. And with what money? I haven't paid them yet... but if they come today they're going to hear from me. They're Mexican. I think they're the same ones that gave me problems not too long ago.

-      Be careful with those people. I don't like this at all. Amadeo, hurry, you have to go to sleep. Luigi, ever since you bought this land, life has become increasingly hectic. By dawn, everybody in the house is already gone... I shouldn't have to continue having kids to have somebody to keep me company.

Virginia knitted as she spoke, just as her mother had taught her many years before.

-      If it wasn't for you, I would have never come to America, let alone buy land. You support me... and it seems like you're good at having children, no? In any case, tomorrow I'll be back for lunch. Maybe I'll stop to pick up Amadeo at school so we can arrive earlier. Don't you ever think about Italy? It came back to my mind today when they told me about those three drunkards. Think of how many people are starving over there, and here there would be work for everybody. I heard from that family from Torino today, mother, father, and two sons, that were with us on the boat. I don't remember their names. Now the sons are probably around twenty years old. They opened a tailor shop in San Francisco a little while back where they make clothes, and not only for Italians. And they have great success, they told me. That's the kind of people we need, workers without strange ideas in mind. They struggle, but now they have a job, they make money, even the sons, if they're serious, they'll go far, you'll see.

The evenings went by like this, chatting, then, after having fed the little ones, they sat at the table. They ate lots of vegetables, the pasta that their Mexican maid had learned to make with flour and eggs was not half bad, sometimes chicken. Almost never veal. Good wine was a rarity; it had been about ten years since the first vineyards had started to produce a decent wine, but it was still very crude, with a rather high alcohol content. Their friends in San José were the best, but the quality, despite their best efforts, was modest, nothing to do with the Italian wine they still remembered so well. At sunset, they all went to bed.

3

Luigi and Amadeo were riding in the cart driven by the former. It was almost noon and the high sun still could not completely melt away the haze that rose almost every night. The mountains that surrounded the plain of San José protected it from the thick fog that often enveloped San Francisco, and the sun was much hotter than by the sea. Perhaps due to the climate, the countryside was much more lush and the well organized fruit and olive tree plantations, which father and son observed from afar, were a vibrant green.

A little further on, two men were walking on the side of the road. They had two large crooked straw hats that they had clearly made themselves, and one of them leaned on a stick. Despite this, his stride was uncertain, and even from far away you could tell that they were swaying as though they were battling ocean currents in a walnut shell. When they heard the cart, they stopped and looked with dark faces.

Luigi turned to Amadeo: - There they are, two of the three from yesterday. They're still drunk.

Then, speaking to the two: - I was looking for you two, and that other guy Miguel. Yesterday, instead of coming to work, you were getting drunk in the saloon. I don't like those who get drunk instead of working. If it happens again, I'll fire both of you. And tell your friend too. In any case, I'm keeping a dollar of your pay. Now go to work.

He threw the half of the cigar that he was chewing on the ground, looked at them defiantly, and tapped the horse, who resumed his trotting. Amadeo turned and saw them, shaky on their legs, watching them leave.

-    That is no way to act - his father continued. - If Mom and I had been like them, we would also be farmhands by now. They're wretches, they drink and beat each other up. That's all they know how to do. How about tonight we go tour the fields? What do you say?

-    Yes, when?

-    Before dinner, I'll come get you.

It was never hot in the house. The air, barely nudged by the breeze, maintained a pleasant temperature even during the hottest days. Amadeo was in his room and tried to read a book, but he was distracted. He looked out the open window often, moving the white curtains aside.

Finally, when the sun began to set, Luigi arrived. - Come, Amadeo, put on your hat. I'll wait for you downstairs.

He did not have to wait. Amadeo had already run to say goodbye to his mom and was ready for the stroll with his dad. For his age, Amadeo was already a big, strong boy and was used to the open air and tiring games. He often went swimming in the river, he took long walks, he climbed trees, and every once in a while he even rode horses, but he was not very good and he did not like it much, especially because the horses at the barn were beasts made for working, not riding. The horses that pulled the cart could not be touched.

They headed towards the fields. Almost all the farmers had left, normally they worked from dawn to early afternoon, when the day started getting hotter. Only a few came back in the late afternoon, those who took care of the irrigation or the harvesting of particular products.

While they walked, Luigi taught Amadeo how various vegetables and lettuces were cultivated, how they were picked, the diseases, the good and bad types of insects. It was like a school in the open air and both Luigi and Amadeo loved those moments.

- Look at those two still there. Who knows what they are doing.
- Aren't they working?
- Look at them, does it look like they're working? They are two scoundrels, I have to get rid of them or they'll corrupt the others.

They went up to them.

- Señor, por favor.
- What is it? What are you doing here?
- Señor, no is fair that you not pay a dollar.
- What are you trying to say, that I'm unfair? With people like you who only think about drinking and not about working?

The one with the stick had come closer and was facing Luigi, although unstable on his legs. His words came out with difficulty, getting muddled on his tongue.

- No, señor, you have to give a dollar to us, one for one, we worked.
- You drank, not worked.
- No, you give me dollar.
- Start working instead of complaining.
- No, you give me dollar.

The voices were becoming agitated and aggressive. Amadeo was frightened, but he saw that his father was very sure of himself.

- No dollar if you don't work.
- No, you give me dollar - the man repeated for the umpteenth time. And he brandished the stick like a club.

Luigi defied the worker by stepping towards him. - How dare you, scoundrel!

And those were his last words. The stick hit him forcefully on the neck, just behind the head. Luigi's eyes widened in shock, his mouth wide open searching for air. He fell on his knees and then fell to the earth face down. Without a word, without a breath, he was dead.

Amadeo stood dumbstruck, frozen for a few seconds. He looked at the two who, frightened by what they had done, turned and ran, throwing the stick to the side.

Amadeo kneeled by his father's side and understood right away that he was dead. He took his head in his hands and cried as the blood ran onto him, his shirt, and his pants. He was desperate. His beloved father, his friend, his guide, his life coach, the man who he wanted to be when he grew up, now lay in his arms, dead, forever dead. No more walks, no more lessons, no more school. He was dead. In his arms.

-    Dad, Dad, please answer me… tell me it isn't true… answer me… please… answer me… it isn't true… it can't be… wretches, killing… for a dollar… for a dollar… it can't be...

He collapsed by his father's side.

When they found them, Amadeo was still hugging Luigi and he kept crying. Virginia came, who immediately thought that Amadeo was also injured, but then she heard him repeating in between hiccups - Dad, answer me, I'm begging you… don't leave me… those wretches have gone away… answer me please… they killed him… for a dollar.

Amadeo was 7 and Virginia was 22.

4

Virginia, all dressed in black, sat at the table with her head bowed and tears streaming down her face. With her, the trusty Bruno with his wife Maria tried to alleviate her pain.

-    Yesterday I wrote a long letter to my parents and I also included a letter for Luigi's parents. I asked my parents to stay close to them and to bring them the news. I hope they survive this tragedy. In last year's letter they had mentioned some aches and pains from old age but you know, the truth is never told in letters. I had to tell them this though.

- You were right not to write to them directly. It will certainly be a great comfort to have your parents nearby.

- Ever since we left I think they see each other often. A while ago I sent a few pictures, the one from when we opened the hotel, a few of the little ones. Look, this one is the last one I sent. I made myself a copy.

- How beautiful you both are here, you did well to send it to them.

Bruno, more realistic, already thought about the future: - Have you thought about what you'll do now?

- What do you want me to do... I have three kids... this farm... lots of people who work. I even thought about selling everything and going home... but I feel like that would betray Luigi's dream. He wouldn't have wanted to. I didn't mention it in the letter... I'm desperate.

She kept crying, and the two looked at each other. Maria got up, came closer, and hugged her in silence. Then, overwhelmed by sorrow: - You know, we never had kids. God knows how much we wanted them. Your children are wonderful and here we feel like this is our home too and like you are all our family. Sometimes I think about the luck you had having a family like yours, happy, hard-working, united. This is a tragedy for us too...

Bruno, with his head bowed, almost speaking to himself: - Luigi was a special person. In these past few years he managed to pull together a great fortune, it would be a shame to abandon everything now.

- But how can I do it alone! Amadeo is a child, he can't help me! And all this land with over twenty people who work on it... they'll steal everything from me. I want to leave...

- We've known each other for a long time and I've worked for you for four years... I can take care of it for a while... if you trust me... and Maria... we live close by... she can help you too... we won't abandon you.

Amadeo was at the door listening. He came closer and tenderly hugged his mother.

- Mamma, I'm here...

Virginia raised her head. She looked at him lovingly, hugged him, and cried.

5

There were many. Most of them were workers, almost all of them friends, at least those who were not traveling, even a few ship owners of the ships Luigi had supplied. And then there were the women, many of them, the mothers and wives of those who had worked for him, those who had appreciated and benefited from his work and his humanity, and the people closest to the family, old friends still shocked that such a tragedy had struck. They heard of them, of accidents or attacks, but they always concerned strangers, or they happened in the city, while San José was still a cheery island where people worked and lived in peace. The Italian community was very large, but there were also French, a few Germans, and a second generation Chinese community, the children of the workers who had built the railway and who lived separately like in an enclave. The Mexicans were unskilled laborers and were a separate group entirely.

They lived farther away, almost in the city, and every day they moved where there was work.

The distraught Virginia stayed at home, supported by those few women who, almost every day, came to see her, some to help with domestic work and others just to say hello and enjoy the peace and tranquility of that home. They had tried to dress in dark colors, like they did back home. Black clothing was certainly not scarce, but many, especially the men, wore their work clothes. Many women cried, but many men also wiped away their genuine tears. A melancholy, orderly procession climbed the steps of the house to greet Virginia who, seated in a chair next to the coffin, held Attilio's hand while she thanked everyone, keeping an eye on the little one in trusty Maria's arms. Amadeo, standing still behind the coffin, observed everybody who came in, his eyes dry and his face tough. He was standing as if to say, I'm here now to protect my mom and my brothers. My mom is not alone, I'm here. The people who passed looked at and greeted him as if he were a child, but AP was no longer a kid. He had become a man. He even knew the names of some, others he had seen before, but most were strangers to him. He watched them one by one, maybe subconsciously, to measure the good that his father had done and for the gratitude that these people expressed, and from those expressions of pain he seemed to gain strength and determination.

When the parish priest of the Italian church of San José arrived, he greeted Virginia and her sons and he blessed the coffin. Then six of the most loyal workers hoisted it onto their shoulders and brought it to the hearse. The procession began moving and everybody followed it. First in line was Amadeo, standing tall and proud, closely followed by Virginia and Attilio and then everybody else. Little George had stayed home with Maria and Bruno.

PART IV

1
San José
1877

The months went by and autumn brought the first rare rains. A light and constant drizzle had drenched the fields and now the sun, which was coming back out, made the colors of the countryside shine.

But those colors did not erase the pain that lingered in the house. At night, Amadeo stayed close to his mother. He never left her alone. At the farm, the work continued under the guidance of Bruno, who spent his days supervising like he had seen Luigi do. Business had slowed a bit because Bruno did not have Luigi's authority or charisma, nor did he have his organizational skills, but they stayed open. Even Amadeo, when he was not at school, surveilled the work, curious and proactive; he was starting to put what his father had taught him into practice.

He reached the cart driven by Lorenzo, a young countryman who, other than cultivating his small farm, took care of transporting the vegetables for the Giannini's almost every day.

- He's a good kid, - said Bruno, turning to Amadeo. - Great worker. Honest. He is very useful to us now.

- I know him, he has worked for us a long time. He was one of the first to arrive after Dad's accident and then he never left so he could help us.

Bruno turned towards Amadeo in surprise: he was convinced that he was speaking to a child, but this was not a childish observation. "He knows everything," Bruno thought with admiration, "he observes everything and makes no incorrect judgments. Above all, he never speaks out of turn."

Lorenzo returned with a full cart, stepped down, greeted Bruno, and then approached Amadeo.

- Hey AP, how are you doing? And your mom?
- Thanks, Lorenzo, you always think of us. Mom is not well, she is very sad… but we'll make it.
- Good, AP, that's the spirit.

In the meantime, Bruno counted the bags and the crates and recorded them in his notebook.

- Lorenzo, did you do the math?
- Yes, yesterday they took everything, and if I had more I would have sold that too. Here is the money. Everything is written down.

Lorenzo reached into his jacket pocket and handed Bruno a small package.

- Thanks. And when will we do the calculations together?
- Saturday, I'll come on Saturday when we wrap up the week. In the meantime, you can hang on to the money. I don't need it.
- We'll see each other tomorrow at the same time… What do you need?
- The usual, potatoes, lots, peppers, beans, tomatoes, cucumbers, and salad. And all the fruit that you have.
- Okay, I'll have everything ready for you. Bye.

Lorenzo tapped the horse and left.

2

In the house, Maria had to insist on getting rid of the mourning clothes and making the environment a bit less depressing. It had taken her three months, and another three to manage to talk about something other than Luigi's death.

Virginia tried to numb her pain by constantly working in the house and, on occasion, in the fields. She always found something to do and didn't delegate any tasks to others, especially if the work was difficult. She was wasting away, and had completely lost the will to live despite still being very young.

Finally after a long day of hard work, Virginia went to rest for a moment in the armchair where Luigi always came to see her. Even Maria moved to the living room and came to sit next to her.

- Virginia, I'm sorry to speak to you so honestly, but I see you getting increasingly quiet… by day you are completely dedicated to your sons, at night you help Bruno with the calculations. You never take a minute for yourself, you never rest. Your only distractions are going to the cemetery or to church. You can't go on like this.

- What do you want me to do… this is my life now… I always think about Luigi… and to avoid thinking, I work myself to death… but even like this I can't do it. - She dried her eyes with the apron that she had still not taken off.

The woman looked at her with tenderness and compassion. - I understand… I can't argue with that… but life goes on and you have three sons to take care of… you are so young… you need a new husband.

- Oh please! What husband?! And it's true that I am only 22 years old, almost 23, but look at me. I look at least 40 and I have three little boys. Who would want me? Turn on the lamp please… I can't see a thing.

The woman came closer and turned on the gas lamp.

- When will they bring us the gas! These lamps make us go bug-eyed. Don't think of yourself as something to be discarded. It's true that you haven't looked after yourself in six months and you look like an old woman, but at your age it doesn't take much to become beautiful again. And then, believe me, there are many men out there who…

Virginia was not in the mood: - For goodness' sake! I don't even want to talk about it. And the men that I know are either married or are workers who linger around here. Tell me of one who would suit me. One who isn't solely interested in my property and who wouldn't get drunk and run away with another woman after a year… Come off it, please, leave me alone.

- Yes, you're right, but if you really want a name... that Lorenzo... the one who transports the vegetables... he comes around here every day... a good-looking young man, seriously... he always jokes with Amadeo and they always talk... and I've seen how he looks at you... even Bruno told me... but you never look up, as always... one of these days I'll tell Bruno to send him inside with an excuse so you can see him...

- No... no... the last thing I need is a man in my house! I have my kids who keep me company. Forget it... it's late, go upstairs and give your husband some food. We'll talk about it another time.

Maria looked at her with compassion. Then, she reluctantly got up, set the table, rekindled the fire with a couple logs, and went to call the boys for dinner. She wrapped herself in a woollen shawl, black, as was used in Italy, said goodbye, and left to go home.

3

At the door at the top of the steps of the house, Virginia, still dressed for mourning and with her hair in a bun at the nape of her neck, poked her head out to call the children. - Attilio, Attilio, come, it's ready.

Attilio was carefully treating a wound of a chicken that, at the first distraction of the little boy, ran away.

- I was taking care of the chicken. It has a cut on one of its legs.

- Are you sure that it needed to be treated and that the chicken wanted to be taken care of?

- But if it's hurt it will be in pain!

- Not necessarily. Animals are different from us, and chickens' legs are always injured and I can assure you they don't suffer from it.

At that moment, they saw Lorenzo coming through the

gate with the empty cart. After having walked up the path to the entryway, he stopped in front of them.

-   Good morning, Ms. Virginia. It's a pleasure to see you.
-   Good morning, Lorenzo. I still have to thank you for the flowers you sent me.
-   I didn't know if I could dare, but I thought that without your poor husband nobody would have remembered your birthday.

Attilio hugged his mother's legs, who in the meantime petted his head gently, and then turned to Lorenzo.

-   Is it true that wounded chicken's don't suffer?
-   Yes, Attilio, chickens always get hurt by running around and they don't even notice.

Then, addressing Virginia: - I hope they brought you joy.

-   Poor Luigi, he always remembered. But yes they made me very happy, thank you. And thank you for everything you do for us.
-   Oh no, don't thank me. It is I who should thank you. If I don't work, I'm not well… And I also wanted to tell you that Amadeo is a great kid. He's quick, you know? He already has a clear idea of what he wants. These past few days we've been thinking of changing the way we work, because with the method we are using now there is too much pain for too little gain.
-   Listen, we were just about to eat. If you want to join us, I can add a spot at the table.
-   Ma'am, I'm all dusty. I'm embarrassed, and I was looking for Bruno to discuss tomorrow morning's deliveries.
-   Come, I'll give you some water. Bruno should be here any minute. You'll wait for him inside.

From that day on, Lorenzo often came for dinner or even just to say hello to Virginia, and when he arrived the children ran to him and he played with them. It was a discrete way to get closer to Virginia. He came very often, always very well-behaved, and he became a regular at the house. With great joy, Maria and Bruno finally saw a glimmer of hope for a change in Virginia's mourning.

4

San José
Christmas 1877

The Day of the Dead had passed, and small sweets were wrapped at home to give to the children in the neighborhood, a Sicilian tradition that had been adopted long ago even by those who were not Sicilian. The house had been filled with children, laughing and screaming as they had helped put on the candy crowns, but despite the cheerful atmosphere, that period, full of memories and regrets, had been bleak.

Then came the months of November and December, always meteorologically depressing, culminating in a harrowing Christmas. Friends came to visit them and keep them company every day, but sadness enveloped the big house, now without its owner. Amadeo had been on vacation for a few days and was now back in school. The countryside, asleep in the winter cold, waited for the warmth of the first sun that would present itself in just a few months, driving away the fog and the rain.

Some hunting friends had brought two wild rabbits and left them with Maria, who cooked them for Virginia and the children. From the kitchen, the aroma of rabbit casserole gave a true sense of comfort that reminded them of their origins in Italy. Maria often told the children about the celebrations and processions, the traditional dresses with rich fabrics and embroidery, the Christs carried on their shoulders, and then the life of the village, the food, the closeness amongst neighbors, the hard work, and the lifelong friendships. Amadeo listened with curiosity and even Atttlio always asked Maria to tell her stories. In those days, however, the stories were sad and even Maria was pensive.

While she ironed, Virginia listened distractedly to the constant chit chat between Nina and Maria, Nina speaking an Italian mixed with Spanish and Maria tolerating the chatter that did not interest her in the slightest but at least helped distract her. It was hot in the kitchen; the stove was on full blast and Virginia shuttled between the stove and the table where she was ironing, switching a cold iron for a hot one. Every once in a while, Maria passed by the table to take the ironed clothes and store them away. In the meantime, Nina continued talking.

Lorenzo finally arrived. He had the gift of bringing a few minutes of peace to the family. The children ran to meet him. It had been a few days since they had last seen him, but Lorenzo had stayed away precisely because he knew those days would be particularly sad and he did not want to disturb the intimacy of that first Christmas of mourning.

After having greeted everyone and having played with the kids for a few minutes, during a moment when Virginia was distracted, he approached Maria and spoke to her in a whisper.

- Maria, can I talk to you? It's about something very important to me.

- Come back here, no one can hear us.

They made up an excuse and moved outside to go to the shed.

- Listen, Maria, I wouldn't want to do anything foolish and so I'd like to get your opinion, since you know the family best.

- Sure, does it have to do with Virginia?

- Yes, of course. I'd like to marry her. Do you think that would be wise? How would she react if I asked?

- I see you circling around here and even Virginia has noticed. A while ago I spoke about you, a few days before she invited you to dinner. At first she did not seem to agree, but then I saw that she invited you and I also see how she welcomes you home every time. By now almost a year has gone by, she'll have to make a decision. If you like, I can try bringing it up, in the next few days, calmly, to see what she thinks. I'll talk to Bruno about it too, but he'd better keep quiet. He often behaves like a chatty countryman.

Maria was very practical.She knew Virginia well and cared for her immensely. She would have never done anything that would make her sad, but she realized that if she wanted to stay in America she had to remarry. Something told her that Virginia had already made her decision.

5

San José
1878

A year had passed since Luigi's death. There was a big party at the estate. Virginia and Lorenzo had gotten married.

There were about thirty guests, almost all of them Italians from the vicinity, the parish priest from the local church of the Virgin Mary, who had also wanted to attend the party after the ceremony, and many children who were running around.

The house had been decorated with white flowers, Virginia's favorite, and tables had been set up inside for the guests. The party was much less lavish than what the Italian community usually put together for weddings, out of respect for the memory of poor Luigi which encouraged more somber tones. There were still accordions that had moved Virginia, as well as the toast to the newly weds which made everybody raise their glass.

Virginia, beautiful in a dress made by a tailor they knew, tried to hide the melancholy and the memory of Luigi still fresh in her mind behind many smiles, but she was also happy. In the months since she had invited Lorenzo to dinner for the first time, she had grown to know him, appreciate him, and, in a certain sense, even love him, certainly not with the passion of her first love, but in a more mature, calm way. She looked at him tenderly, appreciating his dedication and his love for her and her children. Lorenzo was delighted by Virginia's sons and considered them as his own. They felt the same way and for some time now they treated him as though he was their real father.

In the late afternoon, a few started leaving the house, not all quite stable on their legs, their shirts open, with toothpicks in their mouths. The local white wine had finally improved. Lorenzo, who had just finished the umpteenth lap around the tables in Virginia's company, took a tipsy Bruno by the arm.

Some excellent cigars had arrived as a gift from someone they knew. Lorenzo took one out of his jacket pocket and split it in half. He offered it to Bruno as they observed the children chasing each other at breakneck speed in the garden. Lorenzo, as if to seal that pleasant moment, spoke.

- This cigar is pretty good, maybe a bit strong, but very fragrant. Take some before you go, there are too many for me. I don't smoke much. Come, let's go sit under the trellis.

He could tell that Bruno had something to say, so Lorenzo brought him away from the guest's path. Virginia, who had come looking for them, saw that they were getting comfortable, grabbed a bottle of fresh white wine, and brought it to them with two glasses.

The two looked at her lovingly and Lorenzo got up to kiss her forehead.

- Your company clearly did her good - said Bruno, watching her walk away. - She's been revived over the past few months. Listen, Lorenzo, you're a good guy and I know you will treat her well as you have up until now, so I won't give you any advice. That's all you need! But regarding the farm, allow me to tell you that you'll need to take the reins now. My job here is done. I am old and tired. I've done what I had to do, now it's your turn.

-    Oh no! Dearest Bruno, you're neither old nor tired, and we need everyone. In the coming days, we'll discuss it in more detail. If anything, we would reorganize the labor to give you a bit more free time, but that's it. You and Maria are much too important to Virginia… and to me.

Bruno secretly dried his eyes. The wine facilitated his getting emotional. But at the end of the day, that was what he had wanted to hear, and Lorenzo was truly a great guy. The two concentrated on the cigar and bit by bit they finished the bottle. It had been a good day.

PART V

1

San Francisco
1882

Moving to San Francisco had been a very difficult decision, and not only for Virginia. Lorenzo was also very attached to that house and that land. The love that Virginia had for her children had pushed her to overcome the obstacle of feeling like a guest in a home that wasn't hers and of working on a farm that she only partly owned, which was no small feat. Luckily the birth of two children, Harry and Florence, had brought more joy to the big home and it seemed that serenity was finally taking over.

Amadeo was now 12 years old. He had gone to the Notre Dame School of San José and now attended a local preparatory school to enter in the two-year economics and commerce course at Heald's Business College of San Francisco. This had been one of the reasons that had pushed them towards the city. Even Lorenzo's work was carried out less and less in the countryside and consisted more and more of maintaining relationships with customers. The city of San José itself had expanded so much that their farm, once far from the city center, was now about to be surrounded by houses.

Certainly, from the windows of the new house on Green Street, they could no longer see the fields and the fruit trees, or smell the sweet aroma of the country. But when it rained the mud did not get everywhere. Water came from the faucets and it was no longer necessary to go to the well. The light with gas lamps did not create the awful smoke that gave them red eyes and a runny nose. Everything was more modern, including the sewers and the new cable cars, the great novelty of the city, and the first rail trams that had once been horse-drawn and instead were now pulled by long cables placed in a slit in the middle of the road and driven by steam engines.

The house was large with wide windows that overlooked one of the parks that urban growth had respected, as Virginia had wished. It was also fairly close to the offices of Lorenzo Scatena & Co., the company that Lorenzo had created for the distribution of their goods. Lorenzo could even go to the offices by foot, first taking a nice walk and then taking a cable car, instead of using the cart that he happily left with Virginia.

Even Virginia went to the offices often. She had become a good accountant and had a very modern view of work. It was she, for example, who had suggested to entrust the cultivation of vegetables to other landowners so that Scatena would only deal with the distribution. In truth, she had remembered an idea that Amadeo had suggested a while before, an idea that was not viable in San José, but now, in San Francisco, had been put into practice. After the wedding, Lorenzo added his land to that of the family, so in San José they had large fields to cultivate and many workers. Being able to draw from other producers, as suggested by Virginia, allowed them to significantly increase their turnover.

In the evening, seated around the table, they commented on the day's events while Virginia came and went from the kitchen.

Amadeo spoke the most out of everyone. He was the most enthusiastic, curious, and eager to work. When he was free from his studies, he willingly accompanied Lorenzo in his visits to clients.

-     Dad, isn't that Bartolomeo, the one you were speaking with yesterday from San José?

-     Yes, he has a field not far from us. Yesterday he told me that there are two families he knows well, honest people, that would like to buy a plot of land next to his. They're Italian too, from Veneto. They left from Le Havre in France and they just arrived. But they don't have enough money. He told me that if we help them, then they'll sell us their produce. We can keep an eye on them and monitor how they work. At worst, we'll take back the land. But they seem like good people. Maybe we can do it.

Virginia always followed discussions closely, even when she seemed busy doing other things.

- And where did you meet Bartolomeo?
- I found him waiting for me outside Amadeo's school. He told me he just happened to be passing by, but I think he was waiting for me.
- Let's think about it. We've never lent money to strangers. How much do they need?
- I don't know. Bartolomeo told me what they'd like to do, but not how much they need. He told me that he's going back to the market again tomorrow. I could send him a message and ask to see him.
- It's a new idea, and what if they don't give it back to us? What if they sell their produce to someone else?
- I don't think Bartolomeo has dishonest intentions. We've known him a long time. He spoke about these people with enthusiasm, and not only about their agricultural capabilities.
- Let's think about it. This solution could be the future. It seems to me that it could be a new way to work: we finance farmers who then sell us their produce. Let's be cautious, but I'd be for it. At the end of the day it's not that different from what we are doing now in San José, but instead of renting out our land, we fund their purchase. I say we give it a shot, if the sum is not too high.

Work discussions with Virginia were always marked by a cautious optimism, and Amadeo listened very carefully.

- Tomorrow I'll send Bartolomeo a message, then we'll see. Maybe in the coming days we'll go meet them. We'll ask Bartolomeo to accompany us. We'll do something.

Then, turning to Amadeo: - So tell me, how's your school?
- It's wonderful. I have a ton of friends and they teach us so many things, like how to write well, arithmetic, geogra-

phy... I like the school a lot, almost more than the one in San José. The teachers say I'm the best, but if they saw what I'm capable of doing with new cultivations they would be flabbergasted, forget about math.

Virginia was always careful not to show favoritism among her children.

- Good, Amadeo. I'm proud of you. And what do you guys think of Attilio, who told me he wants to become a doctor?

In the meantime she had hugged the little one, who by now was almost as tall as she was.

- Good, that way you help people get better, there are lots of illnesses in these parts. But it's best that you finish this school first, then we'll look for one to help you become a doctor.

Attilio was very proud of his decision, especially because he did not particularly like the countryside and farming.

2

The summer was unusually hot and humid. 80 degrees in San Francisco was an exceptional occurrence. It had been raining for almost a month and, when the sun came out, the evaporation created an unbearably sticky humidity that only the evening breeze could send away, providing a bit of refreshment.

The Lorenzo Scatena & Co. offices were located on the first floor of a stone building that, despite the thick walls and large windows, did not stay cool. On the contrary, it was suffocatingly hot.

Lorenzo climbed the wide stone stairway and entered the office space where his employees had taken off their blazers and were hard at work, then he slipped directly into Amadeo's office, the door of which, as always, was wide open. Amadeo was also just wearing a shirt and had rolled up his sleeves. He was concentrating on a big book.

-   Hi, AP. What horrible heat! It's a strange season, but experts say it should rain. Let's hope. Have you done the calculations?

-   Yes, I just finished them. If you have time, I can summarize the week for you. So, as of yesterday, we sold 327 dollars of vegetables, minus the spending of 261 dollars leaves us with 66 dollars of profit. Potatoes have gone down in value a bit, but ours haven't. They are the best and clients are willing to pay for them. The price of all fruits has gone up. We should look for more pineapples because they are in high demand. Other than that, we're doing well. I got two more clients that I met today, good people. I didn't have to work hard to convince them. We still have 12 farmers that owe us a total of 1,750 dollars at an average tax rate of 6%. Everybody is paying and is thanking us. We've saved 12 poor people from the clutches of loans. To think they had asked them for 5% every week, they can't believe that ours is annual. Speaking of, to thank you for postponing their payment date, the Venetians sent you 6 bottles of wine. Let's hope it's not like last year's…

-   Good Amadeo. It's a pleasure working with you, but it was you who agreed to postpone the date. And as always you were right. So the wine is for you.

-   Thanks, but you keep it. I'll come have some with Mom one of these days.

-   Speaking of your mother, I talked to her last night. I talked about you. I told her that you're the real engine of this company, you're hardworking, and everybody respects you and likes you. Suppliers and clients. If you only knew how many people tell me about you, about how you treat others, the respect that you have… for all those who work honestly… It pleases me greatly. And your mother had tears in her eyes from the happiness.

-   Come on, Dad, stop. I'm just doing my job.

-   No, let me finish. You turn twenty this year and so I thought… we thought, with Mom, that we wanted to give you a piece of the company. I'm thinking 30%. You deserve it, you deserve it all.

- Thank you, but really, I'm just doing my job. I hope to do it well and the respect I have for honest people is the minimum. If you respect others, they'll respect you in return. It's simple. And anyways, when you see a farmer with their hands ruined by work, how can you think that he's dishonest? Somebody who works all day doesn't have time to scam you.

Business at Lorenzo Scatena & Co. was going swimmingly. In little time, they had become San Francisco's most important ship suppliers and the port was the most important port on the West Coast. The nearby silver and gold mines brought in an incredible cash flow, economic and industrial activities flourished, the transcontinental railroad, which was about twenty years old and connected the East and West of the United States, had given a huge boost to trade, and the city was becoming increasingly large, modern, and also dangerous. Crime and lawlessness were everywhere. Every day there were new cases of aggression and violence, especially around the port, where there were many dive bars and swarms of drunkards that often started fights. At times, late at night, some of them were picked up by groups of "enlisters" and forcibly brought on merchant ships, after which they would disappear for a few years. Organized crime was strong, Mexican groups and a large Chinese secret society kept the local police busy and often had the upper hand.

Amadeo had the ability of navigating through the trouble and managing it honestly. For this reason, Scatena was highly regarded in the business world and many people turned to Amadeo even just for advice. Every once in a while, however, he had to stand up for himself: at 20 years old he was almost 6 feet tall and weighed 220 pounds, and if he had to fight, something that repulsed him, he did not fear anyone.

A few months after the aforementioned conversation, Lorenzo convinced himself that the young man's share should reach 50 percent.

After a day spent checking on the cultivations in San José, despite being exhausted, he passed by the office to discuss this decision with Amadeo.

He found him washing himself in the bathroom sink, which was highly unusual, and in fact Amadeo, shirtless, was treating a cut on his arm and he had a large rip in his pants.

- AP, what happened?
- I fought with a guy.
- What guy?
- I don't know, I was talking to the Guazzone brothers to set a few things straight when a guy came and accused me of selling him bad stuff. But I never sold anything to that guy. He's one of the Mexican's henchmen. He came to cause trouble, I told him off, and he attacked me. He had a knife. But I had my hammer.

He raised his fist.

- We beat each other up, but I think he got it worse. It drew a bit of a crowd. The police came, then they stopped him and brought him away. I only have this cut. I think his nose is broken. Look at what he did to my pants.
- Be careful, there's somebody who is jealous of our success and hires Mexicans to scare us. But you don't get clients through bullying.
- Don't tell Mom, otherwise she'll worry. I'll go get changed now, since I've been invited to a party.
- Finally! You're always cooped up in the office. I thought you didn't have friends.
- When you're not around I run away to have fun… to throw a few punches… No, I'm kidding… Of course I have friends, and lots of them, it's the women that I'm missing…
- I wanted to talk to you… but it's not urgent. But you're not giving me the full picture, about the ladies…

3

To enter the party you had to walk through a gate guarded by two men in long black shirts with gold buttons. At the end of the path there was the house, an elegant stone structure of impressive dimensions, which was surrounded by a large garden with tall old trees. A marble staircase led to the entrance, where guests could already be seen greeting the hosts and helping themselves to various drinks. Outside, large torches lit up the main path, while inside everything was lavishly illuminated by large chandeliers. A pianist played popular melodies of the times and his music traveled all the way to the garden. Many guests, elegantly dressed, wandered around greeting each other warmly. There was a lot of joy and friendliness.

By now, Amadeo had abandoned his two friends to greet many of the guests. In fact, he knew almost everybody and almost everybody knew and appreciated him. There were many good things to drink and to eat, mainly Italian products, wines, prosciutto, salami, and, in a corner of the garden, even a full calf cooking over a formidable spit. Many of the people were on the terrace overlooking the garden below and the big fire next to which the spit turned. They waited with a certain impatience for the lady of the house to announce the beginning of the real dinner.

There were a few couples dancing and many young people, including the children of the hosts' friends. After having greeted and exchanged a few words with almost all the parents, Amadeo went to see what people his age were doing. They were joking amongst themselves. He greeted them, listened to their stories, and told some of his own, but his interest in that type of conversation wore out quickly. He politely distanced himself to go to the table of wines. While he asked the waiter for a drink, a girl approached him, a discreet beauty with smiling eyes, wearing a puffy cream colored dress that emphasized her slim body and face. She looked at him with curiosity and, very naturally, spoke to him first.

- Hey, are you Italian too?
- My parents. I was born in San José. What's your name?
- Clorinda.
- Clorinda - it's the first time I hear a name like that. Do they call you Clorinda at home?
- Of course they call me Clorinda. My father would never allow my name to be mangled or abbreviated. Clorinda was his favorite aunt, a spinster who spoiled him until he was 20 years old. I never met her because I was born here, while she stayed in Italy. She died many years ago. I feel like I've seen you before, but nobody's ever introduced us. What's your name?
- Amadeo Peter. But it's so long that everybody calls me AP.
- Now I understand, I've heard about you. You're the one with the vegetables by the ships… who last week got in a fight to defend…
- Drop it. I don't understand what they gain from mistreating people. He was a poor guy who lives by working intermittently. He wasn't hurting anybody. There was no reason to treat him poorly, they were beating him up for no reason, just for fun. And for that I ruined another pair of pants.
- Why another?
- Because this morning I also got in a fight and they cut my pants with their knife.
- But then you're the troublemaker!
- Not at all. I'm a good guy. I'm very laid back and I mind my own business, but when they make me mad, I react. But let's stop talking about my brawls. I also think I've seen you before, maybe down by the port, and if I'm not wrong you were with your father. What does your father do for a living?
- He's a banker.

-   What's your full name?
-   Clorinda Flores Cuneo. My father is…
-   … the president of the Columbus Savings & Loan Bank. Now I understand. So this is your house?
-   Yeah. My father organized this party to find me a husband, he says I'm getting old and that I have to hurry. In his day, girls my age already had two children…
-   Excuse me for asking, but how old are you? You look like a little girl to me.
-   Thank you, but I'm already 24 and maybe my dad is right… I need to hurry. Listen, I have to leave you now, I have to dedicate myself to the other guests… and I also need to look for a husband.
-   Alright, but don't disappear. I'd like to talk with you more.
-   I'm in my own home. I certainly won't leave.

The festivities no longer interested Amadeo. He looked for her with his eyes and followed her discreetly. Every once in a while he lost her and then had to search for her again. But the house was big and after a while he grew tired and looked for a place to relax.

Bit by bit the guests left and the servants began to clean.

Amadeo had found a nice, comfortable sofa that was tucked away and, partly because of his fatigue and partly because of the wine, he had fallen asleep sitting all crooked. Clorinda came and shook him gently, smiling. Amadeo awoke in shock.

-   Good morning AP, or rather, Amadeo Peter. Did you sleep well?
-   Oh God, I'm sorry. I must have fallen asleep. What time is it?
-   Just past two. You're the last one.
-   No, luckily. You're still here. I stopped here on purpose. You promised me that we would have continued talking, but instead you went to your friends and you didn't even so much as look at me.

- Are you always this direct?
- Yes, always. And I almost always get what I want. I'm stubborn.
- And what do you want now?
- To talk to you, like I said.
- Make sure my father doesn't see us, otherwise we're both in trouble.

4

Amadeo and Clorinda got married two years later.

Clorinda was the second of eleven children of Joseph and Maria Cuneo, another three had died shortly after being born. Four years older than Amadeo, she had experienced the various fortunes of her family. Born in Volcano, in the hills of the Santa Clara Valley, on the border of the mines, she had always been accustomed to helping her mother raise her numerous children. Born poor, she had lived through her family's economic growth, but she never forgot her origins. When her father decided to leave the mines and the great store in Volcano to move to San Francisco, Clorinda was only eleven years old. In the new city she began to attend the local school and, in her free time, she helped her mother raise her little brothers. When necessary, she also helped her parents in the shop near the port that her father had opened with great success. From that moment, the Cuneo family's life began to change because, along with the growth of the city, their economic conditions had drastically improved. Ten years later, Joseph Cuneo was one of the best known people in the city.

For Joseph, there was certainly a hint of paternal jealousy towards his eldest daughter, but in reality there was, above all, a natural inclination to not allow his children to drain the fortune that he had so painstakingly accumulated. Joseph had done a bit of everything in life since he arrived in the United

States at age fourteen. From farmer to gold miner, from merchant to real estate agent, he had lived and worked in New York, Virginia, and Baltimore. After Baltimore, he landed in Volcano, where he bought two gold mines, and then in San Francisco, where he consolidated his real estate holdings, becoming the owner of over 500 properties, as well as the founder and the largest shareholder of Columbus Saving & Loan Bank.

At the beginning of their relationship, Clorinda's father was not at all pleased that his daughter was seeing that Italian who, at the end of the day, despite being highly regarded and having a successful company, was a greengrocer. But with the passing of the months, he realized that young man was particularly intelligent, even though his ideas were a bit too liberal, and that he had a rare personality. Amadeo was deeply enamored with Cloe, as he had started calling her to the great disappointment of her father, and he would have married her even sooner if the old Mr. Cuneo had not been so firm. Joseph had to see him often to convince himself that Amadeo did not want to marry Cloe for her wealth. But Amadeo was not interested in the money, as he insisted upon during a private meeting with his future father-in-law.

A few years later, however, when he founded the Bank of Italy, Amadeo had to admit, a bit begrudgingly, that his marriage had helped him enter the closed world of important Italian-Americans and make a substantial leap that he would have probably been incapable of doing on his own.

5

Although only a few hours had passed, Amadeo was so excited that he could hardly remember the ceremony. He only remembered his mother in tears with a glowing face and the annoyance he felt when all those people came to greet him so warmly entering the church. Then he remembered that the door had opened and he had finally seen Cloe, on her father's arm, approaching the altar.

The stunning, radiant sun was dazzling from the big church door that made her shine as though she were on a cloud. The veils of her dress had puffed up and, illuminated by the sunlight, surrounded her like a celestial halo. Amadeo looked at her and was stunned. His eyes filled with tears and his hands began to sweat. This was something from their wedding that he would forever remember clearly.

The ceremony finally ended, despite the length of the sermon of the bishop, who had come just for them, and Amadeo felt as though he had awoken from a trance. He would remember not the wide stairs covered in flowers at the exit, nor the celebratory bells that, from two bell towers, made deafening rings rain down, but only Virginia's emotional hug and the joy of being able to greet everyone while holding his beloved Cloe by the hand.

They then joined their friends, many of them Scatena clients, and many notables, friends of old Mr. Cuneo, at home, where sumptuous refreshments were served, accompanied by an orchestra. The lavish reception had been a demand of Cloe's father who, as president of one of the city's most important banks and of many other businesses, could not refrain from displaying his social status at the wedding of his first daughter. Amadeo and Cloe would have very happily avoided it and would have preferred a toast among family and a couple days of vacation, just the two of them, but they had to succumb to the requests of her father. Virginia and Lorenzo had also willingly accepted the decision of a high class wedding: they still remembered the endless amusement of the wedding parties they attended as children in Italy. Even in San Francisco, the Italian community and the others, from Chinese to Irish, loudly celebrated that special day.

The Cuneo's grand home was glamorously decorated.

From the large gate to the staircase of the entryway, bouquets of white flowers happily contrasted the evergreen plants that framed the driveway. The tall trees were prepared to be illuminated by huge torches which then continued to the stairway in front of the house.

Inside, the rooms had been emptied to have large dinner tables and in the main hall they had made room for an orchestra and a dance floor.

The ladies wore the latest fashion. Some of the women had changed, as was common in those times: a more modest dress for the ceremony and a more colorful, low-cut one for the party.

For the dinner, Cloe had to fight her mother to get a dress that was simple, like she was. When she finally managed to take off the puffy wedding dress, she donned a suit, a white and beige jacket, and a skirt with few embroidered details. She finally felt at ease.

A large tent that could have protected the guests in case of bad weather had been set up in the garden. When Cloe and Amadeo arrived in the cabriolet carriage, as young people used in those days, which was also decorated with ribbons and white flowers, the guests had already invaded the house and food and drinks were happily being served in the garden. Their arrival was greeted with applause, congratulatory yells, calls, and whistles.

Waiting for them at the top of the entryway staircase were her father Joseph with his wife Maria and her grandfather Frank, and not far from them were Virginia and Lorenzo, while the many siblings were having fun with friends in the garden.

The waiters were busy serving drinks and appetizers that the guests enjoyed immensely. A big fire cooked numerous skewers that spread an inviting scent.

After the time necessary to greet all the guests and to drink the aperitifs, dinner was served while the orchestra played the most well known tunes of the times. The cutting of the cake in the center of the garden signalled the beginning of the dances.

Obviously, Amadeo and Cloe were the first to dance. Amadeo was fairly uncertain of the moves he had to learn not long before. Dancing was not for him, and when the room filled, he politely asked Cloe to sit down. The polonaise, waltz, and a new dance that had recently become popular, the Boston two-step, which particularly amused the youth, came one after the other. Amadeo, linked to his Cloe's arm, went around waving, talking to the guests, and clinking glasses. But he couldn't do it anymore; it was not his lifestyle, and he was not used to it. He took refuge on the terrace, where Cloe followed him.

- This is our party…
- It seems to me to be more of a party for our guests. Let them have fun. We're fine here, the two of us.

Leaning on the balustrade, they hugged each other and watched the guests concentrate on circling around each other from the large terrace window.

- Look at the elegance! And what jewels!

Amadeo, surprised by these words, looked at his wife, hugged her even tighter, smiled and kissed her on the cheek.

PART VI

1
San Francisco
1900

Relatives and close friends of the two families joined in the dining room of the Cuneo home, including Clorinda's parents, the hosts, Virginia and Lorenzo, Amadeo and Clorinda, and two couples of friends. After dinner they had gone upstairs to better observe the New Year's festivities of 1900. From the terrace they could see an extraordinary spectacle, streets lit in celebration, where thousands of people sang and danced to music. It was a blend of different melodies that they sometimes could recognize and at other times would confuse. You could hear the accordions, the mandolins, the drums, but then the shrill sounds of trumpets that dominated the scene also arrived. The chants and choruses, not always in tune, tried to make space for themselves in the chaos.

Downstairs, the hall was heated by a wonderful fire in the grand chimney, and the table, from which the men had just gotten up, was elaborately set and showed the signs of a dinner not yet finished. The waiters were in fact bringing the festive desserts with grapes and nuts that would be eaten at midnight, as per Italian tradition.

Some of their children ran around chasing each other and running their hands along the sweets to their mothers' great chagrin. Others, the youngest, had already fallen asleep on the sofas, exhausted from the tiring evening. The ladies had stayed seated at the table to discuss the latest fashion trends and talk about children and also to comment upon the recent distressing news of the plague that had hit some Chinese people in Chinatown. It was news that alarmed everybody, especially those who had frequent contact with the people at the port, where the first warnings had been given.

In the meantime, the men had already helped themselves

to some liqueurs and were savoring their cigars, while from the terrace they commented on the party below.

They also were discussing the recent news, especially Lorenzo who very often boarded the ships to check his cargo and talk to the commanders.

- I don't think there is much to worry about. It seems that it's limited to Chinese communities, and in fact nobody is taking Chinese people on board anymore. It seems that the epidemic comes from rats and I know that ships are now doing a thorough disinfestation. They still don't know if it passes from man to man, but if that's the case then tonight's celebrations in the streets could be very dangerous.

Cloe's father, who had already proven to be a great drinker at dinner, held a glass of Italian grappa that he had brought specifically for the occasion. Even Lorenzo had not held back on the wine and, with his glass in hand, observed the city below.

The rat issue was abandoned.

- I wonder how they'll celebrate in Italy. I telegraphed my relatives. I hope they received my well wishes. They are still way behind in regards to telecommunication.

- Look at the fireworks. It's my first time seeing them. They're beautiful but they also scare me a little. Listen to those explosions, they sound like cannon fire. And the light, magnificent. Let's hope they don't set fire to the city… They're almost all Italians down there, look at them, listen to the tarantella… Italy… I almost don't remember it anymore… I'd like to go back… I was still a kid when I left. Who knows what celebrations they'll have in Italy.

A bit because of the emotion, but mostly because of the alcohol, everyone was following their own thoughts. Cloe's father was keeping an eye on the terrace door out of fear that his wife, who had banned him from smoking cigars and drinking grappa, would arrive. He cleared his throat a bit and, careful not to slur his words too much, said to everybody and to nobody: - I almost don't realize it myself, but today we are entering a new century, the 1900s. They say it will be the century of modernity. Who knows what it will bring. With all these new inventions… the telephone, just 10 years ago nobody had a telephone, now everyone has one. You'll see that soon we'll be able to call Italy. And electric lights, electric motors, steam engines everywhere… we're old now, we won't see all the progress, but young people, they'll be the engines of modernity… Amadeo, what do you think?

   -   You're right. I think the next few years will be incredible and every year will be better than the last. There will be lots of work to do. I also think it will be easier to work and the machines will do the difficult work. Modernization is picking up speed. Just look at how much faster trains have become over the past ten years. And ships. Now you don't even see sailboats unless they are in the junkyards to be demolished. With a steamer you leave and arrive whenever you want, you don't need the wind to pick up, and you can run it with half the amount of crewmembers. A few weeks ago they showed me a steam-powered machine, basically a motorised ox that tows the plow. We're not quite there yet, but you'll see that in no time even agriculture will be revolutionized by machines. It would be a godsend for us, plowing a plot of land today takes time and effort, when there is a slightly smaller and more efficient machine, it will take half the amount of time and half the amount of men… We are living in an era of great changes… those who know how to modernize themselves will make a great fortune… out of all those poor guys down there, who are drinking away all their earnings tonight, the best will escape poverty and become wealthy gentlemen.

   Lorenzo pulled himself out from his memories: - I heard that they're trying to launch a new state-of-the-art passenger ship, with three classes, and the highest one will be very luxurious. Going back to Italy will be faster and more comfortable. It will surely cost a lot, just thinking about those old wrecks we arrived in…

Amadeo was still following his thoughts: - People's well-being will improve, but it will take a lot of money… for everything. This modernity… machines have already changed the way we work and they will continue to do so. New jobs will emerge, new professions… just think of the mechanics, those who plan, build, and also those who will have to do maintenance for the new machinery. Specialised artisans, engine manufacturers, electricians… Many jobs will disappear, but new professions will be born and the best will become increasingly rich… wealth will be the method of judging people, not honesty, intelligence, or righteousness anymore… it'll be wealth. If I have to speak frankly, though, becoming a millionaire doesn't interest me… What do you do with that much money? Nobody who is wealthy possesses wealth, it is wealth that possesses people… Look at what is happening in this modern society of ours. Every action is considered worthy as long as it brings you profits, even if it causes a competitor to go bankrupt. In fact, if it fails, it's even better, one less… Sorry, I didn't want to bore you with my foolishness.

His father-in-law turned to look at him with a mixture of admiration and disappointment. The originality of his words had struck him, and the liberal spirit of that boy had once again revealed itself. He gave him a stern look.

Amadeo, realizing that he had spoken too much, left to escape his father-in-law's gaze, going towards the table of wine to refill his glass. Then, returning to the others: - This wine is good, you can taste that it's Italian! Now, let's toast to a new century. I feel that we will be its key players.

With the bottle in hand he went to serve the others and then, raising his glass: - My dear friends, I invite you to toast not only the new year, but also this promising new century. Welcome to the 1900s, for us and for our children.

And everyone raised their glasses and drank.

2
San Francisco
June 1902

The funeral was impressive. The square in front of the church was packed with people, many of whom came from far away, and even more from the city. A large group had come down from Volcano, a village on the hills overlooking the Santa Clara Valley where Joseph and his family had lived for many years and where the majority of their fourteen children were born. A group of immigrants, like the old Mr. Cuneo, came from San Colombano Certenoli, in the distant Fontanabuona Valley near Genoa, in Italy. They kept to the sidelines, but did not want to miss it.

In addition to family members, all the most important figures of the city were in the church. A truck packed with flowers had been unloaded in front of the main door, and the flowers were then arranged on the staircase to form a stunning waterfall of colors. It was a memorable ceremony, which was featured in the local daily news for a few days.

A few weeks before his death, Joseph had spoken with his friend, the lawyer Cuneo, to get some advice. The two friends had the same last name despite not being related at all. Cuneo was one of the most important and influential lawyers in the city. His clients came from the city's bourgeoisie - industrialists, traders, ship owners; the most important real estate affairs were discussed in his office and his advice was always taken. He had held some administrative positions in the city but, before ruining himself with politics, he retired, leaving the memory of an active and righteous person. In fact, many of his friends who came from that experience still asked for his advice.

That day, Joseph discussed his will with his friend: he wanted advice on how to consolidate his estate and secure his heirs. He considered his family and his children, still too young to take care of his fortune. Luckily, his daughter Cloe had married that truly special boy, who Joseph appreciated immensely after having had the opportunity to change his opinion about his initial prejudices.

They spoke at length about that unpleasant subject, making superstitious jokes so as not to jinx it. Joseph mentioned it to his family that same night at dinner, and he even expressed his wishes. Then, still due to superstition, he pushed back the second appointment for the final drafting of the will until the day he was struck down by a devastating heart attack before having written down what he had said aloud.

The lawyer's office was austere, like almost all the offices of important figures in San Francisco. The fact that he too was an emigrant, and a son of emigrants, made it necessary for his personal and professional behavior, as well as the office decor, to be as far removed as possible from the image that Americans had of Italians. Cuneo always dressed in black, with a vest and crisp white shirt, an elegant satin bow tie, and an impeccable top hat that was also black. His office had a majestic quality, with a wide marble staircase connecting the entrance to the second floor where all the associate lawyers' offices were found. The conference room was furnished with woodwork as high as the ceiling, in glossy wood, with darker columns shaping the extensive bookcase that occupied three walls of the room. On the fourth wall, two tall windows radiated a soft light.

Almost all of Joseph's family was united around the table: his wife, Maria, who was almost fifteen years younger, and his children Cloe, Luisa, Frank, and David who were also representing the other six children, still too young. Of the little ones, only the young eleven-year-old Irene had wanted to accompany her mother and stayed glued to her side.

They had gathered at the request of the lawyer himself,

who had felt that it was his duty to inform the family of his friend Joseph's wishes and to hand over the document he had prepared and never shared. The atmosphere was deeply somber and they listened to Cuneo's speech without making any comments.

Cuneo made a long premise and concluded with what had been decided, but not put into practice, by his friend Joseph: the estate was to be divided equally among the children, but held together by an adequate financial structure headed by Amadeo, to whom he also left other shares of the bank, in addition to those he had already given him for the wedding, which would increase his share to 4%.

It was not a quick ceremony because the lawyer wanted to convince the whole family, without any doubts, of Joseph's last wishes.

3

San Francisco
1900

When they were alone, Amadeo and Cloe commented on the meeting.

-   What do you think?

-   How sad! Cuneo and Dad were really the same. Listening to him speak was like hearing my father. Even the intonation was the same, the accent too. But it made me very happy to hear the lawyer tell us that Dad thought of you as a son, the oldest of his sons. He was very attached to you. And to think of the conversations I had with him when I met you! How many times he told me "that Italian greengrocer." He changed his mind quickly. He would have been happy to have you at the bank, but he considered his son-in-law's presence as an issue for the other members. He didn't like it. Remember, I told you about it a while ago. Now his wishes can be put into practice. At the end of the day, you are the oldest of his sons.

-     He got me in a lot of trouble. I'll have to talk about it with Lorenzo and with Mom too.

-     Lorenzo will understand. It's not an insult to leave a family business for another company, which at this point is also part of the family.

-     I know, but Lorenzo just gave me 50%.

-     That was a few years ago. You worked hard to make it what it is today.

-     I have to think about it. I'm honored that your father thought of me, but I also believe I have some moral commitments to Lorenzo.

Amadeo thought about it all night and the next day too, then he discussed it with Lorenzo and with Virginia. Virginia, who was always proud of her son, released him from all moral obligations. Lorenzo struggled to hide his worry about having to work alone, without Amadeo's support. He was comforted by the certainty that, in any case, he would not abandon him entirely. He knew that Amadeo loved that company that had given him great satisfaction and that his heart still lay with Scatena, even though working with the bank and managing the Cuneo family's fortune were no small tasks.

He was partly wrong: Amadeo's heart still lay with Scatena, but his efforts were largely dedicated to the bank. Amadeo went from one place to another for a few months, but then his presence at Scatena became increasingly sporadic. When he met with Lorenzo, he talked a lot about his new job, usually with enthusiasm, and he described it as a wonderful lever for the local economy. But, very often, he came to Lorenzo's office disheartened by the limited visions of the bank's associates and advisors.

-     Lorenzo, I think we should find a solution for this situation which, I believe, is no longer viable.

-     Which situation?

\- I'm a member of Scatena, but I work for the bank, it doesn't seem fair.

\- I don't see the problem.

\- Well I do. I can sense the problem and it weighs on me.

\- I think you've found a new dimension to your life, why give it up? You're a member of the bank, a great bank, you're the sole manager, and you answer only to the Board. Why should it matter to me if you're also a member of Scatena?

\- I didn't explain myself clearly. The bank is not where my problem lies, even though my visions differ from those of the advisors. It's with you, with Scatena, with the employees that no longer see me here every day, and with the clients that no longer know who to turn to. And yet I'm still a shareholder of 50%, it doesn't seem fair!

\- I really don't see the problem. Everybody has the right to live the life they choose. As for me, don't worry. Even if I don't have the cheerfulness I had when I worked with you, I'm doing just fine.

\- Well I don't think it's fair and I wanted to ask you permission to sell my shares.

\- No, please. I don't want another partner here. I'll take them from you. It will take me some time to pay for them, but I don't want other partners in here.

Lorenzo was concerned; that solution would not suit him at all.

\- Relax, I won't sell to any new partners. You know I'm not interested in becoming richer than I already am. I have everything I need for myself and my family. What I'm thinking of doing is consolidating this company by selling some of my shares to a few of the employees. They'll pay me back over the years, giving me an income that will let me live like a gentleman. They'll be tied to Scatena and they'll do everything to make it successful. The other part of my shares I'll give back to you, that way you'll always be the greatest shareholder and there won't be a way to undermine your authority.

Lorenzo was stunned. As always, Amadeo had found an elegant and positive way to solve a problem. The emotion brought tears to his eyes. This was really goodbye to their collaboration.

-    Sounds like a brilliant idea to me. Many of the shareholders, probably all of them, will put their heart and soul into it. As an incentive, this is probably the best they could ask for. And then if they give you a decent income, it won't be too great of a sacrifice for you. How would you like to proceed?

Amadeo pulled a note from his pocket, handwritten but very clear, and passed it to Lorenzo.

-    I already have both the names and the percentages in mind. I wrote them on this sheet. You're free to modify them as you see fit, but I'd say that the structure could be the final one, even with the position changes that I marked next to each name.

-    I should have known that you had already thought of everything! I'll look over it today, then I'll arrange the property changes. If I think any changes are necessary, I'll let you know so we can discuss them. When would you like to talk to the other employees?

-    Let me know when you're ready. I would make envelopes with individual proposals so that we keep our assessments of individuals private, then I'd gather those involved and make a speech, the same one for all of them, also explaining why there are differences amongst them, even if they are not significant. At the end we'll agree on the final official transition with them.

-    Seems like a good strategy to me. Reading the beneficiaries here, I'd say they are a majority.

-    Yes, the productive ones are almost all there, at least the ones who deserve it, and even the differences in the quotas are basically comparable to their differences in salary. I thought to do that because inequalities cause discontent.

-    In any case you should know that the shares that you

say you will give to me, I don't want them, they're yours. If you want I can hold onto them as a trustee, as if they were a deposit, and they'll always be at your disposal.

In a couple of months Amadeo officially sold his shares of Scatena and could then dedicate himself entirely to the management of the bank.

4

San Francisco
1904

In the two years that followed, he was fully committed. In the beginning, he dedicated himself to studying accounting, which was different from what he had learned in school and from what he learned working at Scatena. Then he dedicated himself to understanding how the structure of the bank, the employees, the roles, and the sectors worked. He learned quickly, and after six months he knew everything, maybe still superficially, but enough to make judgements, and so he dedicated himself to the improvements that he intended on carrying out. He reviewed each individual sector, analyzing all the activities in depth, and established new rules and duties. He found problems in every sector that he touched, so he basically had to revolutionize the entire bank. Thus began the first conflicts, albeit small, with some of the advisors, but the benefits of the changes were evident from the beginning, so it was not difficult for him to counter those people who were so attached to the status quo and blind to innovation.

The relationships with clients improved greatly: his main objective was to find solutions for their problems, even at the expense of higher immediate revenue for the bank. Amadeo knew perfectly well that a satisfied client would be much more likely to use the services offered, thus bringing greater profits to the firm in the medium term. But the discussions among the Board of Directors were constant and more than once he was in the minority. He started a gentle revolution that aimed to modernize the bank and differentiate it from the others that worked in the same market. Less internal bureaucracy, easier access to credit, fewer constraints in the warranties, and more counselling services - these were the first objectives of his new administration. On the other hand, the advisors wanted to continue in accordance with the usual tried and true rules, and many of his innovative proposals were refused, politely but firmly.

After two years, Amadeo could not take it any longer and decided he had to solve the problem at its roots.

Amadeo sat pensively at his desk. The sounds of the street, the voices of the vendors, the neighing of horses, the sounds of the wagon wheels, a rare car roaring, and the rattling of the cable car came in through the window. It was a street that he knew very well, as well as its residents, whom he almost all knew individually. He got up and looked out onto that mass of people who seemed to move in a disorderly fashion but who, as he knew well, all had something to do. Amadeo observed them. They were almost all emigrants, mostly from Southern California, Mexico, and Central American countries, but many were also European emigrants, mostly Italians. He knew all the Italians, or at least knew of them, where they came from, who their parents or relatives were. They had em-igrated because life was miserable in their country and they searched for a better life here. An unbelievably full cart passed by, and the two riding it were clearly adventurers on the hunt for gold. He knew some who had come to the bank to deposit nuggets. None of them had really gotten rich. In fact some of them, in a short amount of time, blew their savings and became as poor as they were before. At that sight, he thought back to his father-in-law who had begun his American adven-ture as a gold digger, but who had then moved on to less risky and much more practical activities. He had been right and the bank was there to prove it.

The sun was setting. He had asked for a meeting with all the bank's main shareholders and all members of the Board of Directors because he wanted to make some remarks about the future that he deemed to be very important. He was determined: he did not like the way in which they were managing business, and he did not see growth within the bank. His attempts to make a radical change in the business had first clashed with his father-in-law's family, the largest shareholders, and then with the other members, all very close-minded and traditional.

Not all the children were pleased with the final wishes of old Joseph, who had intended for him to take care of family affairs, and they did not miss an opportunity to point out how much his management tended to stray from the now established common practices of local banks.

He heard a knock at the door.

- Frank, come on in, I'm glad to see you. Thanks for coming.

Frank was the eldest and most listened to son of the family, and also the one who had taken his father's decision the worst. Even though he had to appreciate the work that Amadeo had done both for the bank and his family, he considered his brother-in-law too liberal and too attached to the world of immigrants

Amadeo had him sit at the desk in front of him.

- I wanted to see you before the meeting because I have a few things to tell you. As you know, my ideas on how to run the bank are very different from yours. I had already discussed it a while ago in very general terms with your father, who disagreed about certain points, so I can't blame you for not agreeing either. Although he advised you to entrust me with the management of the bank, that doesn't mean he totally approved of my ideas, I'm sure. He probably hoped that, fully entering into the workings of the firm, I would change, not the bank. But this did not happen. On the contrary, I have become increasingly convinced that I'm right. The world is changing and we must understand it and, if possible, adapt to modernity. Don't think I'm presumptuous. Maybe I look at facts and people more closely and I try to interpret their needs and desires. That is where my ideas come from. I discussed it at length with your sister Cloe, and she agrees with me. I'm telling you this because I decided to leave the bank and make one of my own, made how I want it with the clients that I want. Don't worry, I'll make sure the bank doesn't have any problems. I wanted to tell you personally before the meeting out of the fondness and respect that I have for you. I have plans ready for my replacement that I believe to be best for your needs. Obviously then the Board will decide whether to follow my plans and then make all the necessary decisions.

Frank looked him in the eyes and was silent for a few seconds, struck by his words: he did not expect such a radical decision from Amadeo.

- I imagine your decision is final.
- Yes, you're correct, it's final.
- Of course. I was sure of it. You do realize that your project is in competition with our bank? And your shares, what do you plan to do with them?
- Trust me, I thought about it a lot. No, there will be no competition. We are on two completely different levels, do not fear. The new bank will target a completely different clientele from yours. It will essentially target the clients you have always refused, and it will also operate differently. Regarding the shares, I have to sell them because I'll need a lot of liquidity to finance my project. In the meeting I will ask the president to sell them, the associates obviously have priority. Just so you know, I will only sell my personal ones, not Cloe's. She'll decide when she wants to.

Frank, who worked next to Amadeo in the bank, was torn

between the relief of no longer being under his cumbersome and demanding brother-in-law and the awareness of how effective the work he had done had been.

-   I'm very sorry to hear your decision. You know how fond we, all of us, are of you and how much we appreciated and continue to appreciate your work. Frankly, I think you have a lot of courage, as well as very clear ideas. I would not be capable of such a thing. I wish you all the best, really and truly.

Then he approached him, shook his hand firmly, and left the office.

Amadeo watched the door close behind Frank. "There goes one of the biggest problems I had," he thought: "jealousy and a limited vision of the market." Frank was a good guy though, prepared, and he would take the reins of the bank, as was his right, leading it according to traditional tenets, as the associates wanted.

5

His secretary knocked lightly on the door and entered without waiting for a reply.

-   Mr. Giannini, they're all here.
-   Even the president?
-   Yes, and he seems nervous too.
-   Good, let's go.

He took some papers from his desk, looked at them, flipped through them, but then he put them down. He knew very well what he was going to say.

He opened the heavy mahogany door that divided his office from the conference room and, as though it was the first time, saw the austere, dark boiserie-clad hall and the table of the same polished wood reflecting the serious faces of the advisors. At the head of the table he spotted Fugazzi, the president, with whom he had animatedly discussed the same subjects on more than one occasion. He knew that he appreciated and respected him. In fact, it was Fugazzi himself who, at the suggestion of old Joseph, had made sure that he was appointed administrator of the bank, and Amadeo knew that he had never regretted it. The bank had never had as much success as it had over the past few years, but lately his vision of the future was no longer shared and neither of them gave up their positions, even in the conversations they had in private. Amadeo positioned himself at the other head of the table, but did not sit down. Instead, he moved the chair aside to have more space and to observe everybody's reactions. He looked around and observed them slowly.They were all very serious and eyed him carefully.

- Good evening everyone, thank you for coming.

His tone was low, calm, and confident. A murmur of greetings answered him, but nobody dared speak out.

- As I was waiting for you I looked out my office window and, as I observed the street, I tried to reflect on our society. In recent years, many major events have occurred that are changing the face of this nation. From the window, I noticed that very few Americans are involved in commercial or industrial activities, almost none. Where are the Americans? They are closed in their offices, they have large, prosperous companies that hire hundreds of Mexicans, Venezuelans, Ecuadorians, and Italians, French, Germans. In other words, immigrants. On the street, however, I only see immigrants, who, with great sacrificial spirit, keep small businesses going, such as fruit stands, vegetable vendors, butchers, laundromats, etcetera.

You are all well aware of the fact that my parents came from Italy. Italy is a very distant country, with a thousand-year-old historical tradition, unique in the world, with an immense cultural heritage, but it is also a nation with strong popular working traditions. A thousand years before the birth of America, streets, sewers, running water, laws, the army, cities, philosophy, economics, and art already existed in Italy at unparalleled levels. Three hundred years before the birth of America, there were already universities, hospitals, commerce, and banks in Italy.

Visiting Italy is a discovery that broadens your emotions, stimulates curiosity, and fills you with modern ideas.

Unfortunately I have never been able to see these things in person, but I have studied them on my own, at night, out of curiosity and because I believe that we should not forget our origins. My father, when I was a little boy, told me many things about Italy, especially about work. The work that farmers do in the country, sweating to bring home the bare minimum for survival. He told me about the work at the ports to load and unload the ships, the work in shipyards where workers died building ships and their bodies are abandoned at sea. He told me about the hard work in the fields and in the cities, about honest work and the dignity of working. And believe me, I believe in the dignity of working. I believe in it strongly, just like I believe that work brings justice to society.

Amadeo stopped and observed the advisors. They were all silent and very attentive and they looked at him with a mixture of curiosity and apprehension.

- Now let's come back to us. As I was saying, looking out the window I saw many people. I saw the shops, the carts full of vegetables, the blacksmith, and the laundromat owned by the Chinese. Two weeks ago, an old acquaintance of mine came to talk to me. He has a nice field, very well situated, on the road going to San José. He came to ask me for money because he wants to turn his vegetable farm into a vineyard. His family in Italy has been producing wine for two generations, an excellent wine, and he understood that this land could give him great satisfaction, and I believe him. He asked me for two thousand dollars.

A restrained but significant buzz arose in response to the amount.

-    It's not a large sum, but I also know that this bank is not equipped for this kind of business. This bank has 187 clients to whom we have entrusted over 80% of our liquidity. With this, we have guarantees equal to 210% of the entrusted. We are in an iron cage. The remaining 20% of liquidity is waiting for someone who is at least a second-generation American and who can offer collateral that is twice as much as the loan he asks us for. In fact, I could not give my friend a positive response. I gave him the money personally.

Several voices arose but Amadeo did not give them any attention.

-    I believe, and am firmly convinced, that banks, including this bank, have a social function, that they are the driving force behind the development of this nation. Banks must become the force on which entrepreneurs can rely to start or expand their business. Banks must guide progress, because this will create new opportunities, new jobs for those who don't have one today, and therefore new jobs for the banks as well. If society does not grow, the banks will not grow either. I do not see any bank in this city, or in other states, which is open to finance new businesses, and I think that is a mistake. I am perfectly aware of the risks that will arise, but I have great trust and I am sure that doing this will enable our bank to have the economic and social function that our country needs.

Amadeo stopped to look at the scandalized expressions on the advisors' faces. He had expected it, but hoped that at least one of those old bankers accustomed to having their dividends delivered to their doorstep without ever risking anything - that at least one, just one would have been enough for him, said something in his favor. The year before he had already disappointed the shareholders by proposing to halve dividends to recapitalize the assets. He had gotten his way, but he had also made himself some enemies. The advisors were, of course, also shareholders of the bank.

His brother-in-law Frank, son of the founder, remained silent and did not participate in the chorus of dissent that had arisen. Amadeo knew perfectly well that he did not agree: he could not allow Amadeo to change the state of affairs. Business was going well and there was no reason to change.

Amadeo looked around, observing the dark wood walls and the sad, unnatural landscape paintings and convincing himself he would not succeed. He would have been willing to take even a low percentage for small businesses. That would have been the solution he would have liked to propose to the advisors. 20% of liquidity would have been sufficient. But he felt that the reaction was completely dismissive.

- And what collateral could your friends give us?

Amadeo looked sadly at the advisor who had spoken. He had known him for a long time; his father was one of the first Italian emigrants in the mid 1800s, but maybe he had forgotten. Even his Italian last name had been Americanized. The question was offensive, derogatory, arrogant, and asked by a man over fifty to a man just over thirty as if his "friends" were up to no good.

- None. None like the ones that you mean. The only guarantees are honesty and attachment to the earth. The other guarantees, what you call "real collateral," are small and I don't think you would even consider them.

- And how do you expect this bank, which has enviable tradition and stability, to expose itself to those… those…

- No, I don't expect it to. In fact I'm talking about it to ask for your opinion. But, as I said, I already gave him the loan… with my own money.

Amadeo was still standing and his tone was calm, precisely to counter the advisors' agitation.

- I wanted to add one more thing. I believe that the rates and fees we apply do not favor the development of credit.

They didn't let him finish.

- Do you think we're here to give money away for free?

- That's unacceptable!

- All the other banks charge rates even higher than ours!

A chorus of protests rose up from everyone present. The advisors protested loudly without bringing up any valid arguments. They talked over each other, which resulted in nobody understanding anything. Amadeo watched them in silence, and through the cigar smoke he observed those moustached figures who held confused and antiquated beliefs amongst themselves. The president Fugazzi had not joined their chorus and looked sternly at what was happening.

Amadeo raised his hands to ask for silence. It was not easy, but at the end the shouting turned into a murmur and eventually the murmur died down too.

- Friends, listen to me. I know what you think. I had no doubts about your reaction… my hope… - Amadeo looked at the advisors one by one - my hope was based on the memory of your origins… I hoped to build on the memories of your fathers' struggles… my hope was also to make you understand that if this bank had more competitive rates and guarantees, it would be able to quickly gain many new clients, which would bring more work to the bank itself… but do not fear, things will remain as you want them to be.

The shouting had almost drowned out Amadeo's words.

6

- Gentlemen, members of the Board, please.

The president called for their attention. Everyone immediately fell silent. Amadeo looked at the president and he too stopped talking.

- I believe that Mr. Giannini has finished his speech and I believe I can conclude that the following proposals are to be voted on: lowering the minimum level for funding to a thousand dollars, is that right Giannini? Along with reviewing the policies regarding guarantees and rediscussing the rates and fees that are applied to customers. Mr. Giannini, would you kindly formalize the proposal and all for the votes?

He was an old expert and he knew that, if he had not interrupted that verbal battle, the bank would have suffered greatly.

-   Thank you, Mr. President. Of course what I have said must be put on record. I will personally take out any superfluous parts if they so happen to be included. If the first proposal is rejected, I will deem it unnecessary to present the next one. The first proposal is the following: Do you agree to allocate a percentage of no more than 20% of the bank's liquidity to the financing of entrepreneurial initiatives, no matter where they come from, or, in other words, eliminating the clause regarding American origins, and for amounts up to a thousand dollars?

President Fugazzi took the floor again: Let us vote for the first of Giannini's proposals. All in favor raise their hand.

Slowly, Amadeo observed the advisors one by one: nobody had raised their hand.

-   Thank you, and who abstains?

Only Fugazzi.

-   Thank you, and now the other side. All those who disagree, please raise your hand.

With much embarrassment, they all timidly raised their hands one by one. Only Amadeo and Fugazzi did not.

Amadeo took the floor, sparing Fugazzi from highlighting the refusal.

-   Thank you. The proposal is rejected and I will therefore abstain from bringing the others to vote, as they were contingent on the first. I would like to ask you to wait just a few minutes. I have to go to my office. I'll be right back.

As he left the room, he heard the whispers beginning behind his back. Contrary to what everyone in that room thought, Amadeo was happy with that decision. He had an idea in mind and he would finally be able to realize it. He went in and opened the safe in the wall, the one where he kept the most important documents. He took a large envelope on top of which there was a letter that he had already signed and he could now deliver.

When he came back the buzz stopped abruptly and everyone looked at him.

- Dear gentlemen, following today's Board decision, I feel obligated to resign immediately. This is the letter that I am handing over and that will be recorded in the minutes. My resignation is, of course, irrevocable. If there are no comments, I would like to ask the president to declare the meeting over. I would also like to inform you that I have already prepared the transition to the person you will indicate to me.

- Just a moment.

The president took the floor.

- Dear Giannini, two years have passed since I proposed to hire you as the sole director. I have never regretted it. Over these years the bank has had extraordinary results for which us advisors and associates would like to thank you. However, I must point out that the positions that you expressed today were not shared by me and perhaps by others, and the results of this vote confirm that. We therefore sadly accept your resignation and wish you a bright future.

He wanted to silence the others and dismiss the crisis without further public comments that could create problems amongst each other.

- Thank you for your kind words - said Amadeo. - If the president agrees, I would like to say just a few words. Eleonora, you are free to go.

The stenographer rose from her chair in the corner of the room and, in quick little steps inhibited by her tight, long skirt, quickly exited the room. She would certainly report what had happened to all the employees.

- Gentlemen, as you know, when I married the daughter of your friend Joseph Cuneo, he gave me a fairly large sum of the shares. Then, when he died, I inherited more, so today I own about 4% of the bank's shares. My resignation today is the fruit of a vision regarding the management of the bank that is different from yours. My role here is finished and I believe that my presence as a shareholder is now unjustifiable. I therefore put my shares at your disposal and I ask that the president take care of selling them. I thank you for these years of extraordinary collaboration and I bid you farewell.

He pushed the envelope of his shares in the middle of the table and, walking around the table, shook everyone's hand. Then, without waiting a moment longer, he slipped out the door and back into his office. His soul felt light, as if he had relieved it of a heavy weight.

"Extraordinary collaboration!" he wanted to laugh. He had fought every week for years with those close-minded old men who refused new initiatives and he had to give up so many ideas that now he was truly exhausted. But tomorrow a new life would begin.

He decided to go home immediately.

7

Two weeks had passed since Amadeo had announced his resignation from his father-in-law's bank to his family. He had not wanted to talk much to Virginia and Lorenzo about the disagreements within the bank or his plans. He had simply informed them that he had resigned. Lorenzo tried to ask him to come work for him again, but he received such vague responses that he understood that Amadeo had other ideas in mind.

One morning, Amadeo went to visit Lorenzo at the Scatena offices.

He entered the dimly lit lounge where a few employees were hunched over the desk with all the windows open. He was warmly welcomed; everybody wanted to greet him, and he spent some time asking each one how they were doing. Then he reached Lorenzo's office, knocked, and opened the door.

- It's been a while, it was about time that you came to visit us. If you only knew how much I miss having you here. I miss your strength and your ideas.

- I miss these offices too, and you as well. I can always reason with you and you understand things on the fly. I can't even begin to describe the struggles over there.

- Are you tired of working at the bank?

- Of course not! Working at the bank was perfect. It was the associates that weren't right for me. Every day there was one who came to teach me how to do things or who gave me advice that was the exact opposite of what I wanted to do. Out of respect, I wasted my time listening to them and I even had to thank them for the help they were giving me. But that's not what I wanted to talk to you about.

- I've studied the structure of the bank and its activities - Amadeo continued - and I've drawn some conclusions. You know Columbus has practically no accounts for emigrants? And do you know why? Because the members expect the bank to only deal with wealthy Americans, or immigrants as long as they too are wealthy. Their clients are mainly from the old Protestant groups because they are the only ones who can provide collateral. I wish you could see how many outstanding payments they have. Almost none! Do you realize that the employees are embarrassed to speak Italian? And what is an immigrant who has recently arrived supposed to do? And do you know that the minimum loan the bank agrees to is 5,000 dollars? And that they ask for the same amount in collateral? In other words, they lend money to those who already have it. Doesn't that seem absurd to you? If you don't help those who want to set up a business, open a shop, start an activity, how will the bank grow? And how will the city, the region, or the state? If new initiatives don't take off, businesses will stay the same and the same money will pass through the same hands. It seems like nonsense to me. And this goes for all the banks, not only Columbus, they're all the same. Almost every day our old friend came to ask me to send money to Italy. Do you know how much the bank asks for to send a few dollars to Italy?

-   Of course I know, I send some every year. Up to 20%, sometimes more. And it's not guaranteed, the risk of theft is left to those who send it!

-   Exactly. And you know how much it costs the bank? They organize the shipping with the carrier and the armed guards. The more money they send, the less it costs. The trip by sea costs almost nothing and the trip by land is at the risk of those who send the shipment. Think about the profits that the banks make, just to then keep that money in a safe. Not to mention the Italian ones that keep the money for two months before delivering it.

-   I know, I know, it's truly criminal.

-   And I also wanted to tell you something else. Those friends who came to talk to me often asked me for loans. As I said earlier, they all have an idea in mind: open a store, start a business, construction workers, carpenters, etcetera. And they asked me for 100 dollars, 200, almost never 500. And I had to tell them no. With a heavy heart, I had to turn them away. All the people I know, friends or friends of friends, people that want to work, grow, some of them who have been here for ten years. And there is not a single bank that listens to them. They told me about Wells Fargo, have you heard of it? It's a bank twice the size of Columbus, a giant. They can't get anything from them either, the banks made all the rules together and they don't deviate from them.

Lorenzo looked at Amadeo with a smile: he saw his eyes shining, he understood that there was more, so he settled into his armchair and took a cigar from the box.

-     My son, when you speak like this it's because you have something in mind. If you haven't done it already. Out with it, I'm ready.

-     I see you know me well! It's true, but I wanted you to know before I took the next big step... I've decided to open a bank. But a bank that works as I say, with lots of associates, with tiny fees without the possibility of having more than four or five. A bank that really serves the community, that loans to the poor, not the rich, those already exist. And that charges little. I'm thinking of a bank that has social value too, that makes income to support small businesses, that stays close to our immigrant friends, to Italians. We can't forget our roots. It's true that I was born here, but my connection with Italy is incredibly strong, my mother, my father, my relatives... how am I supposed to forget my origins?

-     I have to admit - he resumed after pausing - I've been busy these past few days... I set up the financial project, carefully assessed the costs and revenues and risks, etc. Then I asked myself where to open the bank and I even went looking for a place. I toured the whole city. I looked at where the other banks are... I know very well where they are but I looked at them in a different light, so to speak, for service to customers, not service to associates. I searched for a popular neighborhood with plenty of commercial activity. I imagined the bank and the people who come in to deposit the money that they hide under their mattress. Do you know how many people hide their money in their mattress? That money, instead, should circulate, support collective productivity, and give something back to those who deposit it. But that only happens if you trust the bank. That is what I want, a bank that plays an active role in business activities, not an enemy that just sucks up money. One that is close to you, even physically. Well, after lots of exploring, I found a saloon in North Beach that would be perfect for me. Maybe you remember it, it's on the corner of Montgomery Avenue. Anania Quilici is the owner, he's decided to retire and he would give me part of the premises. I could take over for $1,250 a year. It may not be a noble palace, but that's what I want, a strategic point that everybody knows because they used to go there to drink. In the beginning we'll share the space with the saloon, then Anania will leave us everything.

- That's a lot of money, but you've already signed the contract, right? You seemed so calm the past two years, I was starting to worry. What can I do?

- I've decided to put all my assets and most of Cloe's into it. I need help, there are many things to be done and I need someone I can trust. My presence and the fact that I'm risking it all in this adventure is not enough to entice people to buy shares. I also need people with common sense like you, well-known and well-loved, to help me and also fill in for me when necessary.

- I appreciate your compliments, but you know well that I have no banking experience. And I have to support Scatena. The help you're asking for could be very time-consuming.

- I know, I realize that, but, before you pull back, let me finish. I'd like to show you the calculations I made. You'll see that this adventure could become much more interesting than you think.

Lorenzo and Amadeo sat at the table and Amadeo showed him the sums as he had imagined them. There were many sheets of paper and it took them a couple hours to go through all the explanations and questions.

- I see - said Lorenzo as they rose from the table.

- Let me talk with your mother tonight. Actually, come to dinner so we can discuss it all together. You've already thought of a name too, I assume?

- Ah, yes, sorry, I forgot. I want to call it BANK OF ITALY.

8

The wind swept through Montgomery Avenue and many said it would also bring rain. Passersby fastened up their coats and held their hats so as not to have them blown away by the wind. The dust on the road was swirling and flying everywhere. The carriages had all drawn their shades to minimally protect the passengers.

The three-story building that Amadeo was renovating to house his bank was a pretty modest but sturdy building, and in a central position in the popular neighborhood of North Beach, where there were many businesses, almost all owned by immigrants, especially Italians. The cable car that crossed the city ran on a stretch of the spacious Montgomery Avenue. Market Street, with multiple docks on the port at the end, was not far away.

Amadeo had chosen to open the bank sharing the saloon with his friend Anania Quilici, and it was a saloon that, although very well-known, was in a bit of difficulty. A door separated the bar's rooms from the bank's. Inside, they put comfortable but austere benches in the main room. They separated the public space from that of the employees with a counter behind which there were two desks and some cabinets. Next to the counter was the entrance to three offices, one for Amadeo, one for Lorenzo, and a third, larger one for the other employees. In Lorenzo's office there was also the safe that you could see if you left the door open. They had discussed at length, he and Lorenzo, on the choice to welcome clients in an open space, and then they had opted for that solution, much more economical on one hand and much less austere on the other. For those who wanted a more private conversation, there were the offices. Their intent was to make it so that the clients, who were not used to going to banks, would not be intimidated and that they would understand that it was a safe space, and the safe proved it. The entrance at the corner of Montgomery seemed to be made for inviting people in, as it had a welcoming feel and was very visible.

Lorenzo came in climbing over tables and piles of cement, immediately overcome by a cloud of dust.

Amadeo looked at the sign: he had wanted it to resemble the one at his father's hotel. He had gone with Lorenzo, many years before, to see where he was born, in the hotel in San José. It was a nice wooden sign with blue writing framed in gold on a white background, and in a corner he even put a ribbon with the colors of the Italian flag so the Italians, even those who could not read, would recognize it. Even the name, "Bank of Italy," was in memory of his father and their origins.

He wiped his watering eyes, walked up three steps of the entryway, and called loudly:

- Lorenzo!
- I'm here, Amadeo.

Lorenzo came out of a door with a bunch of huge keys in his hand. Although he was accustomed to dealing mainly with agriculture, commerce, and accounting, Lorenzo was available to help with all kinds of grueling work, as in this case. He was happy for that boy he viewed as his own son, who seemed to have a tornado inside him, always active, always moving, always with new ideas. And what ideas they were! When he made him a partner at Scatena, the work increased drastically and the earnings soared. Amadeo was creative with a knack for business and if he was convinced of an idea he would not stop until he reached his goal.

- Amadeo! I wanted to give you the latest news. This morning I found 4 new partners and another 2 will come speak with me this evening. With these 4 we're at 31, that is if, when everything is ready, they sign. Somebody who knows and trusts you would want 20 to 30 shares, not 5 or 6. I told them we'll see at the end, when we break it all down. But they insisted. For now there is not a single American. But you're all white! How can you breathe in all this dust!

\-   Dust? What dust? It's just a bit of wind, it doesn't bother me. It doesn't surprise me that there aren't any Americans. They don't even come to North Beach. But we don't need Americans, we are enough. As for the friends, don't worry, that's fine. In the meantime we have to start the company by depositing capital, then we'll work out the distribution. I'm writing the charter with very clear rules. For example, the president and the advisors will not receive remuneration. You'll see, when they find out, they'll flee, nobody will want to be on the Board.

\-   I don't think so. Just the honor of working with you moves mountains.

\-   I hope you're right. Did you see the construction work? It looks like it's going well. Did you talk with Anania?

\-   Yes, I bumped into him by chance. He told me he wanted to come see the work they were doing. He asked when they'll be done, because he'd like to reopen the saloon, even though he told me he has no desire to anymore.

\-   Well, when he wants to leave we'll take his premises too. And the safe?

\-   Come inside, I'll show you. It's the most beautiful safe I've ever seen. We set the combination and these are the keys. One for the cashier, one for you, and one for me.

Seated on the steps of the entrance, the two lit their evening cigars while the wind swirled dust all around them.

\-   I'd love a beer.

\-   You have to be patient. When the bank is open, we'll have beer too.

Lorenzo turned to look at Amadeo. Through the puffs of smoke he saw his eyes full of dreams and determination. He smiled.

\-   Our members told us that they'd like to come visit tonight. They want to come see where they are about to put their savings.

- Good, everything is almost done. Let's just hope they don't all come together.
- Now all we're missing are the clients.

9

It had not been easy to put together all the members of the bank. Amadeo's idea was that nobody could be defined as the "boss" and claim total control. Setting the rules before starting the adventure was his way of putting his foot down, and he had not started reserving shares for the associates until he had written a charter the way he wanted it. The rules were very simple for him, but very difficult to make the others understand. Only Lorenzo had accepted it without further discussion. The revolutionary concept of "widespread shareholding" was tricky and the inherent uneasiness surrounding an institution like a bank was an obstacle for the partners who were artisans or small entrepreneurs. His proposal was to have multiple small shareholders without more than 100 shares a piece out of the total of three thousand and for an amount of no more than one hundred dollars.

When he thought the right moment had arrived, he armed himself with his patience and began visiting all of his friends, Italian and non-Italian, who he had met when working for Scatena and by whom he was greatly appreciated. He met with all of them and many participated, some with fifty, some with a hundred, but the majority participated with five or ten dollars, and this made him happy. When he had all the shares reserved, he held a big meeting in Quilici's saloon, adjacent to the bank, and the appointments for the Board of Directors were proposed. In the other banks, the Board members were also the shareholders, but in this case, with such a large shareholder base, this was not possible. The few who knew the realities of banking were amazed that the system had been modified to the point that there was no real owner of the bank. Even the nominations for the Board were an unprecedented novelty. On that occasion, Amadeo repeated the fundamental points for the management of the bank, namely that even the smallest loans would be made, even twenty-five dollars, that the bank would be equipped for the transfer of emigrants' money to their families at home at rates half that of the other banks, and that he would personally take care of the guarantees to be requested.

It was a heated meeting. People talked over each other, the beer flowed freely, but Amadeo skillfully managed to have everyone agree. The signing of the share certificates was unforgettable, and many of the associates did not even know how to write.

Amadeo and Lorenzo were very patient and after many hours they had gathered the three thousand dollars of share capital and everybody's signatures.

The Board members and the president still had to be nominated. Only then did he mention that the advisors would not receive any compensation, and that the president would not either, even though he would be busy full-time. Choosing the advisors was not difficult. In little over half an hour, they found the names among the most representative members, but then, when they moved on to the nomination of a president, as expected, everybody loudly cheered for Amadeo.

- My dear friends - Amadeo struggled to be heard
- I thank you for the trust you have given me by signing the share certificates and calling for me to be president of our new bank. But believe me, if I accepted this presidency, the message would be clear: this is the bank of Giannini. I don't want that to be the case, I would like this bank to be all of ours. Even though I had the idea, even though I worked hard to realize it, and even though I will continue to work hard to make it a great bank, I think that this must remain the bank of the Italians, of all of you, of all of us, of all the immigrants that

are working hard in San Francisco to support their families here and in Italy. So, don't take it poorly, I thank you again for your proposal, but I believe that in this initial period the bank can do without a president. We will see in the future who deserves this role.

A roar of applause drowned out his last words and the glasses were raised. The position of president was left momentarily vacant, and Amadeo accepted the vice-presidency.

10

As soon as he had joined Columbus Savings & Loan, Amadeo had wanted to do a period of study. He did not need lessons on the accounts, on the contrary. Instead he had observed everything that unfolded in those offices, who the clients were, how and by whom they were greeted, the procedures, the interior design, how the secretaries dressed; and he had come to the conclusion that the bank had to change. He dreamed of something closer to the clients, where people felt safe and were not intimidated. Less valuable dark wood and more smiling faces. He had made it a habit to go down to the bank's lounge to greet clients and in the meantime he checked on how the employees behaved. He knew what the men wanted and how you had to behave with the women. He knew how to dissolve the distrust of those customers who entered the premises for the first time. In his office, he had liquors and cigars to offer those who came to visit him. The clients of Columbus Savings & Loan were almost entirely high-ranking people and often it was he who went to their offices to discuss business. There were very few women. He had noticed that one of the employees had a particularly gallant way of behaving. He moved him to the center of the entrance hall so that he was the first person seen when entering the building. This employee was a handsome man, very capable, polite, available to everyone, and very much appreciated by the ladies. Amadeo had also noticed that ever since he was hired, the savings had significantly increased. The two things were certainly related.

- Lorenzo, do you remember Pedrini, that worker at Columbus who was at the center of the entrance hall? I was thinking of hiring him and putting him in charge of the lounge. What do you think?

- I didn't know he had quit.
- Actually, he hasn't quit.
- But he won't leave that position to come to us.
- He is very fond of me. I'd like to try to make him an offer.
- It won't be easy, and who knows how much he is earning now.
- Seventy dollars.
- A lot, but worth every penny.
- Yes, he was one of the best-paid employees. But you're right, he's worth every penny.
- For now let's focus on opening.

11

Eleven o'clock in the morning was perhaps not the most suitable time to offer wine, but Amadeo had not given up the Italian tradition of toasting to all happy things, and the opening of a new business was certainly a joyful occasion. It was also tradition to invite friends, acquaintances, and previous coworkers with whom you got along well to offer them a good glass of wine, a slice of salami, and a piece of cheese, all strictly Italian products.

The sun was hot even though autumn had already arrived and some sporadic storms had refreshed the air. Many had come, for just a few minutes, but there were still many -

butchers, bakers, farmers, merchants; they had come to shake Amadeo's hand and congratulate him, then they had gone back to work.

At one, Amadeo and Lorenzo were waiting for people to arrive, but by now the crowd had subsided. A few stragglers were still inside commenting on their surroundings, sitting on the benches, drinking wine, and smoking cigars.

Amadeo and Lorenzo were at the door. Amadeo was not in a good mood. He had hoped to collect deposits from that first day and he did not dare express his concerns to Lorenzo, who would go tell his mother and worry her.

- What did you think of it?

Amadeo almost jumped at the question.

- What?

- The day. It seems to me that it went well. Lots of people came, lots of potential clients, a few deposits, not many, but today is the first day. We can't expect too much.

- Yes, I agree, even though I was hoping for something more.

- You don't seem convinced.

- Well, I'm never satisfied. In fact, I was thinking about how to gather more. I think I'll go back to writing to people like I did with clients of Scatena. What do you think?

- You'll have to write lots of letters. It's not the way it used to be, now there are many clients.

- Yes, there are many, and I can't even go talk to my father-in-law's friends. It would not be proper, and in any case, I don't think they would listen to me. I have to collect small sums, but from lots of people. It will be hard work.

- You'll also have to offer them money in loans, not just ask.

- That's what frightens me. With the deposits we have in cash, we can satisfy a maximum of ten customers, and I would rather not start using our liquidity right away.

Amadeo continued looking around, hoping that some new

friend came up to greet him, but the passersby did not so much as look at the two austere gentlemen standing at the door. The wind, still hot, pushed the leaves in disarray, sweeping them against the sidewalk and under the front steps. He watched a dog walk by and sniff around, leaving his traces on the wall of the building across the street. The dust that rose with the wind remained suspended in the air and left it cloudy and bothersome. A storm loomed ahead, undecided whether or not not to release itself. Lorenzo and Amadeo went back into the office.

- Do you think you'll go eat at home?
- No, I don't think so. Are you going to Mom?
- I'm actually waiting for her here… because we wanted to ask you if you'd accept for us to entrust you with our savings.

Amadeo whipped around to look at Lorenzo who, one step behind him, watched him with a mix of joy and pride.

- Are you joking?
- Not at all, Virginia should already be here.

It was October 17th, 1904, and the Bank of Italy had just been born.

PART VII

1

San Francisco
1904

After two weeks of work, the total reached 70,000 dollars, not an excellent sum but one that gave them hope. The problem was that Amadeo, immersed in the promotion of the bank, had already granted more than $90,000 in loans, drawing from the funds made available to the bank by himself and Lorenzo.

Lorenzo, however, was worried because he did not want to find himself in a situation where he would have to draw heavily from his and Amadeo's savings if they ever lacked liquidity. And even the optimistic reassurances of the latter could not change that.

- Lorenzo, please, don't worry. Every day I meet about ten people who assure me they will bring us their savings.
- Watching you it seems that everything is going smoothly, but I've already heard that some of the associates are worried. This morning Ambrogio and his friend the butcher came to ask for updates.
- And what did you tell them?
- That everything is going well, obviously. They asked me embarrassing questions with a lot of "they say" and they wanted to speak with you. I struggled to keep them calm.
- Tomorrow I'll stop by. We just have to hold on for a month and you'll see, everything will fall into place, just as we want it.
- I hope so, but go see them tomorrow.

The next morning Amadeo showed up at his friend Ambrogio's workshop. It was a small tailoring shop and his whole family worked there, plus two laborers.

- Hi Ambrogio, how are you? Lucia! What are you doing here at this hour? Your scoundrel of a husband makes you work instead of staying at home to take care of the kids. I'll set him straight…

\-   I'm not the only one he makes work, you know? If you go in the back there's also his mother who sews and can't even see with one eye. Ambrogio is a beast!

Amadeo had entered the workshop smiling and as usual he joked around with everyone.

\-   Ambrogio, come here. I have to scold you, your wife told me to.

\-   Nice going, you joke around but nobody works around here. If I'm not here to make sure they spin the thread, these guys slack off. And those two punks that I hired drive me crazy, I should kick their butts…

\-   Calm down Ambrogio, don't get worked up. Come, I want to talk to you.

Amadeo took him by the arm and they left the workshop. Ambrogio grabbed a jacket on his way out and put it on directly over his tank top.

\-   My friend, how is work going?

\-   I can tell you, since you don't collect my taxes. We're doing well, we work and we don't even have too much of a hard time with our payments. Then, you know that project I told you about…

\-   Of course I know, I remember everything. When do you want to start?

\-   I found a nice shop nearby. If we walk a little further I'll show you, come with me.

\-   Lorenzo told me you're worried about the bank.

\-   Well, you know, the rumors that go around. They say you lent more money than you have.

\-   That's all true. We collected over 70,000 dollars but I lent out over 90,000. To people like you, people who work. Should I have told them no? You asked me for two hundred dollars, do you not want me to give it to you? Do you want me to tell you that I don't trust you? I'll give it to you even if that means I have to pitch in my own money! And the same goes for the others. What should I do? Tell me.

\- Well yes, you're right, but if the money isn't there...

\- Trust me, every day I meet people like you who ask me for money, and at the same time they make it so their relatives entrust me with their savings. There is a lot of money in mattresses... a lot of money. I just have to show that I am a trustworthy person, that I don't throw it away, that I make it circulate well, that I am reliable enough not to lose it. And then, don't forget, Lorenzo and I have built a sort of guarantee fund, pretty solid, with our own money, already at the bank's disposal. And thanks to that fund we were able to lend more money. Don't worry, your money is safe, trust me.

\- Yes, there is a lot of mistrust going around, but everyone speaks highly of you. I knew about the guarantee fund, but now that you tell me about it, I'm much more reassured. Come, look, that is the door of the shop that I was telling you about and the window on the side is also part of the shop. And behind there is a cool, refreshing room for the workers.

Amadeo observed and approved.

\- You can already picture it. I can put a mannequin with a jacket, nice stuff, the kind of stuff that attracts clients. Not like that hole in a wall where I am right now.

\- Very nice. How is it inside?

\- Two big rooms, one with a light in front of it and the other with a large window in the back, and upstairs there is another room where maybe my mother can sleep so she can finally move out. We can't take it anymore. Me, my wife, two kids, and my mom in two rooms... we don't know what to do. This would be a nice solution. I could already get some fabrics ready... If you help me, I'm ready.

\- You don't even have to ask. Whenever you want them, I'm here. In regards to the bank, trust me, in less than a month we will have ten times as much money. Do you believe me? No? I see that you're perplexed, so you know what? I'll bet on it! And you know that I never make bets! But I am sure I'll win because I see how things go every day.

In the following weeks, Amadeo doubled his efforts to find new deposits: he had to keep his word and, if he failed, he risked losing credibility exactly in that crucial moment. Maybe that promise was a bit exaggerated but, as the days went by, he realized that his name was more known and respected than he thought. At the end of a month of hard work, the total reached an extraordinary sum of 700,000 dollars.

Exactly ten times the amount thirty days before.

When he communicated this to Ambrogio, the latter demanded to pay the bet in the middle of the street after having called all his friends and having delivered a nice speech with a pitcher of beer brandished as if it was a trophy. Enthusiastic as if he was the one who had won the bet, Ambrogio paid for beers amongst the laughter of the crowd.

2

Sitting in the representative's office, Amadeo and Lorenzo were commenting on that unusual evening's events. After Ambrogio's animated speech, many had come to congratulate both Amadeo and Lorenzo. News of the bet spread amongst the emigrants and many came to deposit their own earnings out of excitement.

- Lorenzo, I think we will have many customers in the coming days who have heard of us by word of mouth, and you need to be the one who welcomes them. I don't want the bank to be centered around me.

- But I don't know anything about banking. Just because I've been helping you these days doesn't make me a banker!

- Don't kid yourself! You're skilled in everything you do. You've taught me a thousand things and now is not the time to be modest. Know that I trust you fully and that whatever you do is certainly the right thing to do.

- You catch me by surprise, but thank you. I'll try to do my best.

Then he changed his tone, as he did when he wanted to discuss personal affairs, and said:

- By the way, I wanted to tell you something… I talked to Virginia too and she agrees with me… I've decided to sell Scatena.

Amadeo looked at Lorenzo with inquiring eyes.

- Why?

- I feel lost in the office without you. I've missed you as a coworker and as a friend. Recently when I was in the office I couldn't wait to come here to help you. Even though you never asked me to, this is the right decision I had to make. And the bank needs to collect more deposits. In a few days I'll seal the deal and then I can give you what you deserve from the sale of the shares that you had left me as a deposit.

Lorenzo had only said part of what he thought. The truth was that, alone, he didn't have fun any more and he searched for excuses to go back to Amadeo. Being able to collaborate with him excited and calmed him. The sale of Lorenzo Scatena & Co. was a logical consequence of his increasingly important commitment by Amadeo's side.

- Do you already have a buyer?

Amadeo played dumb, but he already knew everything, who the buyers were, who had expressly gone to speak with him, at which price they would buy and when. He just didn't want to take away the joy of surprise from Lorenzo.

- It's almost settled, there were three contenders and all very trustworthy. You know them all, but I've made my decision and in a few days we'll sign the contract.

- So we'll have to hold a meeting of the associates like we did earlier.

Lorenzo looked at him, puzzled.

- For what?

- In the meantime I think it would be best for us to inform our associates of the bank's progress. In these past few weeks many important things have happened. And then, I've thought about it long and hard, I'm going to propose your nomination as president.

- Are you kidding? Me? Who doesn't know a thing about banking?

- It may be true that you don't know anything about banking, but you are the most honest and capable person that I know. And in any case I am vice-president, so there is no need to fear.

Amadeo and Lorenzo were seated in the big office. Night had fallen and they were very tired; the day had been full of emotions and tiring in many ways.

Amadeo wanted to return to his Cloe and Lorenzo to his Virginia.

- Amadeo, I'm tired but, I admit, also excited. I'm going home. We'll see each other tomorrow morning.

- Yes, I'm going home too. We'll see each other at six thirty. Don't forget that from now on this is your office and so you can furnish it as you please.

- Thank you. I don't deserve neither the nomination nor the office, but if that's the way it has to be then that's alright with me… I only fear that, now that you've unloaded the hard work on me, you'll have the time to come up with some other idea.

Amadeo smiled. In truth, now he was only thinking about how to strengthen the bank and have it function well, then he would think about its expansion. Of course he wanted the Bank of Italy to become a big bank. He was impatient, but he also knew that he had to take it one step at a time and not rush things too much.

The heat of the day had given way to a cool and pleasant breeze that rose from the sea. Lorenzo and Amadeo's carriages were ready behind the building. When the stable boy saw them coming he removed two sacks of feed from the horses' mouths, tightened the straps of the harnesses, and held the horses still as they climbed in. They had two similar carriages, small, very light with two big wheels and a folding cover that, in case of rain, protected them from the water. The carriages had a single horse that was more than enough.

3

San Francisco
1905

It's not that Amadeo was unhappy, but he wasn't particularly satisfied with how business was going.

In the months after the opening he had struggled a great deal to organize the bank, educate the employees, make the technical arrangements for currency transfers, take care of the clients, and manage everything necessary for it to function properly.

He monitored everything and everyone because the inexperience of some of the employees could create some problems. Even Lorenzo, who put his heart and soul into the project, was constantly asking him for advice and presenting him with problems. Even though he tried to delegate tasks to others, every problem inevitably passed by him and his employees expected that only he had the solution. He could never be far from the bank. He had to be present at every moment, and this bothered him quite a bit because he had always been used to moving around, going out with people, talking, seeing, and understanding the needs of those around him.

In short, he had the impression that he alone had to bear the weight of all the work. However, being a practical man, he tended to seek solutions and apply them as quickly as possible. His belief was that if there is a problem there must also be a solution; if the solution does not exist, then the problem cannot be considered as such.

One morning, after having observed at length the behavior of the employees and the clients, Amadeo called Pedrini into his office.

- What do you think?
- In my opinion, you have to separate some duties by entrusting them to different people and, if I may say so, you should delegate some responsibilities to others. You can't continue doing everything yourself.
- Give me some examples.

Amadeo had developed a very trusting and honest relationship with Pedrini. Now Pedrini was trying to tell him that the salon would operate better if different tasks and responsibilities were given to the same employees. It was a good solution. By differentiating the skills, they could expand the services and be more efficient.

Amadeo was used to sharing even the smallest decisions with Lorenzo, with whom he had an extremely close relationship. So, in the afternoon, he brought Lorenzo and Pedrini into his office and, together, they studied the new placement of the employees, with a new distribution of the tasks. In the following weeks they chose the workers, trained them, and entrusted them with the new duties. They had to change a few things, but in the end they realized that it was a step in the right direction. Work flowed better and the clients no longer had to spend half the day doing an operation that should take half an hour.

The first step had been taken, now it was a matter of seriously dealing with the expansion of the client base. Their closest friends had all been contacted and those who wanted to become a client had already done so. Now they had to think of the others.

Years before, in the early days of Scatena, Amadeo had thought of writing a letter to potential clients in which he complimented their products. He had written them all by hand, about a hundred, and the result had been extraordinary. Of course, discussing produce and discussing money are very different things. Moreover, at that time there was no advertising and his letters were an absolute novelty, while now there were often small sections in the newspaper inviting people to buy various products. That was not what he wanted to do. He didn't want the name of his bank to become confused with shaving cream or a cough syrup. Furthermore, he was firmly convinced that the inhabitants of San Francisco were still hiding their savings at home because they ignored the existence of banks or because they were suspicious of them. He had to entice those people to have trust, even though he realized that talking about money with many of those people could have a counterproductive effect. He had to think about it for a long time.

Amadeo slept little and woke up very early in the morning. He liked laying in bed with his eyes open, thinking and making plans. Those were the most productive moments for him. Looking at the ceiling, he reflected on the problems that beset him. He had learned that other banks, two in particular, were trying to counter his growth by spreading defamatory rumors and slander, which were difficult to counterattack due to the lack of precise accusations and identifiable accusers. Amadeo felt stuck: his practical disposition and honesty did not allow him to use the same unorthodox practices as his opponents. He was firmly convinced that facts would disprove the slander, but he was well aware that this would take time.

He asked for advice from some of his lawyer friends, including old Mr. Cuneo, with whom he had remained on excellent terms, but he understood that in practice these problems were related to his main dilemma: the growth of the bank, the increase of deposits, and the increase of the clientele in general. Having reached an adequate size, he thought, all these problems would disappear.

Amadeo, however, was in a hurry. He was not capable of waiting for the good work, honesty of his character, and willingness to help the weakest people to take action and form a slow but steady propaganda campaign.

That was one of his main arguments in his discussion with Lorenzo.

- I'd like for us all to realize that the true assets of this bank are not the money it has in the safe, but its credibility. If you are considered a crook, you will only attract clients of your kind, criminals.

- I know, Amadeo. I think all of us at the bank agree, us and all the employees. We bend over backwards to be as kind and efficient as possible with our clients. But it's not enough, who enters the bank is already our client and, no matter how well they might speak of it amongst their friends, I don't think anybody spends their time advertising for us. If I may, I think that there is only one solution to these problems and that it inevitably comes from you: you have to work on a personal level again, in person, to let it be known that things are going very well and that you are not the rogue that our competitors say you are. Only you can do something to stop this disgrace.

- I know. Unfortunately I know. What I don't know is who started spreading these rumors. Do you realize that I wanted to create a bank with widespread shareholding precisely to avoid that it be seen as my bank? And now I have to go back and use my credibility as leverage. Does a life of honest work not mean a thing in the face of some barely whispered slander? In any case you're right, only I can defend my name and the name of our bank. What angers me the most is that I've never done anything to push a client away from another bank to come to us.

The first thing Amadeo did was commission a few interviews with local newspapers in which he told his story and described the birth and goals of the bank. Then he had hundreds of flyers declaring the favorable economic conditions printed, in Italian and in English, and he distributed them house by house to all of South Beach, without differentiating between Italian or non-Italian immigrants. Finally he resumed touring the city and going to visit his merchants and artisan friends. His goal was to understand, through speaking with them, what valid arguments could be used to attract new clients: his targets were all the people who did not yet have relationships with banks.

He spent a lot of time with these people, even hours with some more intimate ones. He wanted to know everything about their work, their family, if they had relatives in Italy, and how they dealt with their money. If they were not Italian, he asked about their country and empathized with them. Amadeo spoke Spanish and French pretty well. It wasn't easy: his figure alone, large and austere, instilled fear, not to mention the social difference that these artisans, modest but proud, felt in his presence. More than once he was "courteously" kicked out, but most of the time people listened to him. They listened to the stories about his family, of his father being killed for a dollar, of the hard work in the fields that he had also experienced as a child, and of his project of creating a bank for the most vulnerable that was different from all the rest. With these arguments he sometimes managed to crack the shell of distrust, but he often had to explain what a bank was, what it was for, who the people who worked there were, and that the money that was deposited there was safe, much safer than it was at home. He was trying to convey a new sense of trust to his client-friends by including them in the success that he had managed to achieve.

In the end he convinced himself that only a proposal for concrete, well-structured action that favored the immediate interests of these people would convince them to overcome their hesitation and enter the bank. The action he had in mind consisted of transferring money to Italy more quickly, less riskily, and less costly. Only four years earlier, the United States had complied with the so-called Gold Standard, which regulated the convertibility of money into gold, but the convertibility was very difficult to implement when states were so far and so different from one another, so money transfers were often directly done with gold coins. The system, as could be easily guessed, was very dangerous and very costly. Amadeo, who was on good terms with some banks in Italy, turned to them to understand how it could be done, keeping in mind that, having many clients among the emigrants, the amount of money to be sent to Italy could be considerable. He thus reached a good balance of costs, speed and safety, which allowed him to offer his customers a service that was unparalleled in the area.

At that point he turned once again to using flyers that had given him excellent results in the past. In these leaflets he introduced the bank and proposed the fast and economical service for the sending of money to Italy. He spoke as an Italian to the Italians and in no time both Amadeo and the money transfer service became the talk of the town.

When the first clients started showing up at the bank, Amadeo realized that the system could work, even though it was very laborious, time consuming, and not resolutive on a large scale.

Amadeo did not stop at these results and he even developed a very original system for collecting savings, playing off of the desire of parents to create a fund for their children. With information he got from the registry office, he came to know the names of the newborns among the Italian immigrants, and to these he gave a "Savings Book" in which he had already deposited a small amount. The booklets were supposed to entice the parents to add more money from time to time to create a nest egg for their child. These families became clients of the bank and the booklets remained active for decades.

The results of all these acts proved him right. In that year, he collected more than a million dollars in deposits. It was a highly respected result that made the Bank of Italy the number-one bank among Italian immigrants and one of the most well-known banks in San Francisco. The client base was growing, and now it was a matter of consolidating the obtained position, constantly improving the functioning and efficiency. After all, it had not even been two years since the opening of the bank: they had already come a long way.

PART VIII

1
San Francisco
1906

He watched it in anguish, terrified. He watched it grow closer, a stampede of galloping horses running madly towards him. It was an immense stampede in which the colors blended together, surrounded in the cloud of dust out from which their heads struggled to emerge, with their eyes white and dilated in panic and their long teeth behind which a furious neighing came out. The horses were out of control and collided against each other as they ran, growing closer, and closer, and closer. The sound of the hooves beating against the ground was deafening. The earth trembled because there were so many, heavy and close. There was a lot of dust and it was covering everything, the streets, the houses. You could even smell them, an unpleasant scent, and you could also smell the sweat of the horses. Amadeo was frightened. He looked around, horrified, and heard screams. He did not understand. He wanted to flee but he could not move.

Sweating, panic-stricken, he suddenly opened his eyes.

The earth really was trembling. It was not just a dream, it was an earthquake! A deep, dull roar, loud and from under the ground, followed by another roar and then another, very loud, accompanied by the sound of glasses and dishes breaking. Everything was moving as though two hands were shaking the house. The floor jerked and the walls seemed to crumple up. The chandelier swayed dangerously, the windows slammed, the glass panes exploded, and the cracks chased each other on the walls that were rapidly crumbling.

The bed began to slide, and Amadeo jumped off just in time. He understood immediately that the earthquake was incredibly strong. Yelling, he dragged Cloe with him and rushed into the children's room. He found them terrified and in tears, on their knees and clutching their pillows in their beds.

-   Hurry, hurry, down the stairs! Cloe, leave it, come down, come! Quickly!

He took the youngest under one arm and the other by the hand and, despite the darkness, ran down the stairs as quickly as possible, while rubble and pieces of the wall fell and brushed against them. Their beautiful house was falling apart, even the staircase threatened to collapse as they were running down, dressed in what they had on them, grazed by bricks that rained down all around them. With a final push, they climbed over the rubble and managed to throw themselves onto the street.

It seemed as though the ground had not yet stopped shaking. A few seconds after the first tremor, there was a second, very strong one, and then other minor ones. About two minutes had passed and the streets were filling up with debris. It seemed as though the startling movement was continuing, making the buildings collapse like houses of cards. Eaves, balconies, everything was falling. Wide cracks had opened in the walls and cut through them as though they were made of paper. Four or five story buildings were crumbling in devastating succession among the clouds of dust. Jets of water flowed from broken tubes, creating crazy streams that ran in every direction. The dust that rose from the rubble made everyone cough and enveloped all the surroundings like a thick fog. From a distance they could see an explosion and a massive fire, probably caused by a broken gas pipe. Not far, a fracture had sliced the street in half, separating the two lanes, almost like the work of a crazed axe. You could see men, women, and children fleeing blindly, and horses, free or attached to carriages, out of control, in the dust and the smoke of the first fires.

The earthquake seemed to last for hours, but the ground only trembled for 60 seconds. It was 5:12 in the morning on April 18th, 1906.

***

Amadeo looked at that apocalyptic sight in disbelief, holding Cloe and the kids tightly. Breathing heavily out of fright, he stood in the middle of the wide street hugging his wife, who was hiccuping through her tears, and his terrified children, watching the beautiful and modern city of San Francisco that, illuminated by the macabre light of the fires, fell apart one collapse after another.

Around them people were fleeing, screaming, and crying. A woman desperately running bumped into them and almost knocked them over. From some nearby buildings, flames began to arise and illuminated the first bodies of the victims. The fire was growing with a deafening crackle amongst the houses. Some of the walls were oscillating, unstable, while others were collapsing noisily. Pieces of crushed brick and cement had rolled up to them as they were hugging each other and observing in silence. The dust slowly settled on the rubble and covered the ruins, the streets, and the people in a thin film.

Even they were completely white. Amadeo looked at Cloe to see if she was hurt. He couldn't even speak. He looked at her, looked at his children, and hugged and kissed them, even though he was shaking with fright. As he ran his fingers through Cloe's hair, with dilated eyes, he burst out into tears and hugged her tightly.

- We're safe, my love, we're safe. God protected us. Now we can rest assured, we're safe, we're safe.

In the dim light of dawn, Amadeo looked at the tremendous destruction that surrounded them. He heard the cries of those who were stuck under the rubble, but he also felt his partner's rapidly beating heart and her trembling. He did not know how to calm her down, as he too was shaking and hiccuping. His mind, usually quick-thinking and decisive, could not reason at that moment. He was devastated. A salty taste lingered on his lips, a mix of tears and cement that had settled on Cloe's face and hair.

Finally Amadeo managed to recover and with difficulty he broke away from Cloe. He looked at her again to make sure there were no wounds. A patch of blood was spreading on her nightgown.

-    Let me see, you're hurt! This blood...

A cut on her thigh, maybe from when they were running away, but not serious and not very deep. Amadeo pulled off his shirt and tore it to form a kind of bandage that he wrapped around her. In taking off his shirt he realized that he too was losing blood and that his back was in a lot of pain. He recalled a sharp pain from when he was coming down the stairs. A few moments more and they could have been knocked down by the pieces that fell from the ceiling. Amadeo acted like it was nothing and hid his bloodstained shirt from his wife.

-    Wait for me here. I'm going to try to go back into the house to get a few clothes. Sit down and don't move, I'll be right back.

-    No, don't go, it's dangerous. Don't leave me, please. Oh God, what is left of our home?

-    It's gone, it's a catastrophe everywhere. But let's focus on us right now, we'll think about the house later. Don't worry, I'll be right back.

All that remained of the house were two half-ruined walls and a mass of rubble, but there was no fire and the strength of the foundation had given them the time to save themselves.

Amadeo climbed over the rocks and rubble and delved into the disaster. There was the kitchen, still partly standing, and the pitcher of water was miraculously safe, still on the table, intact and full. There was the dining room, the nice dishware, the French plates, the crystal chandelier, all destroyed. Amadeo observed the destruction, fascinated by some of the oddities, asking himself how the heavy wooden table had ended up on top of the nice antique French cabinet that they had bought just a few months ago. The table was split in half, but the cabinet had survived. It was a hundred years old and it had passed this test as well.

Climbing over the ruins, Amadeo looked towards the upper floor. It was almost all gone. Everything had crumbled, stone by stone. From one demolished wall sprouted their bed, entirely crushed with only a corner visible. They would have suffered a nasty ending if they had not had the necessary quickness. There was the chair with the suit from the night before. They had gone to listen to Enrico Caruso sing *Carmen* at the Odeon Theater. Now that suit was ripped and covered in dust. There was the closet, or rather, half of it, snapped like a twig even though it was made from sturdy, solid walnut wood. What remained was still standing, but a large cement beam had fallen and sliced a part of it. He almost had to break the hinges to open it and his back immediately hurt. He gathered what was inside, even some things that at first glance seemed out of place, and he put everything on the floor. He tried to remember where the shoes could be, since his feet were wounded and Cloe and the kids were also probably barefoot. He turned around and saw them. Cloe was sitting on the stone where he had left her, hugging the kids with her eyes wide open. She was shaking all over, and it made him pity her greatly. He tried to search faster until he found a pair of slippers, made of padded leather, and shoes from the night before. He gathered all that he could, other things for the children, and, climbing over the rubble, went back to them. Then he returned to get the jug of water and he very carefully brought it to Cloe. For now that was enough.

Not even an hour had passed since the earthquake and there was a lot of shouting, crying, screaming, people calling out, people asking for help, the chilling sizzle of the fires that were increasingly growing amidst the rubble. People running and crying, women in despair, cries of pain, tears of children.

2

The rescue squads had worked all day and now the first, tragic night had arrived. Thousands of desperate people were still looking for the little they had left. Discouraged, in tears, they wandered through the rubble and, as much as possible, tried to help each other. Many of the fires had not yet been tamed and others broke out suddenly. The wooden houses in the outskirts of town had almost all gone up in flames. It was said that 50,000 homes had been destroyed solely by fires. The dead were not counted, some said 200, others 400, and many were certainly still under the rubble. The streets were almost impassable and sewers spewed out mice and muck everywhere.

With the arrival of the new day, the military arrived to look for more dead and wounded among the rubble, and also to fight off the increasing number of looters. On the main road numerous horse-drawn carts carried the victims. Someone slept in a corner, exhausted, oblivious to the noise and the people who worked around him. There were cries and wailing everywhere. A motorized vehicle carrying two people, certainly important, circled through the debris.

Amadeo had brought Cloe and the children to safety with the few things he had managed to recover. They found shelter on Van Ness Avenue with Attilio, a doctor and Amadeo's brother, whose home, for unknown reasons, had remained almost totally intact.

Later, with Lorenzo, he went to the bank to see how to recover the safe.

It was not a simple task, as it was entirely submerged in debris. Besides, it would have been too heavy to move.

They organized with a team of laborers and began digging to free it from the rubble and to get closer to it.

By nightfall, finally, they had succeeded and were now concerned with looters.

Seated on two stones, tired and covered in dust, they had gone more than a day without eating or drinking since they did not trust the water that flowed freely from the pipes.

Lorenzo was dejected.

- What will become of this city?
- It will go back to how it was before, even better.
- Everything is destroyed. It will take a lot of time and a lot of work.
- Of course, but believe me, these tragedies stimulate rebirth. This morning I met Mayor Schmitz. He was also at the concert the other night to hear Caruso, and he told me he wants to get started immediately, and do you know with what? With the cable cars - certainly with the homes and the sewers, but also, immediately, with the cable cars. He understands that this city needs to move. It can't wait around and lick its wounds. Everybody needs to know that modernity is stronger than nature. He has many ideas which I share. When he came he told me: "Amadeo, I'm counting on people like you. I know you will be the first in line in the reconstruction of this city and we will make it more modern than any other." There are many nasty rumors about this mayor, but he has clear ideas.
- What do you intend to do?
- Reopen the bank as soon as possible. We cannot forget the people who have lost everything and have only their bare hands to survive.
- And how do we do that? The bank is gone.
- For now, we get the safe. Then tomorrow I'll explain what I'd like to do.

In the darkness of the night, Lorenzo and Amadeo cautiously opened the safe and, with the help of Gaetano Morabito, an old friend from the times of Scatena, they loaded the gold bars and the bags of money onto two carts with which Gaetano had arrived. They covered them with rocks and debris and they set off towards Amadeo's dilapidated house.

When they arrived, they brought the carts next to the chimney that was hidden by two very solid stone walls that had been left partially standing. They emptied the carts and hid the gold bars and the money on the inside of the chimney and then covered everything in rubble.

Then, completely exhausted, they went to sleep.

3

It was twenty minutes to 6, the sun had not yet risen, the air was crisp, and they had not slept for more than four hours. Amadeo was talking to a couple of policemen who had spent the night guarding the closed safe, which was still under the rubble, surely not easy to transport or to open and, although nobody knew it, empty. Amadeo had thought that, with all the hunger that was around, it was best to divert the attention.

-    I was telling our friend that we will need him again in the afternoon.

-    In the afternoon?

-    Give me a minute to say goodbye and then I'll explain.

One of the policemen was coming back with a pot of coffee and two metal mugs. Amadeo thanked him and then shook their hands and went back to Lorenzo.

-    They were very grateful. They wouldn't stop thanking me. You did well.

-    I gave them 5 dollars, not exactly a fortune.

-    They earn 15 a month so imagine their joy.

-    What do you want to do in the afternoon?

-    Come, let's sit here. Let's drink some coffee. You see, Lorenzo, talking to the mayor got me thinking. Schmitz has a reconstruction plan in mind. Our duty as a bank for the people is to be first in line to help when no one else will.

-    What do you mean by that?

-    Giving money to the poor.

-   Are you telling me you want to throw away all our money?
-   No, I'm not throwing anything away, on the contrary. Even more will come, you'll see.
-   And how do you plan to do that?
-   Listen, here there are thousands of people who now have nothing, no house, no money, no job. They're desperate, but ready to work twenty hours a day to rebuild what little they had. So I thought, if you agree, that this afternoon we take our money and we reopen the bank.
-   You're crazy, look at it, our bank. Only rubble, it's even hard to get to the safe.
-   Actually we won't open it here, we'll go to the port.
-   The port? And what is left at the port that could be useful for us?
-   Come with me.

A couple of men whom Amadeo had asked for help had arrived. They took a cart and moved towards the port. They looked for a place that would not block traffic, but that was clearly visible. At noon they had prepared a counter with two planks supported by two wooden crates that were almost the same height. Amadeo was visibly satisfied and sat on one of the two available chairs.

-   I don't understand: what do you want to do with this counter?
-   The bank. We'll reopen the bank here, amongst those who are working. They should bring the sign soon, even though it's a bit beat up, and put it up here. But I was thinking that, maybe, it would be good for people to know that our bank is already open and that it's stronger than the earthquake: we'll write "business as usual" underneath. Nothing has changed for us. So they know, those from the other banks, who are licking their wounds, that we are the first in line when people need it most. Now I'd like to go see Cloe and the kids. I'll be back in an hour.

Lorenzo looked at him, perplexed: the past two days had been full of emotions, but he had the feeling that this was just the beginning.

4

It was April 23rd, five days after the earthquake.

Amadeo stopped the wagon to look. The sight from the high street was distressing and busy at the same time, with the destroyed houses whose debris still blocked half the road, some desperate people wandering through rubble, and the workers who loaded barely filled carts by hand and left slowly, pulled by tired and suffering horses.

Washington Street Wharf was in the distance and the sea was shimmering happily, brushed by the fresh breeze. Docked at the pier were some boats with their sails tied and a couple of considerably sized steamers that were unloading. Lines of dockworkers went up one walkway and down another, carrying bundles of products that came from who knows where. In the middle of the dock, a row of carts dumped debris into the sea to form a small peninsula that would soon become a new dock. And in the middle of the heavily trafficked pier you could see a stand like the ones used to sell vegetables, with a big sign that, from that distance, was difficult to read: "Bank of Italy," and underneath, "business as usual."

- Who knows if people will understand - Amadeo thought.

He looked around. Many poor souls were still in what had been their home a week before and were searching, maybe with their wife and children, for some small things that had been spared in the disaster. He approached one of these men.

- Good morning, was this your home?
- Good morning, yes. There's nothing left.
- What did you do for a living?

-    Purveyor at the port. I brought meat to the ships. A small gig, but it wasn't bad. Now I have nothing.

-    You have no money?

-    What money? I always invested it all in my business. I even had calves in a barn outside the city, all dead, everything destroyed. I had just finished the house a year ago. Nothing left.

The man sat down and burst into tears.

-    Come to that counter down there before nightfall. I'll see how I can help you. You'll see a sign that says "Bank of Italy." I'll be there soon.

-    Who are you?

-    Amadeo Giannini, of the Bank of Italy.

-    But I know you, you were… Scatena…

-    Yes, you remember correctly, that's me. Come, you can trust me, I'll be waiting for you.

Well over an hour had passed, in fact, it had been three, and Lorenzo was very worried.

-    Amadeo! What happened? How come you're so late?

-    Don't worry Lorenzo, nothing happened. I didn't know how to warn you. I went around the ruins and I talked to some of those poor people. Because I thought that we can keep the bank open all we want, but if we don't let people know, it isn't any use. Did you bring the money? Yes, I see our friends over there. The first should be arriving in a bit.

-    The first what?

-    The first people we'll lend money to.

-    But without anything? Guarantees, nothing?

-    What guarantees can they give us, if they have nothing left? We'll have to settle. The promises of good people are like a contract.

-    I don't understand anything anymore.

-    Go get a log book and sit next to me. I'll show you what we'll do.

The sun was about to set and nobody had shown up yet. Lorenzo was nervous and chewed his unlit cigar until it was a lump of tobacco, a sign that he was very worried. Amadeo had written some notes in a log and was now waiting at the table looking at the port.

The two policemen strolled around trying to look dignified, but they were visibly embarrassed. Nobody had come up to them, not even to ask for information, not even to say hello. No friend, no acquaintance, it was just the two of them.

It was then that, finally, the very man Amadeo had first talked to, the purveyor, walked down the street. He approached with caution, observing the policemen out of the corner of his eye. He was very apprehensive.

- Good morning, you told me to come before nightfall…
- Good morning to you. Good, you did well to come here. Tell me about your business, what you did…
- I had calves in a barn that I built a few years ago and, when they order meat, I slaughtered a veal or two, then I cleaned it, made the pieces, salted them, put them in straw, and delivered them two or three days later, or even the same day if it was urgent.
- Would you have worked today? Is there anybody who would buy the meat?
- I actually needed to deliver some veal in two days, but how can I?
- Do you know where you could buy a calf?
- Yes, I think so. In truth, I hadn't thought about it.
- And how much does a calf cost?
- It depends on the weight. Let's say between 12 and 14 dollars.
- How much money do you have left?

The man was standing at the counter and looked at Amadeo with a mixture of fear and disbelief. He had still not understood why he was asking all those questions. He looked first at Amadeo, then at Lorenzo, then back at Amadeo, and then bowed his head and began to cry.

- Be strong, this is no time to cry. I told you, we are here to help, believe me.
- Thank you. And sorry. I think 4 dollars and fifty cents. But I don't have any debts, I've never had any debt.
- What is your name?
- Emanuele Vinciguerra. I come from a town near Bergamo in Italy.
- I know where Bergamo is, my parents are Italian. Lorenzo, write down our friend's name. And where do you live?
- Where you saw me digging, but I don't know if I'll ever go back. So much work to build that house, my wife was so proud of it… now nothing, nothing.
- How old are you?
- 42.
- Children?
- Three.
- Lorenzo, please write down that we will loan 25 dollars to Emanuele Vinciguerra so he can go back to work, buy his first calf, and start his business again. He will come back to the bank in a year and will return 27 dollars to us. Emanuele, do you agree?

25 dollars was more than twice the monthly pay of a worker.

- But I've never taken money from a bank. Banks ask for collateral, but I have nothing to give as collateral.
- You have your work, and that is enough for us. If you agree, sign here, next to your name.
- Oh Lord, nothing like this has ever happened to me. What do I need to do? I'm confused.
- There is no need to be and I guarantee there are no tricks. If you don't want to give us back the money, you can easily disappear and we will have lost the money. But I know you won't do that.
- Oh my God! Thank you, how can I thank you? Imagine what my wife will say!

- To thank us, stop by every once in a while to let us know how your business is going and bring us back the money in a year. But remember, if you are in difficulty, we are always here to help you. Now go home and tell your friends that we will be here tomorrow and the day after tomorrow too, until we get the bank back on its feet.

Lorenzo looked at Emanuele as he walked away crying tears of joy and continuously turning around to wave and thank them. When he disappeared from view, he turned to Amadeo.

- Do you intend to do this with many people? Do you realize what you're doing?
- If we don't do this then this city is dead.
- But if we do this, we and all those who gave us money to invest will die.
- Don't be pessimistic.

The next day, two people sent by Emanuele presented themselves and Amadeo asked them the same questions and lent them some money. Then another two, then one with his wife, but Amadeo was disappointed. He had hoped that more would come. Some people had told him that it was not a bank but a market stand and they didn't have time to lose. But what could he do? They certainly could not build a bank in a few days. Amadeo made a decision that left Lorenzo flabbergasted.

- Maybe I've misunderstood. You want to put the money on the counter as if they were artichokes for all to see.
- Yes, we'll make some nice piles of bills and blocks of gold so everybody can see that we are here to lend money, that we are really a bank and not a vegetable stand.
- You are starting to worry me.
- Do as I say and you'll see. One more thing: the policemen around here make people nervous. Maybe it would be best for them to go a little farther away, or, even better, not come at all. We don't have much money here anyways.

People started arriving on the third day. They approached and saw that the money was really there, that it was really a bank. Amadeo always asked his usual questions, he looked them in the eye, he saw them cry, and then he helped them. And those who waited saw those who got a loan. A young man who had heard that the bank lent money easily came too, but when Amadeo, not convinced by his story, asked him to show his hands and the boy proudly showed him his well manicured hands, all hell broke loose. Amadeo stood up suddenly and threatened to beat him up if he did not leave immediately.

5

Those were hectic days for the whole city and also for Amadeo. Wherever you looked there was construction. The rubble seemed to disappear as the new pier at the harbor continued to expand, and other docks appeared out of nowhere. Some businesses had reopened but, unfortunately, many hearses were still passing through. It was said that the death toll had passed 2,000. A catastrophe.

Amadeo was thirty-six years old, 6 feet tall, and had a thick mustache and sparkling eyes. He continued being a bright visionary and knew where he wanted to go and how to get there. He knew that the other banks would not have reopened soon because, besides the buildings, their records had also been destroyed, while Amadeo knew his clients one by one and knew what their financial position was. From the beginning, with the help of Amadeo and Lorenzo, his employees had begun rewriting their records one name at a time.

His long day was split between checking on the reconstruction of his home, which Cloe supervised with great firmness and determination, the construction of a temporary headquarters for the bank in his brother Attilio's house, where the three families were temporarily living together, and the work at the port, which was becoming increasingly busy.

The success was enormous. More and more people came. By now there was a long line of people waiting and almost all of them received a loan. Not all of them knew how to write, many signed with a cross. But how valuable that cross was!

After a few days, when it became known that the bank had started to piece together the clients' accounts, a rumor started to spread that the safe had been transported to a secure location, and so new clients who no longer knew where to hide their savings began arriving as well, trusting the only operational bank, the Bank of Italy, with their money. The clientele transformed; it became American as well. Of the two million dollars of deposits that Amadeo and Lorenzo had moved from the safe to the chimney the night after the earthquake, over five-hundred thousand had been given out as loans, and the cash would have become a problem had it not been for the many new clients who arrived to deposit their savings. Amadeo was always first in line to welcome them, which instilled a sense of trust and optimism in them. The neighborhood of North Beach was the first neighborhood to be rebuilt and all that activity attracted many new entrepreneurial initiatives that lasted for years, making San Francisco the first commercial port on the West Coast.

A couple weeks after the bank's reopening and after realizing the mass of clients that was literally storming them, Amadeo gathered the bankers of the city together to share his experience. From the makeshift stage that had been built in a room of a not too run-down hotel, he watched the small crowd that had accepted his invitation. He had known almost all of them for years. Even his critics from not too long ago were there, as well as the most powerful people of the city, the great bankers, the merchants, the shipowners, the manufacturers. That group could be instrumental in the reconstruction.

Amadeo was very excited about this opportunity, and he hoped for a positive reaction, especially from the bankers. His hopes, however, were quickly crushed. It was a very animated meeting: on one side there was the old guard, frightened by the problems and incapable of handling the emergency, and on the other there was Amadeo, who tried to push his colleagues to be more courageous and to open themselves to the city that had fallen to its knees. Amadeo was very well-known, but to many he seemed too modern and liberal. He was listened to carefully. Many agreed that they too should contribute to the reconstruction. But in the end the bankers, all in agreement, decided that they would reopen their banks in November, six months later.

After his fairly long introduction that was optimistic but stern, Amadeo left the floor to the others, looked around in disappointment, and closed the meeting with a sentence that made the blood of those present run cold: - In November there will no longer be a city to rebuild and your banks will be gone as well.

6

In October, the reconstruction of San Francisco after the earthquake of April 18th progressed at full speed. Over forty thousand people were working around the port and in the North Beach neighborhood. The traffic of the carts and trucks was so hectic that it became necessary to build a railway to transport the debris intended to fill the new piers of the port. The San Francisco Examiner, the most important daily newspaper of the city, wrote: "North Beach was the first neighborhood to recover… those businesses that once thrived have all re-opened, and many new businesses and private homes have been built in the surrounding area. Its residents have set up 542 new structures in just 4 months."

Six months later, the wooden houses that had caught fire had been replaced by imposing stylish structures, just like the majority of the destroyed buildings, and to Mayor Eugene Schmitz's tram line, that had started running again just ten days after the earthquake, another two had been added.

The Bank of Italy, founded by Amadeo Peter Giannini, was recognized as the main driving force behind the reconstruction and not only within the Italian community but also in all the surrounding areas. In fact, the Italian neighborhood led the reconstruction of the entire city.

Some time later, the San Francisco Call, an important daily newspaper of San José, wrote: "the majority of the cargos of lumber that were transported to North Beach were paid for with money that the Bank of Italy had made available. The loyalty and trust of the Bank's directors and the good faith and energy of the homeless were at the heart of the first major financial deal after the calamity."

While the Bank of Italy had already been growing rapidly before the disaster, its growth skyrocketed after the earthquake. At the end of 1905 the Bank accounted for assets of about 1 million dollars, while at the end of 1906 these rose to about 1.9 million. Deposits went from about 700 thousand dollars to 1.3 million, and loans from about 900 thousand to almost 1.5 million. A resounding success.

It was only then that Amadeo P. Giannini decided that he would be a banker for the rest of his life.

PART IX

1
San Mateo (California)
December 31st 1906

Virginia got up early. She had been like that ever since she was a child. She woke up in time to help around the house before going to school and now, even more so, ever since the earthquake, her sleep had become even lighter, guarded, and more apprehensive. At the crack of dawn she was the second in the family to get up. The first was always her son Amadeo who, when it was still dark, already had something to do, because now he was full of new ideas and the hours of the day were never enough. Now that they all lived together, and even though the house was very large, it was inevitable that the other occupants were woken up.

Virginia fed the two dogs and observed them as they roamed the garden sniffing here and there. The big house in San Mateo where she and her husband Lorenzo were guests had been purchased by Amadeo immediately after they had realized that his beautiful old home in San Francisco was not in a state to be put back on its feet in little time. In any case, the fear had been so great that Cloe would have likely not let their children sleep in that place. The new house was not far from San Francisco and was big enough to comfortably host the whole family. It was a two-story villa, solid and luminous, with big covered terraces that let them enjoy the coolness of the shade, and it was surrounded by a large garden.

- Look how beautiful they are.

Virginia turned to Cloe, who had just come down, still in her dressing gown. The two dogs, of an indeterminable breed and undefinable color, were intently sniffing the most remote corners of the garden.

- They always keep track of what goes on: the cats that stop by, the new family of squirrels, the blackbird they always chase. They look like our husbands when they read the morning paper. They keep themselves informed.

Cloe smiled.

They went to the kitchen to set the table for breakfast: it was almost time for the house to come to life, even though it was a holiday.

\-   When are you moving?

Finally Virginia, after eight months, would be able to move back into her reconstructed house.

\-   I'll start packing today and tomorrow I'll go to Attilio's to get the rest. I think I'll be done in a few days. Then, finally, we'll go back home!

Amadeo came downstairs, fully dressed. He had already been out for a long walk to patrol the area all the way down to his farmer friends.

\-   Good morning. What are you doing dressed for work?

\-   I'm going to the Bank. I have a few things to do.

\-   But today is a holiday, Saint Sylvester's Day, remember?

\-   There's no rest for the wicked, money never sleeps!

\-   If dollar bills already suffer from insomnia on their own then you certainly don't have to be there to keep them up!

Amadeo looked at her with a smile.

\-   You're right, let's let them sleep longer.

The smell of eggs and bacon had taken over the kitchen. After Lorenzo arrived, they all decided to forget about the bags and the bank and to take a full day off.

In the middle of the afternoon the guests began arriving for that evening's party. The earthquake, fortunately, had not struck any of them. That would be the first New Years of their new life and they would not have to mourn anybody. To the childrens' great joy, they were putting together a big party. Everybody was coming, even the uncles Attilio, George, and the young Harry, Lorenzo and Virginia's son. Amadeo and Cloe's sons were going wild. Mario, Lloyd, and Virgil were teasing the two girls, Agnes and little Claire, who crawled behind them to take part in their rampages. The dogs chased them happily, multiplying the chaos that reigned in the garden and in the house as well. The women tried to prepare the food amongst the screams, and tried in vain to calm that wild crowd.

The day was clear and the sun was beating hard, but the cold could still be felt. Amadeo and Lorenzo sat in the garden pretending to keep an eye on the little ones.

-    We got really lucky. Today we are here, all healthy, to celebrate…

-    You're right, it's wonderful. Look at the kids playing.

-    Yes, and then tonight they'll all have a fever. I can see it already.

Lorenzo understood immediately that it was not the kids' fevers that troubled him.

-    You look worried, what's wrong?

Attilio, his brother who was a doctor, also arrived.

-    What were you talking about?

-    That tonight the children will have a fever.

-    Kids' fevers, they pass.

-    But Amadeo was saying something else.

-    Yes, indeed. I'm worried. I was thinking that everything is going too well here. San Francisco is getting rebuilt, new businesses are everywhere, new homes, merchants are rejoicing, the Bank is thriving. But what is happening in the east? I have worrying signals from my informants. I know the banks have had a slowdown in lending, which means businesses aren't growing and more houses aren't being built. If they go into a crisis in the east, we will be affected, too. I was thinking of taking some time off to go see for myself.

2
East Coast
1907

Organizing the trip took over a month in order to contact people and confirm all their meetings. After all, Giannini wasn't that well-liked on that side of the continent, so he had to seek out friends and friends of friends.

Cloe, however, was thrilled. Vacations with Amadeo were always wonderful: even if he worked a lot during the day, he was always free in the evening and very often he would take entire days to be with her. They visited museums and art galleries or simply strolled through the cities. Amadeo was curious and Cloe even more so. While on vacation Amadeo was very talkative, telling her about his work and asking for opinions and advice.

They went to New York, Philadelphia, and then Chicago. To conclude, Amadeo decided to extend the trip to New Orleans, which was not initially in the plans. They returned in May and, in those three months, Amadeo had gotten a good idea of the economic situation in that part of the country. And he was not at all comforted by it.

Upon his return, Amadeo explained many of the impressions he had gotten during the trip.

-   In addition to what I already wrote to you, I wanted to tell you that I noticed that the financial workers were incomprehensibly euphoric while, on the contrary, the economy is slowing down. Risky speculation, monetary exchanges in total confusion, forecasts of not only companies but also banks collapsing.

Those attending the meeting were very attentive, especially Lorenzo and J. Fagan, but so were Pedrini and the other members of the Council. They all, however, were familiar with their Bank's performance and had begun to sense the oncoming difficulties. Amadeo's words made them more alarmed than they already were. J. Fagan, who held the position of Board member to the Bank of Italy as well as chief clerk of Crocker National Bank, was well aware of the problems that were afflicting the American economy, even though they had not yet fully manifested themselves in California.

Amadeo wanted to get everyone's opinions so he could make the final decisions. He then concluded: - I am convinced that immediate action is needed. We must remain as liquid as possible so that we are not too exposed in the event of a crisis. Let's reduce the loans to the essentials and only do them with great care. Another thing that I would like to see done is that we buy gold, everything we can find. And not only that. For those who want liquid money, let's convince them to accept paper so we can keep the gold and silver coins to consolidate the Bank.

Fagan requested the floor. - I've also gotten the same impressions from other sources, so I'm afraid I have to confirm that we can expect a recessionary period in the near future. In this regard, however, I would like to point out that, while it is true that we are expecting a period of difficulty, the tightening of credit and the increase in interest rates could aggravate the economy's performance and therefore also the Bank's.

- Dear Fagan, I agree with you. For now, the recession is showing its first signs on the East Coast so we still have some time to take action before it shows up here as well. I agree with you that rising rates could have a negative influence on the economy, but let's not forget that there are more than 30 banks around here. We are only one of them and our main task is to safeguard the Bank, the depositors, and the shareholders. I have to think first about our goal and then about the national economy, but I am absolutely certain that if we are healthy in a crisis we can do much more than 10 crippled banks. Always remember: it is better to have a solid Bank than big profits.

The economic earthquake began in the autumn with a banking crisis in Egypt that set off a monetary panic and caused the bankruptcy of one of the major banks, along with other minor ones. Egypt was followed by Japan, and then by Germany and Chile. By the end of the year, the panic spread to the eastern United States. When it arrived in California, of the local banks only the Bank of Italy found itself safe, well-capitalized, and with many gold reserves, some of which were made available to prevent the bankruptcy of their friend Fagan's Crocker National Bank, while other banks had serious problems and others failed. The Bank of Italy was thus able to be in the front line to provide relief to companies in crisis.

In New York a few months earlier, J. P. Morgan had gathered all the great bankers and the industry elites in the rooms of the Library, his magnificent office, so that they could find a way out of the recession together. J. P. let them work for a few days, staying out of their quarrels and bickering until it was time to find the solution that suited him best: the establishment of a national bank rescue fund in which the Treasury made available first 25 then another 30 million dollars. The fund bailed out the eastern banks and J. P. Morgan took credit for it.

From this crisis, Amadeo learned that the Bank should open branches in all states. But, at the time, this was forbidden.

3
Denver
1908

The Grand Ballroom of the Brown Palace Hotel was more than lavish. Crystal chandeliers reflected flashes of light on the attendees, walls covered in rich fabric muffled noises, and some paintings were reminiscent of Colorado's bygone days. Amadeo was sitting in his armchair far away from the other bankers, nearly at the back of the room. Bankers from all across America had gathered in Denver at the American Bankers Association's annual meeting and were listening to reports. But not Giannini. He was despondent at the thought that America's most important banking institution had not yet realized that last year's crisis had been more than a wake-up call and was far from over. He had no friends in that room, only a few people who respected him and many more who hated him. He was not a friend of the big East Coast bankers like J. P. Morgan or Rockefeller, who were refinanced many tens of millions of dollars by the Treasury the year before. He was not even friends with Theodore Roosevelt, the young and aggressive president of the United States who had supported them and was also present. Amadeo did not approve of the fact that he was a Freemason and used Freemasonry for his own purposes. He also did not like the fact that he was an avid hunter. But he did not speak of these things.

On the stage, they were still discussing what banking methodologies were being used in the various states. They had already talked about it months before and, as always, had not decided a damn thing.

Amadeo just wanted to go home, but he was waiting for the report from Woodrow Wilson, president of Princeton University and a person he held in high esteem. He hoped that, with his intervention, he would reopen the possibility for banks to open branches in other states. Amadeo was a proponent of it and knew that Wilson viewed this reform favorably.

Businesses were closing and unemployment was rising, but this problem did not seem to bother the eastern bankers whose mindsets were far from the tragedy that was still afflicting San Francisco. On the other hand, Giannini, with his Bank of Italy, continued to finance small business owners by becoming the third-largest Bank on the West Coast in terms of the amount of loans. But his efforts, while considerable, remained very localized.

Lyman Gage, a wealthy retiree who had moved from New York to California and who shared Amadeo's worries, came to sit next to him. Gage, after a lifetime in banking, had served as President McKinley's Secretary of the Treasury and was one of the few who supported the need for banks to open branches in other states. They had met two years earlier, at that historic bankers' meeting a few days after the earthquake, and then saw each other a few more times. They weren't exactly friends, but they had great respect for each other. The mere fact that Gage had come to sit next to Giannini was proof that the New York bankers' alliance was beginning to falter.

They stayed silent until the end of the report.

- What did you think?

Gage looked at Giannini with a vague, enigmatic smile on his face.

- It seems to me that they are unable to learn from the past. Two years ago, banks that weren't capitalized enough passed through a financial crisis. The small ones went bankrupt and then so did the companies that were their clients. And not a word of alarm was heard in this room, quite the contrary.

- You're right. I wanted to tell you that I greatly admired your policy of grabbing as much gold as you could. You were right last year and thus saved not only your Bank but the economy of a large part of the city. But it seems to me that you were the only one.

- It was just luck. I had a hunch.

- You're too modest. But you can't deny that, with this "hunch" of yours, you also allowed Crocker National to save itself. It was unforgettable.

Giannini turned away, a little annoyed. He didn't like compliments.

- Look, Wilson's getting on stage. We'll talk about this later.

The applause quickly faded and the silence invited the speaker to begin.

-    Dear bankers, dear friends, after many years of working in this environment and serving as president of my university, it seems to me that the time has come to speak clearly
to each other. Our banks are this nation's most envied and
least loved business tool.

Gage looked at Giannini with amazement and comment-
ed under his breath: - He's off to a strong start, it seems to me.

-    It seems so to me, too. Let's hear where this is going.

Wilson continued:

-    The banks of this nation are detached from the people
and the people think banks are owned not by themselves but
by some hostile power.

Gage and Giannini were even more attentive and amazed.
The report was becoming an indictment of the profession, an
accusation of being blind to the facts.

Wilson spoke and the audience was left speechless.

-    If opening branches in other states is managed efficient-
ly and economically, it can guarantee resources to the banks,
which will then make them available to the areas where entrepreneurs have their credit restricted by local banks. This
change could restore confidence in the banks in less than a
generation. After all, what have you done with your management? Local banks were created by leveraging local resources, but only a few of those resources have benefited the area.
Any community remains poor when closed in on itself, especially the banking community. You have built this community
in the most unlikely and arduous of ways.

Wilson continued his criticisms. There was a brief, cold applause when he finished, followed by a hostile silence. Many
of the attendees quickly walked away.

Gage and Giannini stood up. The conference was over and
there was nothing more to say. Wilson had cast a chill on the
room and nullified any other intervention. They headed toward the refreshment room, where many of the attendees, in
groups, were commenting animatedly on Wilson's positions.

The two friends stood to the side.

- I already know what you want to tell me, but tell me anyway.

- What can I say, I have already experienced this situation two years ago, after the earthquake. You were there, too. My colleagues' lack of foresight amazes me every time. I can see the big bankers obviously agreeing to open new branches in other states, and they'd better! They expand and become more and more powerful, but they hold so tightly on to their wealth. The small ones, on the other hand, believe that by doing so they will lose their autonomy, their prestige, which is obviously local, and, above all, their profits. Their social function, instead, is never taken into consideration.

- You're right. I noticed Forgan, the one from Chicago First National Bank, applauding thunderously. And he's the smallest of the big ones, so imagine the others. However, you do know that the majority of associates here are small.

- I know, and frankly I can't get over how small they are. Mentally, that is.

- You're meaner than Wilson.

- No, I'm just being realistic. Still, we have the example of Canada: their banks with more branches have withstood the crisis of the last two years better, yet they have been hit as hard as we have.

- You're not afraid of losing control of your bank if it expanded into several states?

- This is the future. Do not be afraid of it, but guide it with conscience. I am absolutely convinced that an integrated group of branches could counteract a crisis that isn't even imaginable today. Think about the support that the group could give to an individual branch in case of difficulty. Think of the farmers in the plains who might finally have a bank that is not just local and therefore not subject to the same momentary difficulties as its customers.

- I wouldn't know how to argue with that.

- Yet all we have heard here are protests against the Treasury.

- They didn't understand that the Treasury supported the national banks, and it left the local ones to their fate.

- Indeed, that should be all the more reason. But these bankers are too protective of their local power. They feel they are kings in their own homes, and if they go out they are no one.

They told each other everything. They were in agreement, and their seats were comfortable, so they let the silence be the backdrop to the wisps of blue smoke rising from their cigars, each focused on their own thoughts.

Most of the participants were preparing to go to dinner, forming groups that were similar in size, in place of origin, and, above all, in beliefs. Amadeo declined some invitations, freeing the others from his uncomfortable presence. At the end of the day, he did the right thing by coming. These were the typical occasions where nothing ever happens, but sometimes all it takes is a single intervention to make it clear that something is about to change. There was no time to waste. They had to prepare to be the first.

He went out into the street and headed for his hotel. A walk would do him good, as it was not far away and would allow him to clear his head. The air was fresh and his mind was hard at work. He went over Wilson's words and their possible implications. If widening the Bank had reduced its power, it would not have been a problem. However, he was absolutely convinced of the contrary. He wasn't afraid to take on such a big step; in fact, it was exactly what he wanted to do. He realized that being small was dangerous in his industry, and the experience he had just had confirmed that. But he also had to convince his colleagues that this was the right way, and that wasn't going to be easy. He had to understand better and make a plan.

When he arrived at the hotel he telegraphed Lorenzo at the office that he would not be returning and then the president of the Commercial Bank of Canada that he would be visiting him in two days. He waited until morning, instead, to phone Cloe.

4
Hollywood
1909

In the car, as they arrived at the appointment, Amadeo told his cheerful wife the reason for their invitation to the opening of a new cinema. Cloe was eager to see this novelty that was not a theater and the figures that were not real characters.

-    I believe this will be the future of entertainment. Think about how you can replicate the same show at the same time in another city. Without limits. It's not like the theater where what you see you can only see there at that moment.

-    You sound so excited that I bet you've already financed them.

-    Of course, and I'm sure it will be successful. But you'll see.

They arrived at their destination and Amadeo helped his wife out of the car. The road was unusually busy and drivers did not have much respect for those who were walking. They would honk at any hindrance from either another car or, worse, a pedestrian. A car brushed by them and then stopped just ahead.

-    Look how rude they are - Cloe muttered angrily.

-    It's the price of progress.

-    I don't believe that. And then going just to stop right there in front.

Even the sidewalk was jam-packed with people. The two who had almost run them over just before stood in front of them in line. They were probably also invited to the opening of the Nickelodeon room. The new screening room that Sol Lesser and three other friends had decided to open was a complete novelty for Los Angeles, the first in the entire region, and they said that it would screen new films that were coming out. Not very many to tell the truth, but curiosity was high and people were flocking in masses.

The facade of the building was illuminated with hundreds of colored bulbs to outline a large gothic gate with a huge "Nickelodeon" sign above the entrance. More colored bulbs all around made the theater's facade very visible even from a distance.

Cloe and Amadeo waited patiently in line for the guests to enter and take their seats. In the meantime, they commented in amazement and amusement on the new trend of using so many bright lights to attract customers.

- Mr. Giannini!

Amadeo turned to see who was looking for him.

- Sol, since when do you call me Giannini?
- I'm sorry, you're right. Mrs. Cloe, how are you? What are you doing in line? Come with me.

The gentleman in front of them, the one who had grazed them with his car, stopped Sol by the arm.

- We have an invitation, too. Where should we go?
- You have to wait here in line. We will open soon.

He firmly but courteously released himself from the man's grip.

- Come, Amadeo. I will accompany you.
- What aggressive people out there - Cloe reiterated, still angry.
- I know who he is. He comes to nose around. He wants to make a screening room, too. But thanks to you, I got there first.

Sol escorted Cloe and Amadeo to the center rows, the ones for the important guests. Then he went to open the doors and the room was full in a few minutes.

Amadeo, turning around, saw that all the seats were occupied and many people had to stand.

The lights went out and the pianist began to accompany the projection of the film. Shortly after, a man wearing a tiny strip of fur jumped from a jungle tree hanging from a vine and appeared to fall into the room. Cloe jumped in her chair and many of the amazed spectators sprung to their feet. A roar of astonishment drowned out the pianist.

-    Cloe, stay calm, it's fake!
-    But what a fright!

The audience followed Tarzan's endeavors with loud comments and applause. The sight of the monkeys elicited endless laughter and a thunderous applause broke out at the moment of the kiss between Tarzan and Jane.

Amadeo smiled happily, but Cloe was uncomfortable.

-    Doesn't it seem a little risque?
-    You mean the nearly naked man?
-    Yes, and then that very explicit kiss.
-    I told you before, it's progress.
-    Like the ones who run you over with a car?

Sol picked them up at the exit.

-    Come with me, let's go drink to this evening's success. I would have never imagined…
-    Bravo, you really made a beautiful thing.
-    Thanks to you! How do I repay your trust?
-    Keep me in the loop on your activities. Filmmaking interests me.

5

San Francisco
1910

It was a delight to walk around San Francisco. The city was alive, pulsating, orderly. People were busy and stores had paying customers. The cars, which were more and more numerous, were honking their way through. Amadeo observed his city enthusiastically, looking at the massive stone buildings and sidewalks that finally protected pedestrians from cars. The billboards made him aware that he too had done something to help that progress.

He rounded the corner of the Bank, almost bumping into a passerby, and was struck by a rather excited and unusually loud clamoring.

- ... because they are certain that they are always right! But when they come home they ask us what to do and how. This is a situation we can no longer accept. We demand our rights just as we accept our duties. We don't feel second to anyone! Anyone!

A roar of applause drowned out the woman's last words. She was dressed in a long black skirt and a black men's jacket over a white shirt with a kind of rosette at the neck, almost like a tie. Other women were dressed similarly and carried a large sign that read "NOW IS THE TIME" in big letters. Many people, curious passersby, had stopped around them to listen to what that lady standing on the stool had to say. The women applauded, the men a little less so.

Amadeo stopped and listened. He knew immediately that these were suffragettes, the activists who demanded the right to vote for women.

- But I would like to ask you all, do you consider it fair that we—we who share life with you, who are by your side in good times and in bad, who support you when you struggle, who rejoice and suffer for you and with you—I ask you, is it fair that when it comes to choosing our leaders, we women cannot contribute? That we can't elect our own representatives? We are half the population, we are not a meagre and ill-equipped minority. We are also subject to the choices of our politicians. We are second to no one!

She spoke with a booming voice that would have made

many men envious, and she flailed around pointing random-
ly at people who were listening to her, mostly men, as if she
really wanted answers. The small crowd began to make increasingly loud objections.

- Go home! Go! Go!
- Don't deal with things you don't understand!
- Go home! Go home!

Two cops arrived, whistling at the top of their lungs and
brandishing their batons. The crowd began to flee as the cops
tried to stop some of the participants. One fell to the ground,
dragged by her hair. Even some civilians started to distribute
kicks and punches to those poor women.

Amadeo was horrified. - Stop, stop, what are you doing!
Leave them alone! - he shouted, running to the defense of one
of the women.

- Mr. Giannini, Mr. Giannini!

Two of the bank's employees heard the commotion and
went out to see what was going on, and when they saw
Amadeo getting into a fight, they intervened.

- Mr. Giannini, let it go. Come with us.

The two were restraining him.

- The police are here! You don't want to be arrested!
Come with us, let it go.

- But those women are people! They're not animals! The
animals are those cops, damn it. Stop!

- Let it go, we'll figure it out later. Come with us.

And with as much courteousness as possible, they dragged
him inside the Bank. Giannini was furious.

- It's unconscionable. Why do the police beat them?
They were just expressing their ideas.

One of the employees who had dragged him to safety tried
to calm him down.

- They're women asking for the right to vote, and men
don't want to give it to them! But go to your office now. I'll get
you a drink.

Pedrini arrived, alarmed.

-   What happened?

-   There are suffragettes out there and the police arrived with batons. I'd never seen how violently they take them away. It's inconceivable! They were dragging them by the hair as if they were animals for slaughter.

-   And you?

-   I went to defend them.

-   They told me! They had to take you away by force.

-   Yes, I didn't realize the risk in the moment. I understand that this is not the way to help them. But I would like to do something.

-   Calm down now and then we'll think about it.

They remained in silence for a few minutes. Pedrini watched him brooding, visibly shaken. Then Amadeo asked:

-   How many women work for us?

-   None, only men.

-   Why?

-   I don't think there are any banks with female employees.

-   Do you think that's fair?

-   It has always been like this everywhere. Look at public offices, too: women clean, but there are no employees.

-   Yet women do so many things. Look in the countryside, they work as hard as men, if not harder.

-   I'm well aware of that, and maybe that's what made us think there was equality, but this is not the truth.

-   What do you say if we were the first ones to hire women?

-   You know how much criticism we'd get!

-   But you know how many endorsements are from women, too. In fact, I'll tell you more. We're going to make a branch where it's all women, specifically for women. It seems to me that this could be a good step to help the movement. And you'll see that we'll be successful.

After a few months, one of the branches in the center was

closed for renovation and when it reopened, all the staff were women. In the meantime, the city was filled with posters advertising the first bank for women, the first bank that guaranteed gender equality. Immediately the anti-suffrage committees organized pickets to block the entrance to the bank and for several weeks it was very difficult to work.

Pedrini was worried, so he went to talk about it with Amadeo.

-    They've been picketing us for three weeks and won't let anyone in. Instead of drawing in women, we're losing men. We should do something about it.

-    But we're already doing it.

-    What are you saying? What are we doing?

Amadeo looked at Pedrini with a smile.

-    Nothing. We're not doing anything, or rather, we're letting them do it for us. How many articles have come out in the newspapers?

-    Many, it's true.

-    All publicity for us. You'll see that when they stop, we will have achieved our goal.

Giannini was recognized as an early advocate of universal suffrage even though he had not even made a statement about it. Some time later the branch became one of the most active in the city and in 1911 California granted women the right to vote.

PART X

1
Favale
1912

When he told her, Cloe hugged him in excitement. And now that he had kept his promise, they had finally managed to carve out four months of vacation time to spend in Italy.

It was a tiring journey, but Cloe was happy and Amadeo could finally see what was left of his family. The first interaction with his town, Favale di Malvaro, had not been welcoming. They looked at him with suspicion, a little astonished by that man with the austere figure who asked around for news of his family in a very awkward Italian.

-   All the Giannini's are dead, even the kid. Try asking barba Tumasin. - he said in Genovese dialect.

There were perhaps some of his mother's family left, barba Tumasin told him. He was the very old keeper of the cemetery who was also the keeper of the village's memories.

Word of their presence spread quickly, especially since this gentleman and his wife seemed to be very wealthy. In fact, the village had never seen such well-dressed people.

It took the mayor, who was warned by an excited Favale resident, little time to figure out that the gentleman was really the American son of the Giannini's and De Martini's who had emigrated many years before. He welcomed them and made himself available, if a bit wary.

The plan was to stay just a couple of days, visit the cemetery, see the surroundings, and look for relatives. And indeed the relatives arrived. Relatives so distant that they didn't really understand to what degree they were related. Instead of the planned two days, they had to stay longer because the lunch invitations kept streaming in and new relatives emerged every day. Cloe had to visit house after house and listen to many stories of people whose photographs told her absolutely nothing. Among other things, conversing was very difficult. It had been almost thirty years since she had spoken Italian only rarely, and she had a hard time following conversations that, in any case, had little Italian in them.

They were in the town square when they saw an old man struggling to walk. He approached them with tears in his eyes and embraced them, first Amadeo and then Cloe.

-    You helped my son. After the earthquake. He had lost everything. Now he is back to work and sends me money. Thank you, thank you, thank you.

And, wiping his eyes, he walked away on his frail legs.

Amadeo and Cloe remained silent, moved by that gesture. Not even they had realized that the help given in San Francisco could reach this place so far away. The country of his father.

Amadeo had arrived very sympathetic towards these people who, after all, were akin to him. But after a few days, he became impatient to leave. He discussed it with Cloe and they decided to go, but to leave a good memory.

-    What do you plan to do?

-    Let's organize a big lunch in the square and make the musicians come, too. Like how it was done a hundred years ago.

That same evening they went to the village tavern, called the mayor and the parish priest, and knocked on the houses that overlooked the square. The next day they needed tables and plates and glasses to give food and, more importantly, drinks to all those who had come.

The festive atmosphere infected everyone and more than a hundred people came. They arrived bringing their chairs, as they were used to doing for village parties. Some came with bottles of wine, others empty-handed. But big pots of pasta and minestrone came out of the tavern's kitchens and vegetable pies and stews came from some kitchens of the nearby houses. In the center of the square, the mayor coordinated the traffic as carefully as if that was the decisive moment of his career.

The accordion players arrived, and Amadeo looked at them sentimentally: he knew Favale's accordions, the emigrants in San Francisco played them and he remembered them from when he was a child. The parish priest gave a blessing, and he even tried to say a few words of thanks to the son who had returned home, but, fortunately, it was very brief. Even more simple was the speech of the mayor who, considering the presence of wine and food on the table, mumbled a few words then dived into his plate.

- Luckily hunger got the better of him - Cloe commented in a low voice.

At the end of the meal and after much music and singing, Amadeo stood up and asked for silence. In his Italian with a strong American accent, he said the usual things that should be said at those occasions, thanking the mayor and the parish priest and saying that he left a certain amount of money to do some work in the village. Then, after a moment of emotion, he concluded: - Even though we live on the other side of the world, our hearts, mine and Cloe's, are here with you. I promise that we will be back soon and so will our children because we, like you, are Italian and we are from Favale.

A roar of applause drowned out his final goodbyes and everyone wanted to go and hug him. None of them could imagine that it would be a promise kept for the next seventy years, until their last daughter, Claire Hoffman, became too old to travel.

2

It had been a beautiful trip. Visiting the historical cities they had only read about or heard about—Florence, Rome, Naples, and Pompeii, then further down to Calabria and then

Venice— had filled them with pride that they already carried in their hearts but was now confirmed by visiting for themselves.

In Milan, they allowed themselves the luxury of renting a car that was every millionaire's dream, American or otherwise: an all-new Isotta Fraschini. They took it to Genoa, where the ship would sail for New York.

The train ride had not been comfortable and they thought that taking a luxury car from Milan to Genoa would be better. But they hadn't dealt with the roads, especially the Giovi Pass. It is a winding ribbon of beaten earth with potholes and obstacles of all kinds, all ups and downs, bottlenecks and cliffs, and full of very slow carts and trucks. The dust raised by the wheels of the few cars sometimes clouded the view of the driver who, although locked in his cockpit, wore a leather cap and goggles. They stopped in Mignanego, a small village right at the top of the Giovi Pass, to rest the car after the arduous climb, but more so to rest Cloe's stomach.

When they arrived at the Federico Guglielmo Pier, the dock was already packed with people. They had to make their way through families of emigrants and accompanying relatives, carts loaded with all sorts of goods, and horses that were ill-suited to this commotion. The crowd was particularly noisy and the honking of their car trying to make its way through added to the confusion. They finally arrived at the foot of the gangway, where a sailor gave them a military salute and took care of their baggage.

The sun was shining through the ship's windows on the upper decks, the impressive wall of the "Duke of Genoa" steamship blocked the view of the city, and its two huge smokestacks filled the air with black smoke.

At the top of the gangway, the commander, the first officer, and the purser were waiting for them, all very elegant in their full dress uniforms. They approached Cloe and Amadeo, greeting them with great courtesy. The commander did the honors. The purser accompanied them to their cabin.

As they walked along the bridge, the purser explained that the ship was refurbished after the hardships of the Italo-Turkish War, during which it was requisitioned and dispatched for troop transport. The first class area was especially renovated, and some technological innovations were added to make it safer and more comfortable.

- We have some distinguished guests on this trip. I believe one of them is an acquaintance of yours, Mr. Rockefeller, who honors us once again with his presence. When he travels to Paris, he often uses Italy as an embarkation port.

- Of course, I know him well - Amadeo said. And, to himself: "Unfortunately."

Amadeo could not stand him and he was distressed by the idea of having to make the trip with him. He lowered his gaze: from the dock and to the walls of the "Duke of Genoa," hundreds of people were shouting their goodbyes to each other. On the one hand he was delighted by such festivity, but on the other he was annoyed by the excessive noise. He was reminded of the journey of his parents, emigrants of another time, and a twitch of affection squeezed his heart.

3

They stopped in Naples for just a few hours to allow other passengers to get on and off and to replenish supplies. Amadeo and Cloe decided not to disembark, but admired the view of Castel dell'Ovo and Vesuvius from the port. Leaning against the railing, they observed the bustle of people and goods.

- Look, that gentleman by the car is Rockefeller.
- Is he leaving?
- I don't know, maybe he's arriving.
- He didn't show up on the ship.
- No, he didn't. Who knows what he's doing in Italy.

They went to the upper deck to enjoy the sun.

The next few days of the trip were still very enjoyable. The perfect weather and the classy Italian cuisine made the voyage delightful. They were invited almost every evening to the captain's table or the purser's table.

-   I didn't see Rockefeller, didn't he get on board? - Amadeo was curious.

-   Yes, he reserved two connecting cabins. He uses one as his office and the other as a dining room.

-   It's strange that in all these days he has never shown up, not even once - Cloe interjected.

-   I think he takes advantage of the proximity to the coast to send radio messages to his offices. Now that we are passing Gibraltar, he'll probably take some time to relax.

They crossed the Strait of Gibraltar at noon on a sunny day. On the right-hand side, the Rock, imposing and threatening, stretched out towards the sea. On the left-hand side, in the distance, you could faintly make out the African coast of Ceuta. A merchant ship crossed their path and the two ships greeted each other with a long whistle.

As predicted by the purser, they met Rockefeller for dinner. He sat at the captain's table, they sat at the purser's table. They greeted each other and exchanged a few polite words.

That was the last night of calm waters. At the crack of dawn, the ship began to jostle its passengers.

The days passed and the sea gave no respite, even though the ship was equipped to ease the movement of the waves and the captain did everything possible to deal with them. Life on board was not pleasant. At mealtimes there were many empty seats and the musical shows did not arouse as much enthusiasm as they deserved.

The sunshine and optimal temperature allowed people to linger quite pleasantly on the outside decks during the day, but the trouble began in the evening. It was not uncommon to witness the occasional bout of seasickness, with sailors rushing in promptly to clean up the mess.

Both Amadeo and Cloe, after the first day of discomfort, got back in shape and did not miss a dinner. At the table, the commissioner commented: - I'm happy to see that the movement of the ship no longer disturbs you.

Cloe was excited about the voyage: - Just the first day. Now you can tell that we've got a rhythm going.

- I'm glad. As you can see, you are among the few.

Not even Rockefeller was seen around anymore.

The ship came into sight of the coast one foggy morning. The ship's loudspeakers announced the approach to Ellis Island.

Amadeo and Cloe were leaning against the rail. As the fog cleared, several boats came alongside the ship. The Statue of Liberty appeared, immediately followed by an outburst of cheers, whistles, cries, songs, and chants. Amadeo and Cloe looked excitedly at the statue and at the people below.

They went down to the cabin to prepare to disembark. They were the first to get off.

In front of the gangway, the commander and his officers greeted the guests. Rockefeller was right in front of them. They had not seen him since that famous dinner after the Strait of Gibraltar. When he reached the gangway, Rockefeller vigorously shook hands with the ship's doctor.

- Thank you so much doctor, I don't know how I would have done it without you. You helped me survive this tremendous trip. I don't know how to repay you.

And the doctor, in English with a thick Neapolitan accent, replied: - I am happy to have been useful to you. But, you know, since the Etruscans invented money, there is a way.

Amadeo looked at Cloe and under his breath said:

- That doctor is the prototypical Italian.

As they shook the commander's hands, their smiles had not yet faded.

PART XI

1
Los Angeles
1913

Amadeo was distracted as he sat comfortably in an armchair in his new office on Spring Street in Los Angeles. Looking out the large window, he let his mind go to the memory of that time, over twenty years ago, when he had seen the valley from the hills. How excited he had been about the orange groves and the care with which the farmers treated the countryside!

The sun was beating down hard. Even though his sombrero protected him, it warmed up his head and made him drip while an unbearable heat rose from the sweaty horse. And yet, the view was breathtaking. At his side was a Mexican farmhand, Angel, who had been working for his company for a long time. He was a trusted person, and very young, whom Amadeo had brought along for fear that his Spanish wasn't good enough.

They took the train almost all the way to Los Angeles, hired two horses, and headed north. It hadn't taken long, and after an hour of galloping they arrived in the nearby hills.

The plain that stretched out in front of them was quite the spectacle, covered with orange groves and meadows where cows and sheep grazed. There were a few roads with scattered houses and the sea was glittering down at the bottom.

Amadeo turned to his friend.

- What do you think?
- Marvelous. We're sure to find the oranges we need here.

They went down to the base of the hill. In the plain, the orange trees were full of fruit waiting to be picked. The trees, well spaced out and lined up like toy soldiers, gave a sense of the care with which the land was treated. The aroma was exciting.

Now, locked in an office on the fifth floor of a gray stone

building on a street full of cars and trams, those memories cast a veil of melancholy over him. In just twenty years, that beautiful valley had become a conglomeration of buildings and roads full of traffic that, day after day and week after week, occupied the valley's beautiful orchards and went down to the sea.

Amadeo took his hat, went down to the street, and went to look at the people, the stores, and the businesses near the bank. Many people were walking on the wide sidewalk, some in a hurry and some with the air of having time to waste. But all were well-dressed, giving the clear impression of a lively and affluent society. Amadeo strolled around, looking at the traffic and at those same buildings he had despised a few moments before but were now putting him back in a good mood. He took off his jacket. The heat and the breeze that swept the streets became pleasant again, and his bad mood melted away in the Hollywood sun.

He thought of calling Cloe. He wanted her to share in his state of mind. He went into a wine store and came across a kind Italian man who, as soon as he realized that this stout gentleman with a smile on his face was the famous Giannini, immediately put him in touch with his home in San Mateo.

Cloe was frightened: a phone call in the middle of the day? Then she was shocked: to call just to tell her he was fine? She asked him a thousand times if everything was really okay. Then she was moved: had he really left his business matters just to call her? Amadeo barely managed to convince her that yes, everything was fine and he was happy and had simply felt the need to call her.

Afterwards, he went back to talk to the shopkeeper.

- Why are you telling me that the wine is too much and of poor quality?

- Because my father made wine in Italy and I worked at Krug in Napa Valley for many years. In Italy, wine is made from just one grape variety. Krug is trying to do that too, but here they are used to putting together any of the grapes they have. They almost never make a selection. The care of vineyards is non-existent. They only think about quantity. Of all the wine I have, I will not sell bulk wine to you. I could sell you a few bottles of Latour's Beaulieu or...

- No Italian wines?
- After vine pests destroyed 90% of Italian and French vineyards, only big companies were saved and Italian vineyards were bought by French and Germans. They were and still are more organized. They made crosses and planted insect-resistant vines. The pests no longer attack the roots of vines like they did to the European vines.
- So the Italian companies... ?
- There are only a few and not high quality, I'm sorry.

Amadeo knew this because it had been a long time since an Italian asked him for financing to purchase a vineyard, and a couple of them had gone badly.

He returned to the office and his mood soured again. Fagan was waiting for him.

- I see you chose the best! - he commented while looking at the bottles, then continued: - From what I've heard, the Italian producers are not doing well at all, not for a while.
- We need to review our positions toward those companies ... If we need to support someone in need ... I want to talk about it with Guerri, who we'll see in a few days.

Fagan answered him absent-mindedly as he looked at some of the papers in his hand.

- Park Bank isn't doing well either, in fact. I would say it's downright bad. I have the reports here and I don't like them.
- I know. And so does Williams, which is why he has summoned us.

Williams was the new superintendent of banking for the Governor of California. He was very in favor of supporting struggling banks, so he called Giannini to propose an acquisition that would allow him to expand in that area and save a struggling bank at the same time.

After a few hours of meeting with the superintendent, they defined the acquisition with a clause that Park Bank would change its name to Bank of Italy. Now it was a matter of working hard to get the bank back on its feet. There was a lot of competition, but Amadeo was confident that he could get all the customers that the other banks were rejecting. He wanted to replicate the success they had in San Francisco now that he had a much stronger position, but the two realities were different. In Los Angeles there were fewer Italians and in San Francisco he didn't have to fight against such hostility. Now a press campaign had begun against the "Italians" with frequent hints of unsubtle racism.

Nonetheless, within two weeks the acquisition was technically completed and the executives, old and new, were ready to work.

Amadeo was pleased. The new bank had two branches, in addition to its headquarters, which allowed it to cover a rather large area.

2
Hollywood
1913

He was sitting in the office in continuous contact with Pedrini, who kept him up to date on all the important events from San Francisco. He was waiting for the new members of the newly acquired bank that he convinced to join the board in just a few days. He chose people who were very influential in the area, such as Secondo Guerri, an Italian and the president of the Italian Vineyard Company, and John Lagomarsino, the president of the California Lima Bean Growers Association. Then he invited a big real estate developer, a big fruit farmer, some hotshot lawyers, the old president, and the bank's chief clerk. In all, there were 21 new board members. All people were chosen according to the rule that it is better to have friends than foes.

When they were all seated around the table in the meeting room for the first board meeting, Amadeo stood up, took the floor, and with his firm and authoritative voice said: - Good morning everyone. I read in some newspapers that our presence here has not been very appreciated. You too have read about the unpleasant attacks we have suffered mainly because we are Italian. Some of you are still Italians, others have Italian origins, but I believe that all of you have sensed, hidden behind the insults, the envy for what Bank of Italy has been able to do in the north. Our success has been based exclusively on the willingness to grow that small business that had no support from anyone—not from public administration, not from private institutions, and especially not from banks. I believe that free enterprise must be the cornerstone of our society and that banks must be able to support this growth by facilitating access to credit and offering sustainable rates. To be clear, I do not believe that we should not have profitability. Quite the opposite, actually. But I do believe that good accessibility conditions can provide entrepreneurs with the tools to grow, and that their growth will be the basis for the growth of our bank as well. You have been asked to serve on this board primarily because of your social and entrepreneurial skills, but also because you know the area well and lead companies or organizations that represent an important part of Southern California's economic sphere. I believe that the reason you have agreed to become members of this board is precisely because you, too, share the goals that this bank pursues.

- Dear friends - Amadeo continued, - "I am by nature very realistic, but also very optimistic, and I promise you that with everyone's help this Bank will soon become one of the most important in all of California.

A round of applause underscored his words and Amadeo concluded: - So thank you for accepting this position, which I am sure will draw the ire of many people, but the best response to criticism will be the results of our work. Welcome and good luck with your work.

Another round of applause closed his short speech. Secondo Guerri asked for the floor.

- Amadeo, thank you for inviting us to partake in this new adventure. I can confirm that you are right that the civil society, as they call it, of Los Angeles does not like the intrusion of foreigners, be they Italian or from who knows where. The banking world has always been very closed-off, as if every day we face the difficulties that come from drought or hurricanes or insects that eat our crops. We are simple people, used to working and taking risks. We all know how common practice it is for loans in this area to be granted only to friends and friends of friends as long as they are backed by some, let's call it, parallel favor. We must end this immoral practice that only rewards a certain type of business community, an entrepreneurship that we are not a part of. And, I say this loudly, we are proud of it. I think I can also speak for the other friends sitting here: we will be the best supporters of this bank and strive to make it great, the greatest. Hurrah!

Guerri began to uncork the first of the bottles he brought to toast. The toasts came one after the other, the empty bottles multiplied, locally produced cigars popped out, and they began to talk about farming, about wine, and no longer about the bank. And Amadeo, at the center, knew at least as much about it as they did.

3
Los Angeles
1913

- Gerardo, how are you this morning?
- I'm well, Mr. Giannini. How are you?
- How many years have you been here?
- I came to America two years ago last month, and in one month I'll have been in Los Angeles for two years. Do you know that I still remember everything about when I arrived? It's always been on my mind. It was such a thrill that the other night I started writing a sort of story about my arrival. But I've only just started it.
- Well done, Gerardo. Do you want to be a writer?
- I'd like to. Being around books and newspapers makes you want to write.
- You do things right, then let me read what you write sometime. And if you need it, I'll help you.
- If you want the story, I have it here. Then bring it back to me because I have to finish it.
- For now, give me my paper.

Gerardo took the newspaper and inserted the pages he had written.

- Here it is. If you don't give me good news, though, I won't give it to you.
- I have nothing new to tell you today. The stock market is not reacting and everything is stable.

It had been two years since Amadeo met that quick-witted and always smiling Italian boy. When Giannini was in Los Angeles, he would pass in front of Gerardo's cart full of books and newspapers on his way out of the house. When he bought the newspaper, he would give him some information about the stock market—things that were simple for anyone who worked in the financial sector, but were extraordinary for the layman. Gerardo, who was a very thrifty boy, invested his small savings according to Giannini's recommendations and slowly accumulated new resources. In just his second year of following the information he received, he gathered enough capital to buy a house in Italy if he wanted to. That was the goal of all emigrants, but he didn't want to freeze such a large sum. On the contrary, he kept his money liquid to be able to invest more and more. He wanted to be rich, really rich. Giannini cared about him and Gerardo knew that and trusted his advice.

-    Mr. Giannini, what do you think about me opening a kiosk for books and newspapers?

-    How many things do you want to be? A bookseller or a writer?

-    Don't tease me, I could never be a writer.

-    And where do you want to put the kiosk?

-    Over there, on the corner.

-    And who would work there?

-    I would. And, maybe, Vincenzina.

-    Your wife? But didn't you want a child?

-    Yes, but not right now. And if we ever do have one, there's also her sister.

-    Well done, Gerardo. You're right. I'll read what you've written in the coming days and then I'll get back to you. If the kiosk goes poorly, maybe become a writer.

Amadeo walked away smiling.

When he got home he called over Cloe.

-    Listen to this, we have a new writer in town.

-    Who is it?

-    Gerardo, the paperboy. This morning he gave me a piece of a story he wrote about arriving by ship many years ago.

Cloe sat next to him, attentive and curious. Amadeo made himself comfortable. The subject that Gerardo previewed had interested him and was full of memories. The writing was clear and orderly, even if a little shaky. Amadeo began:

Even though the morning fog was clearing, it was still impossible to distinguish the line of the horizon that separated the sea and the sky. The colors were enveloped in the cotton wool of that indefinite atmosphere that, in the autumn days closest to winter, blends and softens the colors, bringing them close to gray. The ship was approaching and everyone was out of their cabins. Some were leaning against the gunwales, some were standing up, wrapped in their thick winter coats. They were out there in the cold to see what everyone had already heard about from their acquaintances: the towering, hopeful spectacle of the Statue of Liberty. The ship had been reducing speed for a while now and the engines were almost idle. The fog horn sounded at regular intervals even though the visibility was not that bad, but they were in the river and there was a lot of traffic of ships, boats, and smaller boats.

I was also leaning against the gunwale for almost an hour, but no matter how hard I looked, the sight I saw was just an extensive gray haze. The cigar that hung between my lips had long been extinguished and only the strong taste of tobacco mixed with the burnt flavor of the cigar kept me company. At that time I had just turned twenty, but I already felt like an older, experienced man. I had been working since I dropped out after elementary school, but no job satisfied me. Little money and no future were not for me. I felt that the world had very different goals to offer me. The problem was that I had no idea what they might be. But between the certainty of nothing at home and the hope of a future full of success in an unknown world, I chose the second option without hesitation.

I had read up on what the landing would be like, with the days of quarantine in a sort of prison that was Ellis Island. Then, I would finally take on a new life. I was with my uncle who was fifteen years older than me and also leaning against the gunwale. He was much calmer than me. He seemed to be

waiting without the slightest worry to see the Statue of Liberty emerge from the mist and announce our arrival.
- *Uncle, aren't you cold? - I asked him.*
- *Of course I'm cold, but I don't want to miss the view of Ellis Island. I didn't miss it last time and I don't want to miss it this time either. Are you nervous?*
- *Oh yes, Uncle. Very.*
- *I heard you last night, turning over in bed.*
- *I didn't sleep at all.*
- *Come on! You were snoring like an ox. Look!*
- *Where? I don't see anything.*
- *No, it's nothing. I was wrong. I thought I saw the statue... there it is! Yes, yes. Look! There, right in front of you!*
- *Where... I don't see... Yes, yes there it is... there it is!!!
I see it too... Oh my God, how exciting, Uncle! Here she is!
She's so beautiful!*
- *Look how big... how big... how wonderful! Come here, come on, Gerardo, you don't have to be ashamed if you get emotional. Come...*
I was trying to hide my tears, but then I moved close to my uncle and burst out crying on his shoulder.
- *I've been waiting for this moment for so long... if only my mom could see me… how exciting... how beautiful... how beautiful!*
By now the ship was very close to the statue. In order to look at it you had to raise your head and you couldn't embrace it all at a glance. The fog had cleared but the mist still covered the sea.

- That was well done, - Cloe said, wiping her eyes, - this is a boy who deserves it.

She was moved. She envisioned her parents who made that journey many years ago, like thousands of their compatriots. The story was touching and Gerardo was very talented. After all, he had barely finished elementary school.

***

Although Amadeo paid him many compliments, Gerardo never became a writer. But with Amadeo's help, he opened a bookstore. The following year he opened two more and hired twenty boys who sold newspapers on the street. That group of bookstores quickly grew into a book and newspaper distribution company. In just under a decade, Gerardo became the leading distributor of publishing products in Los Angeles.

PART XXII

1
Los Angeles
1919

There were many concerns that troubled Amadeo. His desire to expand made him impatient to open new branches and increasingly aggressive against the bankers' lobby.

Among his fiercest opponents was a Swiss-Italian-American named Joseph Sartori, a very powerful man who founded one of the first banks in California, Security Trust and Savings, fifteen years before the Bank of Italy. Sartori saw Giannini's advancement as a real danger to his business. His competitor's growth was so resounding that his Bank was beginning to seriously suffer from it. In addition to his Bank, he was very active in numerous other initiatives, especially real estate, which he obtained with very dubious methods. He was involved in the construction of a number of large hotels and was also one of the most active supporters of the construction of the new Los Angeles Aqueduct, the route of which was strongly opposed by Owens Valley farmers because it caused their fertile valley to dry up. But Sartori supported the project both financially and politically, even proposing the use of the army to defend the construction work. His methods were quite rough.

To stop Giannini, he spread rumors that he was tied to the Sicilian Mafia, that he worked for the Vatican, and that he wanted to overthrow the American government. The final slander he made public was that the Bank of Giannini was out of money and that some of his clients were worried.

Amadeo was infuriated by these rumors that, of course, reached his ears. A great supporter of legality, he would never lower himself to deal with Mafia members who needed violence to enforce their own goals. He was now strolling nervously through the room of the house while Cloe watched him very worriedly. Never had she seen her husband so angry.

- I've been investigating for a month to find out who started these rumors. A month, you see, a month thrown away following rumors. And who's behind it? Sartori! And who else could it be! He and that other scoundrel from Mulholland who scammed the farmers in the Owens Valley. Scamming the farmers, you see? Farmers! Who live there, with water! He takes it away from them and doesn't even pay them! Those poor people who have lost everything! And how bold of them to speak ill of me!

- Look, those are still only rumors. If they had something, some evidence or just something true, they would have already sent you the feds.

- That's what infuriates me! If they dragged me to court at least I could take it all apart. But rumors, how do you defend yourself against rumors? They're not accusations, there's nothing written anywhere.

Red in the face, Amadeo measured the room in long strides, gesticulating like a madman. Even Cloe was frightened by it, more for his well-being than for the actual damage these rumors could cause.

- There's only one thing you can do, besides calming down and reasoning coolly.

- Which is?

- Nothing. You don't have to do anything. Or, better yet, continue as you always have. It is only with your work that you can silence these rumors.

Cloe's calmness and good sense had the power to calm him down, too. He sat down next to her and took her hand. He was out of breath. He stroked Cloe's hand in silence for a few minutes until his breathing resumed its normal rhythm.

- Yes, you're right. I don't have to do anything. Be careful, yes, but continue with my work. "In the meantime though," he thought to himself, "I'll have a nice sign put up in front of the branches."

A few days later, in front of the entrance, the words "Over $75,000,000 in assets" appeared under the Bank of Italy sign. Better to have it be known.

2

But the day came when two elegantly dressed individuals came to the Bank and asked for the director. Pedrini welcomed them in his office. The two entered and closed the door behind them.

- Leave it open, thank you.
- No, we prefer to keep our meeting confidential.
- As you wish. Please, tell me.
- I'll get right to the point. We're part of an organization that primarily works in Chicago but we have branches all over the United States, even here in California. Our activities provide us with a certain amount of liquidity which we intend to send to our parent companies in Italy. We know that you have a brilliant system for getting remittances from Italians to their families in Italy.
- Yes, it's true. We are very experienced in that regard.
- We, however, would prefer that these remittances of ours have a certain secrecy. That neither the sender nor the receiver be recorded.
- We guarantee the confidentiality of our remittances, but we must indicate who sends and who receives. All that must be recorded.
- I insist. We give you the money and you send it to Italy. Then these transactions must disappear.
- You caught me off guard. I'm just an executive, I'll have to ask my director.
- Well, talk to your manager then. Let him know that the day after tomorrow we'll be back here to find a solution.

As soon as the two exited, Pedrini called Amadeo.

-     They came. You were afraid of it, and sure enough it happened.
-     As expected. I'll talk to them when they return.

They returned two days later, as they forewarned.

-     My employee has explained to me in a nutshell what you need. Do you still want to clarify some details?

Giannini was told from the beginning everything he already knew.

-     How much money are we talking about?
-     A lot, a great deal for you.
-     I'm really sorry. We never turn down a great deal but if your conditions are what you told me, I don't think we can do anything. I really am sorry.
-     You are Italian. We are also from Italy. You must understand us and help us.
-     I would like to help you very much. But I must tell you something that few people know and that should not be divulged.

Amadeo moved closer to the two and lowered his voice with complicity.

-     We are the Bank of Italy, you understand? Bank of Italy. That is, we are the Bank of the Italians. When we send remittances to Italy, the feds come to check each transaction one by one and want to know everything. Among other things, we are constantly getting checked by plainclothes agents who pretend to be customers. We don't even know them but they circulate and observe everything that happens. They might even be here today, we don't know. Losing a good deal pains me, but our hands are tied. Maybe it's better if you go to an American Bank. They can help you out.
-     We'll see you again soon.
-     With pleasure. If you have any good proposals we are always available.

The two exited, slamming the door. Pedrini came in after a moment.

- How did it go?
- I told them that we have the feds monitoring us.
- And they believed it?
- They're gone for now. I'm furious. The newspapers refer to us as the bankers of the Mafia and these men come in and propose this crap! Don't let me see them again. And let's keep our eyes open.

3

Amadeo spent long periods in Los Angeles because his branches, which he opened in the plains as close to farmland as possible, worked extensively with southern agricultural producers. He had his brother Attilio come to Los Angeles. At this point, Attilio had abandoned his medical profession years ago and was totally dedicated to the Bank. The goal was to increase their work in the agricultural sector as much as possible.

Amadeo's strategy was to obtain substantial federal funding under the Federal Farm Loan Act and use it to support the settlers. He had asked Attilio to join him in Los Angeles because he had a particular talent for dealing with people, whereas Amadeo was rather disagreeable to government officials. This occasion required relying on someone of the highest caliber.

- I've already gotten all the necessary information - Attilio said after listening to Amadeo's line of reasoning. - In order to access state funding, we must amend our bylaws. You know that the settlers use brokers to deal with the banks. That costs them more than five percent, and the brokers are bound to the banks and not to the settlers. That money is all wasted.

- This is a practice that we need to stop immediately - Amadeo said. - Go to New York now and get the financing, and I'll get the new business set up here in the meantime.

For dinner they picked a good Italian restaurant in a garden with a large pergola of orange trees. The two brothers did not have many occasions to be together and Amadeo wanted to be informed about everything.

- Do you remember Sol Lesser? We went to the grand opening of his theater with Cloe a while ago. Do you know how they're doing?

- Of course I remember. We gave them 500 dollars. They were incredibly successful and now they want to open six more theaters.

- Interesting. Stay on them. If they need it, follow them. You'll see, this will be a rewarding endeavor.

4

Attilio returned from New York a month later. He obtained the financing and they were now ready to attack the market of agricultural settlers. In the meantime, Amadeo had taken over six new banks that he was working on for some time and was preparing to acquire four more.

While the post-war economy was faltering and the banks were suffering in the rest of the United States, Amadeo took advantage of these moments of weakness to take over new branches. Technically, these were not true acquisitions, which the law prohibited. It was a matter of having friends purchase shares of the banks and, when it was possible, they would in turn sell them to the Bank of Italy.

After struggling for almost a year to limit the Bank's expansion, the new superintendent Stern decided to widen those narrow legal procedures because he was beginning to appreciate Giannini's strength and intelligence. Most importantly, he had the astounding results of his management before his eyes. This way, some banks would avoid being overwhelmed by economic difficulties.

Amadeo and Attilio left the office and went to their usual restaurant where the food was good and where, more importantly, it was quiet under the magnificent pergola of orange trees. Amadeo was pensive and Attilio looked at him with concern.

- The new acquisitions are taking up too much of my time. I can't deal with anything other than putting all the new businesses together. I'm also pretty tired. Cloe scolds me every night. She says I'm coming home later and later and I don't talk to her anymore.

- And she's right. You should listen to her more. You know she's always given you good advice. But - Attilio continued - I wanted to get back to the subject of Sol Lesser. Over the past year, I've gotten to know a lot of New York producers and I can guarantee you that they're all working like there's no tomorrow. I have the impression, however, that California will soon supplant New York; here there is sun, desert, forests, and the sea, while in New York you have to build everything in the studio and costs are rising. Some have already moved to escape the clutches of the big guys who have monopolized production. In New York you have to go through those three or four people who decide if and when to make you work and at their prices. I started working with Vitagraph and Shenck Brothers, who have moved a substantial portion of their studios to Hollywood. They've both already started working again and their first films will come out before long. By the way, while I was leaving for New York I was given a script of a film by an unknown writer. I brought it to you to read because it seems interesting, it's the kind you like. The problem is that it doesn't involve famous actors and the story is completely different from the usual love stories they make now. In fact, no producer wants it.

- What is it about?

- A child rejected by his mother who is raised by a poor man and living from day to day. When his mother wants him back, the child runs away to return to his new father. It's a very moving story but full of comedic bits.

- Who wrote it?
- Some guy named Chaplin.
- Never heard of him. I'll give it a read.

Amadeo read the script and some time later wanted to meet the author. A funny little man showed up with a lanky gait and a bowler hat on his head that was too small. As he sat down in a chair, he funnily removed his equally funny hat and spun it around so that it ended up hanging from his bamboo cane.

Amadeo smiled. He had never seen such an original character with a serious and sad look, two little moustaches under his nose, and eyes always on the move. His clothing was curious to say the least: his pants were too loose, his dinner jacket fell off his shoulders, and his feet seemed to dance in his shoes.

- Good morning, my name is Charlie Chaplin.
- Good morning, my name is Amadeo Giannini. It is a pleasure to meet you, Mr. Chaplin. I read your script and I confess that I liked it.

Chaplin put aside his character and became professional. Even the tone of his voice changed.

- Thank you. As you may have read, the movie I'd like to make is made up of funny moments, with some other touching and tragic moments. But it sounds like a good story to me. I've even thought of a title: "The Kid."

They discussed it for a couple of hours. Chaplin confessed that he had nothing to offer as collateral and that other banks would finance him, but at rates of 20 or 25 percent. He was very disheartened. Amadeo listened carefully and then made his offer: the Bank of Italy would finance the movie with an amount higher than what Chaplin requested, which he would pay back with 20 percent of the box office. No interest, but profit sharing. If it is successful, great. Otherwise, the Bank would lose its money.

Chaplin rejoiced, never having expected to receive $50,000 without interest. He sprang from his chair to hug his benefactor, hopping in his oversized shoes, twirling his cane, and whistling a very merry tune. The funny little man from just before had returned.

Filming began in July 1919 and the film premiered in January 1921. It was a resounding success. The debt was repaid in six weeks and that film became the most profitable investment in film history for many decades.

In New York, Attilio was also working very well. One evening, at the table, Cloe wanted him to tell her about his experiences in the world of cinema—the love affairs, the actors, and especially the actresses who hung around him. But Attilio was much more pragmatic. He was a banker, even though filmmaking had become one of his main enterprises.

- Schenk came again. He is the smartest of them all. He knows how to present his projects to you. He inundates you with his words to convince you to finance him.

Amadeo knew him very well.

- He's good though. He's done a lot of things and done them well. He has never let us down.

- Sure, but you have to keep him under control. He tends to spend more than he should. Maybe not in film production but...

- In his life of luxury?

- Very much so. Anyway, he came and asked me for another 300 thousand dollars, in addition to the 600 I had already given him. I asked him for collateral for this. He was shocked and offended: "But you've never asked me for collateral. I always pay you back on time. Why this change?" he said, flailing about and walking around the office nervously.

- What did you do?

Cloe and Amadeo were amused.

- I let him blow off steam. Then, when he finally sat

down again, I told him: "Dear Joe, you have to admit that 600,000 dollars without collateral is already a lot. Another 300,000 seems excessive. You know, I told my boys that, without collateral, I wouldn't even give that kind of money to Rockefeller, Senior or Junior. Not even to Henry Ford and, if I have to add others, not even to J. P. Morgan himself." He walked away offended, but I know he'll be back.

Cloe wanted different kinds of stories.

- What's new in film?

- Go see a Walt Disney film. He does stories with pretty interesting animated drawings. I haven't seen any of them yet, but I'm told they've already screened a couple of his shorts. He comes from advertising and seems to be very talented.

- I've heard about him. Cloe, when we go to Hollywood let's look for something of his.

5

The news coming out of Europe was certainly not reassuring. The Great War had just ended, leaving behind 20 million deaths and a devastated land. Emigration to the United States had also resumed on a massive scale from many eastern countries such as Poland and Slovakia. Poorer countries such as Greece, Spain, and Portugal along with less poor but more war-torn nations such as France continued to fuel the flow of migration in a major way. In Italy, poverty reached unbearable levels. The young people who had not died in the war were now leaving their homeland, depleting the workforce more and more. The nation was exhausted. The war had destroyed everything, including generations of young people who heroically sacrificed themselves for a new love of country that first bound the nation during Italy's unification fifty years earlier.

The post-war crisis inevitably reached the United States,

first hitting the companies that produced military equipment and then gradually all the others. California was hit some time later and less aggressively, mainly because its primary economic activities were related to agriculture and particularly to the cultivation of cotton and beans. Military uniform production was easily transformed into civilian clothing production, perhaps in lower quantities but at higher margins.

But in 1919, prohibition began to hit hard on producers of spirits, wine, and beer with strong ramifications on the agricultural economy and the value of land. The Bank of Italy was also affected, but it had the strength to withstand it without too much damage.

Amadeo watched with concern as the region's economy evolved with a particular focus on immigration. In the last year, the population increased tremendously and changed demographically: it was time to take action.

Therefore, he wanted to gather all the key players of his Bank. He needed to express his thoughts but he didn't want to abuse his spot at the top of the hierarchy, as he had often done. He wanted to involve everyone in person, listening to opinions and proposing general work assignments that were very clear. He gathered everyone in Bank of Italy's main office in Los Angeles: the advisors, the directors, the chief cashiers, and also some particularly active executives from all the California branches.

The hall was packed with more than 100 people standing and waiting for Amadeo to take the floor.

- Dear friends, I wanted to talk to all of you because I believe that we need to radically transform our attitude toward the area we live in that has changed and is still changing. When I founded the Bank of Italy in San Francisco, I did so because I felt that the local banks were not sufficiently open to the population. With hindsight, we realized that the population that we helped has, over time, become a formidable asset for the city and the area. We obviously benefited from them as well, and it has been a continuous growth ever since. Now it seems to me that, while we make a lot of effort, we are no longer able to engage the real economic players who might have the skills to bring new business initiatives to life. And who are these new players? They are the immigrants who have just arrived and who have fled war in Europe. This time they're not just Italians; they're Germans, French, Russians, Poles, and let's not forget our neighbors, the Mexicans, trying to make their fortunes here, too. What I would like is for many of these people to be hired as soon as possible, and for a proper school to be organized internally for them to learn basic banking practices. At the end of the course, I would like these new hires to be made available to all these immigrants who do not speak our language. I would like our Bank to become the reference point for everyone. And when I say everyone, I mean even those who feel like outsiders in our cities. I would like us to become a place where they can find a sign of familiarity and closeness.

His speech was met with some initial coldness and a sentiment that was perhaps not racist, but the fear that some of them would lose their jobs to new hires was palpable. Some tried to ask questions simply to get more clarification, but no one thought for a moment to expose themselves with arguments to the contrary. Eventually, after numerous questions and just as many convincing answers, everyone realized that Amadeo was right as usual and that no one would be fired, so the meeting ended with a hearty round of applause.

A few months passed. In the California branches, these new employees began to approach their compatriots, who were bewildered in the halls of the banks, to be of help. The Bank of Italy made a massive advertising campaign with posters written in many languages inviting people to approach the bank where they would surely find an official who spoke their language and could help them. The campaign was very successful despite the harsh, scathing criticisms expressed in numerous newspaper articles. Amadeo didn't worry about it and in a few months the Bank became, as he had predicted, the home of many immigrants who had no one else to turn to for help. Amadeo himself became involved in many initiatives to support immigrant communities throughout California.

6

He was talking about it with his friend Sebastiani, a great producer of wine and especially grappa, a great passion of Amadeo's. Napa Valley was magnificent, colored with various shades of green from the new leaves of the vines and trees that were coming back to life. It was a spring Sunday and the two of them were sitting under the pergola of the cellar where Sebastiani produced his wine. They talked about anything and everything as they tasted some good salami and sipped his famous grappa.

Between lines of cigar smoke, Amadeo was describing how the branches have been getting the most bizarre requests since they hired immigrants from many parts of the world that the Bank was not always able to satisfy.

-     Fortunately, my employees include some extraordinary people with astounding problem-solving abilities.

The grappa had loosened Amadeo's tongue, and he also took pleasure in recounting his experiences with his friend.

-     I'll tell you this story that is wonderful and shows the true extent of the steps we have taken. One morning, a young Mexican woman with two men in tow showed up at the Ventura branch of the Bank of Italy. The woman was very excited and happy and ran off to find the official who would understand her. Fortunately that official was also a woman, among the best in the class that all these new employees take. The Mexican woman excitedly tells her that her fiancé had finally declared that he wanted to marry her, but that she would first have to divorce her previous husband. My employee is quite astonished, but also intrigued, so she keeps listening to her. Obviously she points out to her that they're in a Bank and not a matrimonial agency. The woman is undaunted and, strengthened by our advertising, very seriously says,"You are the only ones who understand me and you are important, great, you can do anything. I want you to take care of it!"

-    Funny, it's clear that your advertising has not only hit the nail on the head, it's gone too far.

Sebastiani was amused.

-    Maybe you're right, but listen to how it ends. At this point, my employee is confused and trying to stop the flood of her words. "This really is a Bank, not town hall or church" she tells her, and the other woman is still unwavering. "No, no. I know that you can do it. You must marry us. Now!"

-    And what did your employee do?

-    She also tried to stall because, I've made this short for you, but there was a back-and-forth that never ended with the two men standing around looking intrigued and even embarrassed. Then, to try to calm her down she says "I'm sorry, but it can't be done right now. I have to ask when it's possible. Come by in a few days and I'll tell you when." And the woman asks, "Should we come back tomorrow?" "Not tomorrow, in a few days. Let me ask, when I know anything then I'll tell you."

-    And how did it end?

In the meantime, Sebastiani was slicing salami and pouring drinks.

-    The employee acted immediately. She spoke with the branch manager, then went to find the first Catholic church with a Mexican priest to ask him for information and prepare everything. When the Mexican woman showed up again a few days later, they explained how to do it and gave her a sheet of paper with the addresses of where to go. After less than a month, the woman got a divorce. Shortly thereafter, the couple was married and the Bank gifted them the floral decorations.

- What an extraordinary story!
- If you only knew how much we laughed with Cloe about this new "matrimonial agency" business at the Bank. By the way, I don't even know how they managed to get divorced.
- This is what you mean by integrating with the area.
- Of course integration is good, but maybe there's no need to overdo it. However, I did want to meet the employee to give her an award. She had an unmatched presence of mind.
- Great story. If you want to stay a bit longer, my wife made some tagliatelle.

7
San Francisco

San Francisco's Italian community was well organized in cultural and political clubs and looked to Amadeo as its main protector. From the frequent meetings of these clubs, it became increasingly clear that the problem of monetary remittances from the United States to Italy was becoming significant. It already was at the end of the century, and this was one of the reasons why Amadeo decided to found his own Bank. But despite his efforts and the improvements he implemented, the problem persisted. Even Cloe, who attended the Italian associations for women in San Francisco and knew the concerns of members' wives, raised the issue with him. In fact, it was not uncommon for the ladies themselves to complain about the difficulty of transferring money to their families in Italy. It was therefore a problem that needed to be addressed and Amadeo, as was his custom, decided to tackle it by focusing on the possible solution, not the problem.

He had many friends in Italy. During his travels he met many businessmen and bankers, and he visited them in both New York and San Francisco many other times. He had already done something in years past with these gentlemen, but now the time had come to consolidate the project. At that time, however, he was under some stress because the big East Coast bankers, among whom J.P. Morgan Jr was the most active, were again trying to stop his expansion. His lawyer and long-time friend, Jim Bacigalupi, had been trying for months to convince Superintendent Stern to allow him to take over a Bank in the East. Stern already had to defend himself against the attacks of bankers when, shortly before, he authorized a decisive expansion of the Bank of Italy in California. And now he was under pressure to stop Giannini in the east. Despite all the efforts of his rivals, Giannini got authorization to take over the East River National Bank, his first Bank on the Atlantic Coast.

Now, finally, he could think about Italy.

A few years earlier he had convinced a group of Italian entrepreneurs that if they founded a Bank with the characteristics he suggested to them, it would have the full support of the Bank of Italy and especially of Giannini. Part of this negotiation was carried out by the Italian Chamber of Commerce in New York. In 1917, while the war was still raging, these entrepreneurs founded the Banca dell'Italia Meridionale, the Bank of Southern Italy, with precise collaboration agreements with their friends overseas. In 1919, less than a year after the acquisition of East River and just after the end of the Great War, Amadeo crossed the Atlantic again and landed in Naples.

8
Naples

Italy was shattered by months of strikes and riots. The northern regions were paralyzed by the communist squads that shut down the cities and factories. Instead of facilitating the country's reconstruction, the end of the war had highlighted the very serious economic problems that were causing a dramatic revolt against the king and the government. The newspapers, which had full pages of reports and comments on the demonstrations, were practically split into two factions. The first was led by *Avanti,* the official paper of the Socialist Party, which praised the strikes and the city revolts. The other referred to *Popolo d'Italia,* the official paper of the Fasci Italiani di Combattimento, the new party just founded by Benito Mussolini after he left the Socialist Party a few years earlier. This faction instead condemned the communist violence but called its followers to the fight. Tensions were high and civil war was just around the corner.

The regions of the South—less affected by the destruction of the war, but afflicted by historical poverty—looked fearfully at the conflicts that were destroying Italy from Rome upwards. In Naples, membership of either political faction was rather mild and the Monarchy, still much loved, was rather absent.

When Amadeo disembarked, he was greeted by a city that was decidedly calmer than he expected. The news he was hearing and the newspapers he was reading had shown him a situation that was much worse than what he was seeing now with his own eyes. Of course there were no cars, at least not as many as in California. The "shouters," or newspaper boys, sold not only newspapers but also vegetables, fruit, and cheese, or it was the plumber or the coalman who was "shouting" his profession in the middle of the street. The buildings were mostly still upright, the German airship bombs from the surprise attack the previous year had damaged the Quartieri Spagnoli, and Posillipo and Piazza Municipio still had clearly visible damage, but certainly not comparable with the destruction of the northern regions closer to the front.

Naples, however, was a city that had lost its jobs. With the end of the war, all military contracts had disappeared—from munitions to carpentry, and the entire black market, which had developed in parallel. Unemployment was high and the peasants who left their small farms a few years earlier to come and work in the city now found themselves without work in the factory and without their farms.

Amadeo was happy he didn't bring Cloe. That sight would have distressed her greatly.

9

Rome

His short trip to Rome deeply moved him as he met with some of those entrepreneurs and friends who founded the Bank on his advice. The capital, though far from the war, already showed signs of the poverty that the conflict was inevitably dragging in. But the abandoned countryside, the crumbling farmhouses, and the impassable roads caused him such pain that he abandoned all doubts. When he met the group of friends who founded the Bank, he made them a dignified proposal to take it over, much to the relief of the Italians who already believed they had lost their money.

In order not to alert his American enemies, Giannini had the acquisition of the Italian Bank done by his company, Bancitaly Corporation, which he had founded a few years earlier as a container for real estate and some banking holdings that would later be transferred to the Bank of Italy. These were some of the tricks that he, the faithful Pedrini, and the lawyer Bacigalupi had invented together with the ever-present Attilio, who was a tenacious and imaginative worker. His enemies were growing in number and in power. The usual big bankers were joined by some senior federal officials and new bankers such as Henry Robinson, the new president of the Pacific Southwest Bank who was also a senior member of the Republican Party and a close friend of President Herbert Hoover. The need to use a corporate vehicle other than the Bank arose from the fact that by now the Federal Government had established so many rules to stop its expansion that it had become necessary to work around the law with borderline illegal methods.

Giannini had created the largest Bank west of Chicago and had the highest number of depositors in the entire United States. The operation he had just concluded with Italy had opened a direct bridge for him to become an active participant in the postwar reconstruction of his parents' country.

10
San Francisco

Cloe was waiting for him at home. She was easily convinced not to follow Amadeo on his journey because she knew of the tragic conditions in Italy and also because she was very concerned about Virginia, who had been suffering from a heart condition for a few months.

Since she was a young girl, she overcame all sorts of vicissitudes with extraordinary fortitude, including the tragic murder of her husband. Now, as the years passed, she had become a weighed-down woman, struggling even to get up a few stairs in the house. She had just turned 65 but had aged prematurely in recent months, putting the entire family on edge.

Amadeo went to see her as soon as he arrived in town. As he entered the house, he ran into Lorenzo, who was also advanced in age and was spending more time at home than in the office. He asked about his health and then went upstairs. For the first time he saw her old and forlorn in her chair, which was the same chair she used to sit on to knit in their first real home in San Jose. She was looking absent-mindedly out the window, her hair pulled back on her head, as was the fashion thirty years earlier, a shawl over her shoulders, and only a string of pearls to polish her figure. Amadeo was overcome with emotion. Virginia hadn't heard him coming and she turned around when he called to her, showing her wrinkled face where two dull eyes were looking for him with love. But her smile remained fresh, almost youthful, and her whole face lit up at the sight of her son. She got up with some difficulty, but paid little attention to that strain.

Amadeo came over to help her.

- I'll do it myself, thanks. I'm not dead yet! Come on, let me see you. You've been gone a month. I was just thinking about you and about Italy. How was it? Let's sit here, come, tell me about your trip.

They moved to the couch nearby.

- Bad, it was bad. The war was devastating. Poverty is everywhere.

He briefly described his train ride from Naples to Rome, then told her what he ate and how good the pasta was.

- Just tomatoes, no weird sauce, garlic, tomato, two basil leaves, and a dreamy pasta. Believe me, we don't even know how to boil water here, let alone cook pasta!

Virginia was returning to the energetic woman she once was, able to get excited about little things like a plate of pasta. But then she wanted to know about his work.

- I took your advice. It took a while, but we finally got it done. Now the Bank is ours, not all of it, but in a year's time it will be. And then we'll change the name. I don't like the Bank of Southern Italy. What about the North? I don't want to stay in Naples, I want to open branches all over Italy. It's much easier there, there are no American rules.

-   Do people know that you are behind this? That in a very short time the Bank of Italy will be there?

-   No, not yet. But maybe it's early. Even the name, in my opinion, is stopping the expansion. But still, we need to consolidate it and find people who can manage it well.

-   You're right, the name needs to change. And don't call it the Bank of Italy, call it the Bank of America and Italy. It gives the sense of the close connection between the two nations without belonging to neither America nor Italy.

Amadeo was speechless. He had come to visit a dying mother and found an effervescent mind, capable of astonishing him. There wasn't even any discussion; the Bank would be called Banca d'America e d'Italia.

That was the last time he saw her alive. After a few weeks, while Amadeo was traveling, he received the news that his mother, the pillar of his life, the one who had always fought with him and for him, had passed away one night, in silence and without disturbing anyone.

PART XIII

1
Stanford
1928

- … And now, with great pleasure, allow me to call our benefactor to the stage. In truth he needs no introduction, but I would like you all to applaud Amadeo Peter Giannini.

In the Great Hall of the University of California at Stanford, the voice rang out powerfully, amplified by large speakers. A thunderous applause followed the closing words of the president, the last in a series of important figures who had spoken before him. Now it was the guest's turn.

Amadeo rose from his seat in the first row, caressed the hand of Cloe sitting at his side, and climbed the four steps leading to the stage. The applause continued and he had to work hard to get silence.

In addition to the faculty and the authorities of San José in the audience, there were many students who were the children of the farmers whom the Bank of Italy had helped to expand and become rich.

- You all know that I was born a few miles from here. My first job was in the fields. My father, Luigi, was a farmer and I have always respected and loved this profession. Since I decided to become a banker, my ambition has always been to help my local area and make sure that California farmers could have their own local bank to support and guide them. Today, the Bank of Italy is the first among all the banks in this area to finance agriculture—the first here in San Jose, first in Salinas, first in Marysville, first in Madeira, and first in Ontario. In Stockton we are second by a very small margin. We are proud of that and proud to see that here among you are many children of the farmers who were able to take advantage of the Bank of Italy's presence to improve their circumstances. For this reason I have decided, together with my family, to personally finance the construction of a new wing of this university, which will be dedicated to the study of new crops, new technologies, and the economic questions that will derive from them. To do this, I have allocated a sum of $1.5 million to this university.

There was a moment of stunned silence. None of the previous speakers had mentioned amounts, only a "gift". Suddenly the room erupted in applause with hat tosses and rodeo whistles. Everyone stood and cheered like there's no tomorrow. The president struggled greatly to restore order. When he resumed speaking, Amadeo was moved. He took a check out of his pocket and handed it to the president. The applause started again. Amadeo returned to sit next to Cloe.

- You've done a beautiful thing.
- I think so, too. All this money… We're rich enough. Don't you think?

Cloe took his hand.

A couple of months earlier, the Bank's shareholder meeting had approved both a bonus for President Giannini and the distribution of a substantial dividend, which made many of the present shareholders incredibly enthusiastic.

Amadeo didn't want them to give him a bonus for the work he did the previous year and had discussed that at length during the board meeting a month earlier. When he took the floor that afternoon he was very harsh.

- Members of the board, I thank you for appreciating my work, not only with your beautiful words addressed to me, but also with a significant cash prize. I thank you again but, if you'll allow me, I would like to refuse it. I do my job in a way that seems most logical and fruitful for our Bank. I already receive great financial satisfaction from the distributed dividends and I don't need anything else. In fact, they are far too much for me and my family. You all know how I feel about it. Money is not my priority.

James Flagan, the Vice President and his friend from many battles, responded to him. Although very ill, he had wanted to attend that meeting.

- Dear Giannini, perhaps you forgot to include the salary you receive as part of your income. That dollar a year that the Bank has been struggling to pay you for years.. Surely that's indispensable for your personal life.

The advisors all laughed. Fagan had thus dampened Amadeo's harsh tone and continued.

- I don't want to list all the things you've created and accomplished this past year. I just want to mention your obtaining permission from the Treasury to issue banknotes with legal value. We haven't yet done the math on how much this new business is making us, but the early data is exciting. So, as far as I am concerned, I reject your refusal and, as a matter of fact, I would like it to be endorsed by the other board members as well. Thank you.

The applause that followed confirmed the decision. Amadeo would take a bonus of $1 million.

Back home, sitting at the table, he talked about it with Cloe. She was obviously interested in that news: they could have bought a new house or given it to one of the children when needed or who knows what else.

- That's a lot of money.

- I know, that's why I tried to refuse it. But there was nothing I could do.

- You know I feel the same way, but that's a lot of money. Frankly, I wouldn't know what to do with it.

- We need to use it well. Doing nothing with it would be a shame. We could buy a vineyard and then make our own wine.

Cloe looked at him furtively and smiled.

- Then you go there to prune the vines...! The only thing you can do is to give them back to the city, our city, the city where we lived and that has always helped you in your work.

Make it happen. It will be a thank you for the love we have always had from these amazing people.

2
Los Angeles
1928

In one of his many phone calls from New York, Attilio advised his brother Amadeo to go to the movies and see Walt Disney's latest film, Steamboat Willie.

\-   Go see it. Cloe will definitely like it, it's fun. If I can, I'll even set up a date for you to meet him as soon as he comes to Los Angeles - he had said.

Amadeo mentioned it to his wife who was still very interested in new movies and was looking forward to it. But she couldn't remember who Walt Disney was.

\-   He's the creator of those animated films. We saw one, which I must say was mediocre, some time ago.

Cloe had to think about it for a moment.

\-   The one on the plane with a funny little mouse?

\-   Yes, that's the one. Now he's made this new film, with sound. Attilio told me that it was a huge success in New York.

They commented on the show that evening when they returned from the theater. Cloe was quite critical.

\-   It feels more like a children's diversion than a movie. I would say it's lacking personality.

\-   You're right. The story is non-existent, it doesn't pull you in. But technically they are very well-done. The quality of the illustrations and movements is very good. In my opinion, it can be quite successful. But something has to change.

Two days later, a tall young man showed up in Amadeo's office. He had a good face but rough manners, and was not friendly with his host right away.

Disney briefly recounted his backstory, from movie commercials to early short films. He also added that he was spending more time looking for new financiers than creating new films. However, when he began to explain how his characters are born, his eyes lit up and his speech became much more pleasant. From his words, you could easily understand how much love he had for his creatures and how many incredible ideas went through his head. As if to bring the characters to life, he absent-mindedly filled the paper in front of him with drawings as he spoke. Until Amadeo interrupted him.

- Is it you who draws these?
- Yes, I do the drafts of all the images. Then I have four guys who draw the animation.
- That's an enormous amount of work.
- Yes, indeed. But it's like building a car; you start with the individual pieces that you then put together until the car runs. And seeing the finished work is great satisfaction.
- I went to see Steamboat Willie the other night. Very interesting.
- I'm glad you liked it.
- I didn't like it. It's fun, but in my opinion that's not the way to make animated films. It's fine for children, but it will never attract an adult audience.

Disney looked at him in bewilderment. - I don't understand.

- I've seen a number of character designs, interesting ones. But, again, they work within a story that doesn't hold up. I have no desire to know what will happen after a certain scene. I could watch the movie from the middle and not notice.
- Now I understand. I actually write the stories, and to be honest, they're a pretty homemade way to tie together a number of funny situations.
- Exactly. So, in my opinion, it doesn't work. You should think bigger. Come up with a story that is interesting—not only for children who are much more attentive than we are,

but also for parents who won't come back to see one of your movies. In the movie business, innovations without heart or personality quickly go out of fashion. Your stories are destined to end up like that. If you'll allow me to give you some advice, look for a story. Maybe one that's already written by someone good and try to adapt it to your technique. The story must be good, interesting, engaging, and full of imagination.

- And where would I find it? And how much would it cost me? I'm making some money now with this film but I had to sell my car to produce it.

- Look for a children's fairy tale, a famous one that everyone knows, and make a movie out of it. Take a fairy tale from the Brothers Grimm, so you don't even have to pay for a copyright. Get some ideas on how to develop it, then come back to me and we'll see what we can do.

Disney returned many months later with a rather thick folder of drawings.

- Since we met, I've only been working to follow your advice and I prepared three proposals.

He took the drawings and told the first fable. Amadeo was perplexed.

On the second try, Disney took out the designs of Snow White, the dwarves, and the evil queen.

- This is *Snow White and the Seven Dwarfs*.
- I know the fairy tale, let me see. How long could it be?
- I have no idea. Half an hour? Forty minutes?
- No, it has to be much longer. It has to make sure that you feel the happiness of Snow White and her life with the dwarfs, the sadness of the curse, the search for a solution, and the great joy of love in the end. I believe that an hour is just enough.

Amadeo was already thinking about the film as if it were in production.

- And it needs adequate music, too.
- It's a nice dream, but I don't know if I can make it happen.

-    ...and the seven dwarfs must sing.

Disney was embarrassed. The banker was fantasizing out loud. It was a good sign, though.

-    Bring me the sketches with the rewritten story. I'll take care of the rest, don't worry.

It took eight years and 1.5 million dollars to make the one-and-a-half-hour film. Most of the financing was provided by the Bank of Italy, which led a consortium created specifically for this purpose.

Snow White and the Seven Dwarfs was screened for the first time in December of 1937 at the Cathay Circle Theatre in Los Angeles and was a resounding success. Almost all of Hollywood's most famous actors and producers were in the room, from Charlie Chaplin to Clark Gable and Judy Garland to Marlene Dietrich.

A week later, Amadeo came home with the New York Times. The headline was *Thank You Very Much, Mr. Disney.* A year later, Walt Disney won an Oscar.

3

Amadeo climbed the grand staircase at the entrance of the Los Angeles Public Library. The monumental building was awe-inspiring and the grand staircase had a majestic effect. A clerk was waiting to escort him to Orra Monnette, a petite but smart-faced and bright-eyed man who was one of the Library's board members at the time.

Years earlier, Orra Monnette received a considerable sum of money from his father that came from the exploitation of a particularly rich vein of gold. Orra made numerous investments with that money. One of which was the American National Bank of Los Angeles, which, after a few years and numerous acquisitions of other banks, was moved to the corner of Wilshire and Western Avenues and changed its name to the Bank of America of Los Angeles.

Amadeo looked around, appreciating the richness and beauty of the interiors. Monnette was waiting for him on the marble balcony of the upper floor that surrounded the large hall below and onto which the management and employee offices overlooked. He was an elegant, smiling gentleman, a little older than Amadeo. He took a few steps towards him with his hand outstretched.

- Thank you for coming to see me. I gladly would have come to you.

- I must confess that I insisted because I have never been here and I was very curious. Congratulations, it's a magnificent building.

They walked through the office and continued to talk. Amadeo was impressed by the building's size, its organization, and the amount of books and documents that were being looked up there.

- So the reason you're trying to raise the funds is to expand the Library - he said.

- We no longer know where to put the donations that come in all the time. Valuable documents, entire collections of antique books. It's really becoming a problem. We have to build a new wing, and quickly too.

- It will be an honor for the Bank of Italy to endorse one of these bonds. I have seen something magnificent that absolutely must be supported. Count me in.

The visit had ended, and the two men headed for the exit. Monnette, interested in the fate of the competing Bank, did not miss the opportunity to inquire.

- I know that the Bank of Italy is doing very well and that you're expanding more and more.

- Yes, I must admit that we are doing quite well and we are expanding our influence in the east as well. But you don't know how many difficulties we've had. We have everybody against us.

- I understand you well. When I started my bank, I put

in a million dollars out of my own pocket and my intent was to make sure it was supportive of the area. I wanted to copy you, but at a higher level. When I needed to expand, for a time I was able to. Now, any excuse is a good one to stop our expansion. I try to ingratiate myself with politicians through these charitable actions like the Library, but to little avail.

-   I'd like to talk to you again - Amadeo concluded - who knows, we might be able to agree on some communal project.

4
New York

They met frequently over the next few months. Amadeo had not only endorsed one of the Library's bonds, but had also personally made a donation. Orra Monnette was thrilled with his new friend. He was fascinated by his modern take on business. Amadeo, for his part, had a project in his head and was working on it in secret.

In the meantime, Monnette had managed to move his Bank's headquarters to New York City at 44 Wall Street and developed a good relationship with J. P. Morgan. This friendship could be crucial to Amadeo's plans, and he decided the time had come to take action and meet with the great New York banker.

John Pierpont Morgan Jr. inherited the ability to do business, along with the colossal fortune that he managed, from his father. Like him, he was cynical, opportunistic, and ruthless. His word was law in New York, especially within the banking world. The Morgan family fortune was born in the steel mills and developed in finance, a field in which it had excelled for more than a generation. With this great wealth, he had acquired great power that he used without moral qualms.

The meeting took place in Morgan's office on Madison Avenue. The large, solid wood desk, dark oak paneling, and low lights gave the room a severe elegance. Extraordinary antique sculptures stood out among the few pieces of furniture and paintings of the finest workmanship were masterfully displayed as a feast for the eyes.

Amadeo found an awkward man sitting at the desk. His face was dominated by a large nose that his rather prominent mustache uselessly tried to hide. His thick eyebrows protected his piercing, almost ghostly eyes. At first glance, he knew the man deserved his fame. Instead, he was struck by the beauty of that room. A museum. Wherever he turned his eyes, he discovered extraordinary new details that only an avid collector could have put together. You could see the enormous amount of money devoted to his love of ancient art.

- May I compliment you on this room? I find it unique, extraordinary. Quite frankly, I've never seen anything like it.

- Thank you. As a matter of fact, this was my father's passion and now it is mine too. I devote a lot of time to it and, between us, a lot of money as well.

- This looks like a portrait of him.

Amadeo pointed to a lavishly framed painting that hung on the wall beside the magnate. It was a magnificent portrait of a stern man with piercing eyes.

- It looks like it, but unfortunately it is not. It is a portrait of a Dutch merchant, a certain Nicolaes Ruts. It was done by a young Rembrandt. If you'd like, I'll also show you the rest of the office which is pretty interesting.

- It will be a pleasure! Maybe later, to distract us from our own problems.

- Well, you know I've been getting information about you and the Bank of Italy. It seems to me that you've been doing a pretty good job in California and other states. I also understand that you would like to expand into our neck of the woods. Why? There are already many of us here and I don't see how your policy of low rates and minimal credit can help this area which, again, is already abundantly covered.

-    Frankly, I don't want to expand my Bank. But I would like to take over one for which I am already a shareholder.

-    What bank is it?

-    Bank of America.

-    On Wall Street?

-    That's right. I would like to merge it with my other New York bank, East River National Bank. As you can see, nothing that would jeopardize the status quo.

The discussion went on cordially. Amadeo agreed to sign off on a substantial loan to his host's bank. Then J. P., clearly satisfied, closed the meeting.

-    Well, your projects seem noteworthy to me. Proceed as you have told me, and you will have no obstacles from my end. I would be grateful if you could begin as soon as possible with the financing of my Bank. As we said, this is a fundamental point of our agreement.

They parted with the promise of another very welcome visit to J. P.'s office-museum.

Amadeo agreed with Mannette to acquire a majority stake in the Bank. Soon after, he arranged for the merging of the East River National Bank and the Bank of America of Los Angeles.

The new banking group after the merger was now one of the largest in the entire United States. There were numerous branches in every state, east to west, north to south.

5
San Francisco

The return to San Francisco to inform Cloe that his project had been successful was not a happy one. When he arrived in San Mateo, the atmosphere in the house was bleak.

-    Mario has been sick.

-    What do you mean?

- He got a cut and the blood wouldn't stop coming out. The doctor said that Mario most likely has hemophilia.

Mario was the eldest son who had finished his studies and started working at the Bank. Amadeo considered him his heir.

Amadeo had to sit down on a chair.

- What can be done?
- They are trying to figure out what treatments are best. They will tell us something any day now.
- Where is he?
- Upstairs, in his room.
- How is he?
- You'll see. He's pale and weak.
- I'll go see him.

Amadeo climbed up the stairs with great heaviness. He entered the room and looked at his son lying in bed. He was asleep, pale and thin. He looked at him intently, perhaps for the first time. He sadly realized that he had not been a good father. He didn't play with him as a child, he never paid attention to his hobbies, he never went with him to a baseball game even though Mario loved it. Amadeo was more connected to soccer, as it was played in Italy, but he wasn't even able to teach him that. He barely knew that there was a Ligurian team called Genoa Cricket and Football Club that was well ranked in the Italian league. The few times he came by the house, he spent more time with his Cloe and let the children keep to themselves. But Mario had not been a child for a long time. He had already finished his studies and had been working with him for a couple of years. He realized that what he knew about his son was only related to his work. His life was just the Bank. His actual family was the Bank. Suddenly he felt alone. He sat down next to the bed and, perhaps for the first time, caressed him.

Mario opened his eyes and looked at him, almost in amazement.

- Dad!

- Mario, I'm sorry I woke you.
- Don't worry. I've been sleeping all day.
- How are you?
- I'm weak, but tomorrow will be better. I can feel it.
- Tonight you eat a nice steak and you'll see that tomorrow will be completely different.
- How did it go in New York?
- So far we've done the merger and have no problems with other bankers. Frankly, some hostility as I expected, but Morgan seems to be protecting us.
- Are you sure about that?
- No, not at all. I don't trust Morgan. I'm afraid that shark is planning some action against us. The two banks together are too greedy of a bite and he can buy them in one night with the money he has. We have to think about protecting them. But I already have a plan in mind. Now go to sleep. I'll see you for dinner.

6

Mario was soon back on his feet. His illness remained serious, but did not impede him in any way. With the new medications, he could lead an almost normal life while being careful not to injure himself. He moved around with a cane and an emergency medical kit that he would carry for the rest of his life.

A few days later, Amadeo sent him back to New York with precise instructions. First, he was to found a new company, the Transamerica Corporation, in which he was to combine all the shares of all the banks in their group so that no one would be able to take possession of a single Bank. All this was to be completed as soon as possible and with the least amount of publicity. Mario was appointed the chairman of a board of directors that included a number of New York bankers with ties to J. P. Morgan.

***

After about a month, Mario returned to San Francisco. Amadeo was waiting for him with a bundle of newspapers on his desk.

- Have you read it?
- From this morning? No, not yet. I just got off the train.
- I could feel it in my gut that Morgan was setting a trap for me. He gave me his blessing to settle in New York because he thought he could take over the majority of our banks in one fell swoop and become the largest banking group in the United States. He thought it through. But we were quicker. Read: "we will not allow Italian immigrants to take possession of our banks," "the raiders of Americans' savings," "the collective front of the American banks against the Italo-Californian speculators." Pretty harsh statements. They'll give us a run for our money.

When they came out of the office, they were mobbed by a group of journalists looking for statements.

- Giannini, how do you respond to the Eastern bankers? Tell us how you'll defend your reputation.

Amadeo and Mario tried to make their way through, but the pressure was considerable. Mario took his father by the arm.

- Maybe it's better if you make a statement.

Amadeo stopped. Flashes went off and reporters jostled around.

- I've read the interviews that were published this morning. For now, I must tell you that the instigators of those words reported in the papers are not prominent bankers on the East Coast, but only second-tier figures. We approached that market in friendship with the people who really mattered. We would never have allowed ourselves to seek confrontation with anyone, in fact. Perhaps we organized everything a little too quickly, given that we are used to this and it seems useless to waste time on marginal issues. But I assure you that these journalistic attacks have surprised me because they do not correspond to the truth.

-    And what do you plan to do in response to the allegations?

-    We will undoubtedly meet again with the banking world's key players to try to figure out how to collaborate in a spirit of friendship.

-    What solutions do you see?

-    I can't disclose anything, but I'm thinking of changing the composition of the board to perhaps include more coastal bankers.

-    Will your son Mario remain president?

-    Don't ask me questions I can't answer. We'll see. If necessary he will also take a step back. Again, we moved in friendship and in friendship we want to stay. Now, if you'll allow us, we have a lot to do. Thank you all.

When they were alone, Mario wanted to know.

-    What do you have in mind?

-    I've sent a message for now. You should convene a board soon and see how they behave. I think you're going to have to stay in New York for a while.

Cloe was very worried about her son's health, and she hadn't seen him in a long time. She prepared a nice lunch and was looking forward to spending some time with him. Only their daughter Claire, Amadeo's great love, was home. She had just gotten married and was acting as her father's secretary while waiting for her first child to arrive. Amadeo knew that he had to announce that Mario would be leaving soon and that Cloe would not take it well.

-    I thought that Mom and I could go to Italy - Amadeo announced at one point. - The season is getting nice and so we will rest after our most recent struggles.

He smiled and looked at the reactions of his family members. Claire was shocked, but happy. Mario, instead, looked at his father with questioning eyes. "You're leaving me alone? To face those monsters?" he thought.

-    Mario still has some things to do in New York and in a few weeks he'll be leaving, but we'll leave as soon as we're ready, right Cloe? And we'll be gone for three or maybe four months. We're going to visit our new relatives in Liguria and then we'll go to Rome because I want to see it well. I'm expecting to see some very influential people and I'd like to take advantage of it to visit the Sistine Chapel.

Cloe was uncomfortable. She had never contradicted her husband but this time she would have stayed home very happily, even if the news from Italy was exciting: the reconstruction after the war was proceeding very well and many new things were happening.

-    Who is expecting you?
-    None other than the Prime Minister, Mussolini, a great man. He sent me a message through the Ambassador saying that when I should go to Italy, he would like to meet me. Now I will answer him.

7

Rome

A couple of weeks later they embarked on the ocean liner "Roma," the largest ship of the Italian navy that the whole world was proud of. It had a wonderful first class deck that even had an outdoor swimming pool.

The trip lasted only 12 days, just enough time for Amadeo and Cloe to get used to all that luxury.

When they arrived in Genoa, they rented a car to go see their friends in the Fontanabuona Valley—first in San Colombano, the village where Cloe's parents came from, and then in Favale di Malvaro, where Amadeo's parents came from.

They went to Rome by train, renting a private carriage to

enjoy all the comforts that those carriages had to offer. They got off at the Hotel Excelsior, where they were greeted by a pesky group of journalists who were already waiting for them. The hotel staff had a hard time containing them.

Cloe was quite annoyed.

- If we have to go through this every time we arrive at a hotel…

- They'll calm down, you'll see. Look, I've just been given this invitation, and tomorrow we're at Chigi Palace to meet Mussolini. I'm very pleased. Mussolini is the European politician who has helped his country the most. He is a practical decision maker. I like him.

Amadeo was walking around the hotel room with the card written in beautiful handwriting. The invitation was for lunch at the headquarters of the Ministry of the Interior, where Mussolini had his office.

Headlines in *Popolo d'Italia*, the daily newspaper tied to the fascist party, came out the next day about the great Italian-American banker's arrival in Rome to meet the head of government.

- Prepare yourself because today will be a long and eventful day.

Cloe watched him as he finished getting dressed.

- Are you sure you like Mussolini? There are certain rumors circulating about him.

- I've read about them. Who knows if they are true. Reading the newspapers, it seems that the story of Matteotti's murder is all a political fabrication. The trial is not over yet. He took the political responsibility in Parliament, but maybe he did it to give cover to the fascist fanatics who seem to be the real ones responsible. For now, however, there is still no real evidence.

- I find him disturbing. He seems to be someone who pretends to be a lamb and instead is a ravenous wolf.

- Come on, don't exaggerate. He's a politician and you know how politicians are easily swayed.

***

At Chigi Palace, the Giannini's were welcomed with pomp and circumstance. Mussolini clearly wanted the public to know that a great Italian, the creator of the largest American bank, was his friend and a supporter of his politics. The pleasantries took place in the palace's beautiful garden, where the police were lined up and in full uniform. They moved to the Salone d'Oro, the Hall of Gold, after a brief presentation to the press from the top of a stage surrounded by Italian and American flags. Cloe tried not to be noticed, but stood with her head in the air to admire the magnificence of that room. Then they moved on to the table. The great banker and the great politician, sitting next to each other, had a serious talk. Meanwhile Cloe, sitting next to the American ambassador, tried to keep the conversation going.

When they were finally back in their bedroom, Amadeo was tired and threw himself on the bed fully dressed.

- He didn't stop praising his politics for one minute.
- And you?
- He tried to convince me to support his party.
- How?
- Money, first of all, and then public statements, interviews, nothing particularly engaging. But I remembered your words. I didn't promise him anything, not even advertising the Bank of America and Italy in his paper. Maybe I'll do something in their paper in New York. Maybe.
- What else did he talk about?
- The things he has done. But there is always that strong tone in his words that worries me. He told me about the countryside and the farmers who adore him and the industrialists who support him. But, from the way he talks, it always sounds like he wants to go to war tomorrow. It worries me.
- You look tired. What's wrong?
- I have a little pain in my right arm, but it's nothing.

- Should we call a doctor?
- No, that's not necessary. I just need to rest.

The next day, however, the pain had not gone away. Amadeo was still refusing to be examined when there was a knock at the door.

- A cablegram for Mr. Giannini.

Cloe brought it to Amadeo.

- It's from Mario. "Terrible first BoA board meeting. Received insults and prevented from speaking. Call me. M".
- What time is it in New York?
- I'll call him now.

The operator took more than two hours to give him the line. Luckily Mario was in the office waiting for his call.

- I don't know what to do anymore. I was insulted. Our friends were never able to speak. I myself couldn't get a word in. I tried to assert my authority, but between the yelling and the booing I had to end the meeting. It was a terrible experience. I also heard that they are selling shares and the stock is losing a lot. What should I do?
- We made a mistake trying to stay friends. Now we'll have to go to war, but not right away. Let's wait for them to drop the stock again and then we'll buy. But you wait, let them take the steps they want to take.

8

Amadeo was very worried and in an awful mood, more for the Bank than for his health.

Over the next few days, the pain in his arm got so bad that he could not leave his hotel room. He had chills and a fever and struggled to breathe. The doctor diagnosed him with pleurisy and confined him to bed, forbidding him to get up. But by the next morning the pain in his arm had spread throughout his body so severely that he couldn't even eat.

- Cloe, send a wire to Mario. Tell him I probably won't be able to move for a few weeks and that he'll have to keep me in the loop.
- If only you'd leave the Bank alone for a while. Your son is there. He'll know what to do.
- This inactivity is killing me.

Amadeo wearily began to get out of bed after about ten days of very painful penicillin injections, but he didn't have the strength to do anything.

- As soon as you're a little better - the doctor said - I'll prescribe you a stay in one of my clinics on Lake Nemi. You'll see that you'll regain your strength there.

Sure enough, Amadeo and Cloe went to Lake Nemi the following week. The clinic was new and very well equipped, but Amadeo felt imprisoned.

- I haven't seen a wire from Mario today.
- He may not have had anything to say to you.

Amadeo didn't comment. He had a premonition, but he didn't want to scare Cloe unnecessarily. Two more days passed, and Amadeo insisted to the secretary of the clinic that they check for possible impediments.

On the third day, the wire came.

- It's from Claire. "Mario crisis two days. Now better. Call tomorrow. C."
- You knew and you didn't tell me!
- No, how was I supposed to know this? I was afraid of it, though. He has never taken this long to wire.

For the most part, news from Mario and the bank only came from wires that got longer and longer. Making phone calls was almost impossible. The news was getting worse and worse; the stock was falling and the bank had no proper management. Amadeo was extremely nervous. Cloe was exasperated.

- Please stop stressing. You'll never get better if you don't calm down.

- How can I calm down? They're taking away our bank. They've already taken the value to the minimum. Mario doesn't have the authority to fight those crooks. And I'm here doing nothing!
- You're sick, can't you see? And you're being treated, but treating you is worse than treating an elephant.
- If only I could make a phone call. I have to talk to Bacigalupi, Attilio, and Mario. I can't condense everything into four lines of a wire. Which, by the way, anyone can read.

July and August were a living hell. Arguments between Amadeo and Cloe were a regular occurance. However, the summer heat had put Amadeo back on his feet. On his last visit before leaving the clinic, the doctor was very clear.

- Know that you are not cured. In fact, I can tell you that you will never be cured. Forget about continuing to live the life you've lived up to now. Leave it to your children to continue your work. I recommend you take a nice vacation, especially where it's warm.

His life was in the bank. How could he think of leaving his job?

Cloe was even stricter than the doctor and, contrary to her usual behavior, she raised her voice.

- Now you're going to do what I tell you. No more of these trips back and forth to America. From now on you have to ask my permission to move around. And I'm going with you.

It wasn't a question, and Amadeo fully understood that. He began to think that perhaps the time had come to pass the baton. But not right away, he still needed to settle a couple of things that were close to his heart. The situation for the bank was very serious, almost tragic. A lifetime of work was about to go up in smoke. Amadeo had a thousand solutions in mind, but until he was in New York and knew all the details, he could not make any decisions. There were only two paths: give in to J. P. Morgan or fight him. What to do?

Cloe had no doubts. - I have never seen you give in to or obey anyone. I'd be very surprised if you started now.

Those few words were enough to trigger a radical transformation within Amadeo. Even the disease took a back seat. The only cure that could heal him was a battle. Surrender would have been his death. Amadeo embraced Cloe and gave her a kiss.

It was a couple of days before their arrival and Amadeo was rapidly regaining his strength. His gait was still unsteady as he walked on the deck of the ship and thought about the various alternatives. He had to support himself often to avoid falling, but there was no doubt that the disease was about to succumb to his will. He looked like a lion. Cloe was happy about it. She was meeting the man she loved from better times once again. That illness was forever, but Amadeo was stronger than the pain.

9
New York

-    I want to know everything!

Amadeo arrived at the Transamerica Corporation's New York offices and was now standing in front of Mario and Bacigalupi.

-    You must not withhold even a comma from me. I have been inactive for months, thinking only about the bank. Now we have to fully grasp the situation and take action. And don't talk to me about illness anymore! - His voice was back to being strong and vigorous. The anger that brooded in his body gave him an authoritative tone he had from times past.

They did great work in those weeks. He wanted to have a picture of the banks' situation down to the last detail. He wanted to know everything about all the branches and also who the shareholders of the companies were.

The U.S. economy was going strong. The stock market was at an all-time high, and enthusiasm was through the roof. When he felt ready to take action, Amadeo asked to meet J. P. Morgan again. The appointment was made a few days later.

From the window of his study, Morgan observed the hunch-backed man climbing the stairs with great effort, step by step. He was leaning on his cane and being supported by his son and daughter. Morgan could not believe that the old man was Giannini. He had heard about his illness, but had expected him to be in better condition. Claire stayed in the lobby and the two men were escorted into his office after a few minutes.

Amadeo sat down heavily in the chair without waiting to be invited and skipped the introductions.

-   It seems clear to me that we are not welcome on Wall Street. We're sorry about that, but we didn't come here to wage war. I understand the aversion that members of a tight-knit community feel when an outsider tries to break into the inner circle. I am more sorry that you do not like my son because Mario is a talented banker. He has made no mistakes whatsoever and has been punished for far more than his possible failings. But I can also understand your position and take note of it. What I cannot accept is that, for ideological reasons, a bank should be destroyed. Considerable capital has been burned on the barricades of a stupid war. This, I cannot accept. I can't accept it!

Amadeo caught his breath. Mario was tense and the atmosphere in Morgan's magnificent office was electric. After a few moments, with his head down and a tired voice, Amadeo continued.

-   I will now tell you things that I have pondered very seriously and that have cost me immense pain and great effort. I hope to have found a way to stop the massacre that has been destroying an important banking group for many months. My son will give up the position of president of Transamerica to become vice president. For the presidency I was thinking of Walker, who appears to be a prominent personality and someone you seem to trust. The two will work together, possibly in friendship, for the good of the bank. As for me, this disease of mine is incurable and is debilitating me to an unbearable degree. I have to think about my health. The treatments I'm undergoing are very strenuous and I need a lot of rest. If you need me, just ask. But I'll be staying where it is as warm as possible. New York is not for me. You can only give me two answers: either yes or no. And you have to give them to me now, because I want to leave.

J. P. looked at him and didn't understand. Was the old lion really in that condition? Or was he putting on a clever act? But his elegant suit was meant for someone ten or fifteen pounds heavier. That weight loss could not be faked. The tired, wrinkled face and white hair had certainly not come about by chance. Only his eyes were the same, but otherwise Giannini's mighty body was only a memory.

The proposition was an interesting one. Walker was a very capable and astute navigator of the difficult waters of Wall Street. And he was one of his men, very trusted. The helm would soon be in his hands.

The minutes were passing and the silence was becoming oppressive.

Giannini began to get up, and Mario helped him in strict silence.

- I understand.

And without even saying goodbye he slowly turned around, leaning on his cane and his son's arm.

- Wait.

J.P. stopped him, but Amadeo barely turned his head. J.P. hadn't gotten up when he'd entered, and he didn't intend to get up now that he was leaving. His loud voice rang out for the first time since they had entered.

- Wait. All right. Walker will be president and Mario vice president.

Amadeo resumed walking out. No thanks, no farewell, no handshake.

It took Amadeo a few minutes to get into the car, helped by the driver and his sons. J. P. observed the scene from behind the curtains. He still didn't understand how much truth there was in Giannini's illness. His doubts remained.

- Bettie!

His secretary came in an instant.

- Have someone follow Giannini—the father, not the son. And every night I want to know what he does.

Amadeo's car pulled away.

When Amadeo returned home, he entrusted his cane to Claire and briskly set off to change his clothes. Cloe, who had just returned from her errands, saw him and looked him up and down from head to toe.

- Why that old suit? With all the beautiful ones you have? Look how it falls on you. Do you dress like a beggar if I'm not around? Change and then give it to me. I'll give it to the poor.

- No, Cloe, leave it in the closet for me and don't touch it. And prepare yourself because I won't be leaving the house for a few days and you'll have to run errands for me. Important ones.

Cloe looked at him curiously.

At the J. P. Morgan Library a few days later, a rather unidentifiable man was standing in front of J. P.

- Has he gone out?

- No, never. We haven't seen him in four days. Day or night.

- Who goes to the house?

- The wife goes out in the morning to go grocery shopping. She stays out for an hour or an hour and a half, and then never goes out again. The son goes out in the morning and comes back in the evening. The daughter came once at lunchtime.

- No one else?
- The doctor came once. He stayed for a few hours.
- Anyone else? Delivery men? A lot of mail?
- No one. In the morning they come by to deliver the mail, but it's always the same mailman who leaves the doorman a few envelopes for the whole block. The doorman also collects the newspaper.

J.P. was deep in thought. Could it be that he was really that run down? Everything seemed to indicate yes. Just as well.

In the meantime, Mario had convened the Transamerica board of directors with the sole item on the agenda being his resignation and the appointment of Elisha P. Walker as the new president. With the convening of the council, the period in which Amadeo absolutely had to stay in New York and continue putting on his act was over. That day, finally, the doctor arrived early with a nurse and accompanied Amadeo and Cloe to take the train to San Francisco. The nurse accompanied them to their destination.

Cloe was happy to be done with that terrible performance she was forced to take part in. She was tired of sneaking kilos of documents in her shopping bag and was sick of seeing Amadeo running around the house during the day like a caged lion, working with his son from evening until dawn. But the instructions were mandatory. Amadeo was certain he was being watched and wanted everyone to think he was very ill.

10
San Francisco
1929

Ever since Virginia had left him by himself three years earlier, Lorenzo had given up on life. Amadeo's efforts had been to no avail, nor had those of Attilio who still had a lot of medical knowledge even though he was now a banker. Lorenzo went to the office like a robot. He listened as Amadeo told him about the Bank's successes and sought out, as he once did, his advice to give him some more stimulus and stop that increasingly rapid deterioration. When he stayed at home, Amadeo would visit him. He wanted to keep an eye on him. He felt that Lorenzo was getting out of hand and he didn't know how to stop him. They often sat in silence, but sometimes they recalled the pleasant moments of their long life.

- When you were fifteen, you were so arrogant that you didn't want to go to school anymore. You felt that it no longer had anything to teach you. What a kid!

Amadeo smiled.

- I was young!

- I remember your mother being desperate because she didn't know what to do. You were doing very well at school, but you didn't want to go back. We had a long discussion in bed that night and I proposed the deal: "One try, just one. But if it goes well, let him come work with me." I vividly remember how serious and attentive you were when I asked you to find me a truckload of oranges from someone other than our supplier. And I asked you that because there wasn't a basket of oranges in the entire San Francisco area at that time. It was an impossible bet. And your eyes were sparkling when I said, "If you can do it, I'll give you a gold watch."

Amadeo looked at Lorenzo lying on the bed, fully dressed. Memories were piling up in his head. Hearing them recounted by the man he loved so much was heartbreaking.

- You only knew about the watch. I don't recall you knowing about the deal with your mother.

- No, you're right. I just knew I wouldn't be going to school for a few days. I didn't even realize that was my first major test.

- You were as quick as a ferret and wouldn't let an opportunity pass you by for any reason in the world. When you showed up with a signed order for two trucks from Santa Ana Fruit Company, I was stunned. They became our loyal suppliers from that day on. How many times I've told them this story! And your mother, how furious she was. She really hoped you wouldn't succeed. But a deal's a deal, she had to give in.

Amadeo reached into his vest pocket, pulled out a gold watch tied to a chain, and looked at it nostalgically.

-    Here it is. I've never parted with it since then.

He looked at Lorenzo and his heart ached. He had been able to solve impossible problems in his life, but now he wasn't able to help his second father with whom he had lived an extraordinary adventure of so many years. When faced with a problem, he always had a question in his mind - "What would Lorenzo do?" - and now that same question demanded an answer precisely to help Lorenzo.

He saw him getting older every day, walking more and more wearily and talking less and less. Above all, he lost his geniality. He no longer had that half-smile when he made witty comments or that blissful expression after a sip of good wine. Gone were his jokes, his zest for life. That great man, who was a good, intelligent, tireless worker, no longer had any drive at eighty years old. He had great satisfaction in life; he went from being a cart driver to president of one of America's banking giants and had a wonderful wife who brought him three wonderful children from her previous ill-fated marriage and one beloved child of their own. Now he could leave in peace.

Lorenzo had not been able to get out of bed for the last few weeks. On August 21, after having a cup of good Italian coffee brought to him, he put down the cup and passed away. He had no illness or apparent reason for dying. He simply wanted to reach his beloved Virginia.

It was traumatic for Amadeo. Although he was expecting his stepfather's death, this grief was equal to that after his mother's. Lorenzo and Amadeo had lived their lives together, shoulder to shoulder, from the vegetable and fruit trade to the creation of the bank and the battles to make it truly great. Lorenzo was always Amadeo's calming soul, the one who held him back or urged him on when it was the right moment.

Amadeo locked himself in his office and cried.

PART XIV

1
San Francisco
1930

Walker began his presidency at Transamerica with very conciliatory statements and praise for Giannini. Wall Street's crisis on October 24, 1929 was putting the entire financial sector in serious trouble and the subsequent stock market crash caused a panic to erupt. Walker was also publicly appreciative of Giannini's very prudent work, which had prohibited all branches from speculating in the stock market in the previous months. He had ordered them to hold on to as much gold as they could. Giannini even ordered the closure of the accounts of clients who had thrown themselves headfirst into the game after tremendous stock market performance. This highly conservative policy had saved the bank.

But the day came when Walker began to criticize his management, bringing into question the veracity of the financial statements of the companies that were part of Transamerica. At his home in San Mateo, Amadeo quickly realized that he was acting on Morgan's behalf and that he was preparing even worse criticisms. In fact, shortly after, Walker decided to depreciate the bank's assets by \$1 billion, causing Bank of America's stock to plummet from \$49 to \$14.

Amadeo was furious. Walker was destroying in a few months what was built in thirty years with heart and intelligence. The final straw was a phone call from Mario from New York.

-    Bad news. Horrible, actually. Walker has decided to merge Bank of America with Bank of Italy.

Amadeo had a fit of anger and sadness.

-    He's trying to cover his own mess with our assets. Just wait, he'll make an enthusiastic statement about creating an enormous, indestructible group that can deal with the crisis.

-   He's already made it. It'll be in the papers tomorrow morning. I tried to talk to him last night. He kept me waiting in the lobby for over 2 hours, then I left. I also heard that he intends to cut the next dividend in half. So the stock will lose more and it will be easier and easier for Morgan to take the majority.

-   It will have to be over my dead body. I don't think it will be easy, though. He will be able to acquire a small minority, not more. The time has come to put our plan into action. We have some time, but not too much.

He had the afternoon to clear his head and let the anger melt away. The next morning, his counterattack would begin.

When Cloe saw him, she knew immediately that something was not right. She questioned him with her eyes. Amadeo lost it.

-   Can you believe it? A lifetime of work—the first bank in the brewery, the earthquake, the sleepless nights, my mother putting in her savings, Lorenzo—all wiped out in an instant. He didn't even warn me. He takes our money and expects us to thank him.

-   What are you saying?

-   The Bank of Italy has been merged with Bank of America. The Bank of Italy no longer exists.

Cloe looked at him and felt like crying. A wave of memories swept over her and she had to sit down. When she lifted her moist eyes, she met Amadeo's. They didn't need to speak to tell each other things; their looks were more meaningful than a thousand words.

Amadeo left to walk to the harbor. That was where he had started and that was where his counterattack would begin.

-   Alfonso! My friend! How are you? It's been so long!

Alfonso was an old friend of his and one of the first people who had purchased Bank of Italy stock and then turned it into Transamerica stock. He had a nice clothing store in a central spot on the harbor.

- Look who's here! What are you doing with that cane?
- We're getting old, dear friend. But only physically, not in spirit. The old lion is always on the prowl.
- I heard they're making you mad in the east.
- They make me sick, those crooks. Look how I have to get around! How's business with you?
- There is a frightening crisis. I haven't had a customer in days. I'm afraid the crisis will get even worse.
- You're right, and now I can't help you anymore.
- Why not?
- Because the wise guys in the east ousted me. They took advantage of my illness and threw me out. They said I did a bad job.
- I don't believe it! The nerve! You of all people!
- Unfortunately so.
- Can't we do anything?
- You are a friend so I can tell you that there could be a solution…

Amadeo went to visit dozens of friends like Alfonso in the harbor and then on the streets of North Beach. He went on foot as he had done nearly thirty years earlier. His targets were all the small shareholders from a list he was given during his months of seclusion and whom he now went to see one by one. Those he was unable to contact were notified by word of mouth and then by constant pleas in the newspapers.

When he felt that he had finished with his contacts in San Francisco, he moved throughout California, travelling the state far and wide and organizing meetings in city auditoriums. His illness seemed to take a back seat, and his strength and vigor sustained his labors.

2

Amadeo looked at the rowdy crowd of people. His hopes had been fulfilled.

In Stockton, a beautiful rural town between San Jose and Sacramento, he helped a great many farmers and now they were thanking him. Seats in the theater had sold out quickly and a large crowd was on their feet, waiting for Amadeo to speak.

He began to speak in grave silence. He spoke for half an hour and then concluded.

- You all know that our institution has always been one with a soul. We have always worked for the benefit of our customers and shareholders.Thank you all for stepping in and believing in me.

That was how Amadeo closed his speech in front of the enormous crowd that was first touched and then enraged by Amadeo's words.

One of the organizers had a hard time quieting down the roaring applause and, in a thunderous voice and articulating his words well, he warmed up the audience even more.

- There seem to be two or three New York bankers who think we are a bunch of illiterates. 200,000 investors in California who leave their savings and economic policy in the hands of two or three people from New York! Do they really think they can use Russian dictatorship methods to give orders to our Bank employees without us reacting and organizing to take them out?

A roar drowned out his words. People stood up and were screaming and insulting those bankers known only by name. Amadeo, however, was someone they had known personally and for a long time. Their trust was reserved for Giannini, not those others.

With difficulty, Amadeo took back the floor.

- Friends, I promise you that things will change soon. I

will take back the helm and pull the Bank out of the mud that these fools have thrown it into.

Another roar.

3

When Amadeo was sure he had a sufficiently large number of supporters, he began a campaign in newspapers along with radio spots, posters, and private letters.

"Back to good times" was the main commercial of the campaign and it lasted several weeks. Amadeo was so thrilled that he almost forgot about his illness.

- You caused a panic here in New York. They almost stopped saying hello to me in the office.

Mario called every day and talked about how the banking system was experiencing extreme difficulties. The crisis was eating the banks, the economy was collapsing, unemployment was growing every day, and there were long lines of poor people waiting for a meal from humanitarian organizations.

Amadeo was calm and determined. The news about the country's economy worried him to no end. Now the final act had to begin. He called Mario.

- Now withdraw all funding from Morgan. All of it, mind you, and with an urgent transfer order. This will start to give him some concern and keep him busy for a bit. Call a shareholder meeting immediately and put the appointment of a new president and new directors on the agenda.

- This will be your victory.

- This will be a victory for the Bank and its shareholders. I'm not interested in winning.

Two lists were presented at the meeting: one referring to the East Coast bankers and one referring to Giannini. The outcome of the vote was overwhelming. Amadeo thought he could win by a sufficient margin to beat his opponents, but the victory was extremely wide—far beyond anything he could hope for and, more importantly, it left no doubt as to who was the man the shareholders wanted at the helm. The California shareholders made their importance known.

Walker and his other allies were literally swept away and a new leadership group took over with Giannini at the helm.

Amadeo Peter Giannini, the son of Italian immigrants, had become the greatest banker in the world and he would never come down from that pedestal again.

4
Hyannis Port
1931

The crisis of '29 had devastated America. The industries that didn't completely fail were still laying people off. Trade collapsed, as did the extraction of raw materials. The middle class disappeared for an entire generation. In the United States, 12 million were unemployed. The same banks that had fueled both stock market and real estate speculation were hit and had to downsize. The United States stopped lending to European countries that were still recovering from the Great War and also stopped importing goods and raw materials, thus causing a general collapse on that side of the Atlantic as well.

Crime reigned. Extortion, robbery, and especially the production and smuggling of alcohol became the main activities of the underworld.

America was in disarray and only politics could provide the solutions.

The 1932 presidential election was approaching, and Giannini was approached by potential candidates for his endorsement. But none convinced him.

Some time earlier, he had some business dealings with a very influential figure both on the East Coast and in Hollywood where they had financed movie studios together. Joseph Kennedy came from Boston and was connected to the Democratic Party. He received Amadeo at his magnificent home in Hyannis Port where he was spending a few days on vacation.

Amadeo was greeted by some excited labradors and then by a group of screaming children playing in the meadow. Joseph was waiting for him on the patio terrace. The two dogs followed Amadeo, sniffing and wagging their tails before going to their master's side.

- They smell my own dogs and identified me as a friend.

- You are a friend to us, too. Welcome and thank you for coming all the way here.

The villa was immense. It stood in the middle of a large lawn facing the sea from which a healthy breeze with the scent of seaweed came.

They went into the study where they talked about cinema and the difficult economic situation. As a banker, Amadeo had a perhaps more thorough grasp of the situation than Kennedy and his concern was even greater. He expressed his ideas.

- Some time ago I was contacted by several potential candidates who, of course, asked for my endorsement. But I wasn't convinced. And, by the way, they didn't even make it to the final round of nominations. Frankly I don't feel like supporting Herbert Hoover. The mistakes he made were appalling, and I really hope he doesn't get re-elected. Rather, I believe that you know the Democratic candidate, Roosevelt. He's a decision-maker with clear ideas that he can put into practice without being influenced too much by other leaders. Do you think he is reliable enough?

- I agree with you that the next president must have these characteristics. Roosevelt is a very smart person. He knows how to listen. He doesn't get pushed around and he is quick to make decisions. He could be a good fit for us. Our joint support could be critical to his election.

-    I would not want to publicly express my formal approval right away, but I would still like to meet him — perhaps when he comes to California for his campaign.

5

Franklin Delano Roosevelt went to California on an election tour organized almost entirely, but secretly, by Giannini. At the Commonwealth Club in San Francisco, he delivered his most important electoral speech and listed all the actions he would take to revive the economy. Amadeo was impressed and fully supported him from that moment on.

F. D. Roosevelt won the election by a wide margin, but the American economy took a frightening fall in the four months from the vote to his taking office. While Hoover and Roosevelt were discussing possible government actions, industries collapsed, banks entered into an even worse crisis, and poverty became unbearable. Depositors rushed to the bank windows to withdraw what little money they still had since a collapse seemed inevitable.

In his inaugural speech, Roosevelt tried to turn around the negative sentiment that had spread across the entire population by now: "The only thing we have to fear is fear itself — nameless, unreasoning, unjustified terror which paralyzes needed efforts to convert retreat into advance."

General morale was raised in some part by this speech, but much more so by the economic initiatives that the president undertook in his first one hundred days with strong government intervention to support jobs and a more equal distribution of wealth.

Bank of America was called to bail out some smaller banks to avoid total collapse. Times were so drastic that Roosevelt was forced to stop cash withdrawals for an entire week, following Amadeo's suggestions. In the next three months, he issued an emergency decree that called for substantial financial aid, extra support for consolidation operations between banks, as well as the opening of branches without specific limits and other official aid initiatives. During this same time, he established new, much stricter rules on financial transactions to avoid the excesses of the past.

Among the actions he undertook, he also abolished Prohibition as it was one of the main reasons for the growth of crime without reducing alcoholism. Unfortunately the winemakers were in a drastic situation; most of the vineyards had been destroyed, cellars were mouldy, and companies went bankrupt. When alcohol was deregulated, prices plummeted 90 percent and those producers who were saved were dragged even further into disaster.

The New Deal initiatives ranged from providing the unemployed with public works jobs to protect the environment, coasts, rivers, and forests to tax reforms that increased taxes on the wealthy. New rules were introduced to protect competition and labor unions. An agency for the production of electrical energy was created, which allowed for a pronounced containment of energy costs. These initiatives succeeded in reversing the process of recession by slowly restarting the economy.

The crisis affected banks in a very significant way. Mergers, encouraged by the new directives, reduced in number and increased in size.

After dedicating a lot of time to politics and working closely with the president, Amadeo thought it was time to turn the bank's activities around. Taking advantage of the weakness of his competitors, he focused on the bank's growth. He talked to Mario about it. And Mario was ready.

-    I believe we are making a mistake - he said. - We are

treating our Bank and its customers like all the other banks. In my opinion, we should radically change the way we present ourselves and stop approaching customers as if we were selling any old commercial product.

-   What do you suggest? - Amadeo asked him.

-   Let's take a commercial sector, a sector that's struggling but that we believe has great potential. For example, the automotive industry: it was growing, and now it has been greatly downsized. These days, if you want to buy a new car you either pay for it in cash or companies propose a payment in installments for 12 months and with interest of 20% or even more. Let's try to change the rules, doubling the repayment period and cutting the rates in half. At the same time, we'll support this new initiative with an unceasing advertising campaign.

Amadeo paused to think about it for a moment. - That sounds like a good idea. Let's get back to funding small investments. The auto sector seems like a good start, so we can also help the manufacturers.

- I would add one more thing. You're right that we should go back to making small loans, but let's not stop at those who already have a business. Let's especially help new ventures, artisans, shopkeepers, etcetera. And let's look primarily at their reputation for lending and not just at the collateral they can give.

- This sounds like a good idea too, but let's start with the auto sector first.

After less than six months of heavy advertising with newspapers, radio, and posters on the street, the auto sector was on the upswing and became one of the major sources of the Bank's profits. On the radio every day you heard commercials with a voice saying:

"Just today Bank of America financed the purchase of 270 cars!"

"A car is bought every 5 minutes with a Bank of America loan!"

There was no shortage of political and media attacks at all levels from the usual lobbies of other financial companies that sought to stop Giannini's expansion. Nevertheless, within a year Bank of America became the second largest operator after General Motors' finance company.

A major business magazine wrote: "Bank of America advertises its loans exactly as American Tobacco does to sell its Lucky Strikes."

The ad campaign had entered into everyone's homes, and no one in California or many other states could say they never heard about Bank of America's loans.

6

Shortly after verifying that this operation was succeeding, the father and son got together again to talk about development.

Mario had become his father's closest collaborator, having inherited his imagination and intelligence. He had also taken on his management methods, which were sometimes unorthodox. Although he did not have his father's direct and almost rude manner, his policy of expanding the Bank saw no obstacles and overwhelmed the competition with proposals that bordered on arrogance. He also had the ability to intervene in difficult times for companies to find ways to get them back on their feet.

In spite of his scrawny build, he was very active and was also becoming an exuberant creative. Sometimes his ideas surpassed those of his great teacher.

-    I have prepared a list of businesses for you to consider. It's time to get back to helping both commercial and artisan small businesses and, again, I would publicize this project. As an idea, I would prefer to proceed with new ventures and leave those who already have a business for later. I met a guy a few days ago, a great designer who is passionate about jewelry. He told me that if he had the money he would have started his own business, but now he is a store assistant. These are the people who I would like to help. Or carpenters who aspire to become furniture makers. I think there's a lot of potential in this project.

-    I agree. First, we need to give precise instructions to our executives. Have them be careful not to get the wrong person, but don't have them only consider the collateral they provide. We know that most of these customers don't have much to pledge.

-    And I would add that it doesn't matter how small the request is.

They began a vast publicity campaign offering small loans to everyone. And the response was extraordinary; although the crisis was still very much felt, this new initiative became an integral part of people's lives and millions of Americans benefited from it. Thousands of new businesses were born across the United States.

In the surroundings of Hollywood, where cotton cultivation was still quite important, textile plants and tailor's shops were built. They took advantage of the proximity to the film studios to make new clothes that were modeled after the costumes on the sets. This led to the birth of a new fashion industry that had great success not only in California, but in the rest of the United States.

Cloe was intrigued by the bank's large-scale advertising campaign and was so impressed that she spoke about it with her daughter Claire, who had obviously followed the whole operation for herself. Claire, also enthusiastic about it, wanted to tell her about an episode that had just occurred.

-    We became so famous that a guy showed up in a Hollywood branch who wanted to work in the movies as a snake handler and asked us to finance the purchase of a 7-meter python for him.

- A python?
- A 23-foot monster with a body 20 inches wide that weighs 500 pounds, at least.
- And what would he do with it?
- It seemed like he wanted to rent it for the movies.

7

Bank of America's expansion did not stop there, as families and their newborns were also financed. The most well-liked initiative was the one in which the bank would give a savings account to a newborn with an initial $5 already in it. Mario thought that, in time, these would become their future customers.

During a trip to the north coast of Los Angeles, Amadeo saw the sizable fleet of fishing boats returning with fish. That was the predominant business in the Monterey Gulf. He stopped for a few days to watch the boats return and saw that they were unloading large quantities of sardines that ended up in factories to be canned. He soon became friends with the manager of the most important factory located on Ocean View Avenue in Monterey and he gave him a tour of the production line. The smell of fish was unbearable and Amadeo wanted to leave quickly.

- How do they work with this smell?
- They were born here and this is their life. I would say that they don't smell it anymore and that, if anything, they don't consider it a stink but an aroma.
- All year long like this must be hard!
- No, you're wrong. Unfortunately, sardine season is only twice a year and lasts for two or three months. For the rest of the year, they pretty much only catch other fish for local use. They only make money from sardine fishing. In fact, we close in the dead months, too.

-    I think I understand, and I was thinking about a proposal. Can I talk to you about it?

It immediately occurred to Amadeo that in the months of inactivity both the fishermen and the canning companies must struggle financially, so he thought he would intervene to support them during those months. He discovered that there were already small local financial companies doing the same work, but the intervention of the Bank, which had put itself in strong competition, literally made them disappear in just one year. In the years to follow, Bank of America's presence doubled the fishing fleet, allowing other canning companies to grow and turning Monterey into the capital of sardine canning.

8

San Francisco
1932

It was very cold. The icy wind blew down from the mountains and rippled the sea of the bay with a thousand white sheep. Amadeo, curled up in his coat, wondered why on earth he was in that place away from everything and everyone. He was locked in the car, already almost decided on leaving, when the driver interrupted his thoughts.

-    It seems like it's coming.

Amadeo looked down the street where he saw a truck trudging up the hill. He stopped beside the car and a rather disheveled little man got out of it with rolls of drawings that he struggled to protect from the wind.

Amadeo looked at him in bewilderment.

-    Good morning.

-    Here I am. Sorry for the delay but, you know, we are very busy these days.

-    Tell me.

The engineer Strauss placed the scrolls in Amadeo's car and asked him to follow him.

- Well, you see, here we are on the San Francisco peninsula. The shore there in front is the Marin Headlands, and the channel in the middle is the Golden Gate. But I think you know these things very well.

- Yes, indeed.

- My project involves the construction of a bridge about 230 feet above sea level, supported by two pillars that leave an overhang of about 3,900 feet for a wide passage for ships. To help you understand, this is a sketch of how I think the bridge will look.

- What materials do you want to use?

- Iron and steel for the bridge and stone and concrete for the two bases in the water.

- And how do you plan to get a 3,900-foot road to stand suspended in the air?

- With tie rods, here, you see. These are the tie rods and the bridge is suspended from them.

He showed him a design of a suspension bridge between two tall double pillars that supported two large cables. From those, the tie rods descended to become the supporting structure of the actual bridge.

- Interesting, very modern. Have you ever made a bridge like this?

The engineer had a moment of indecision.

- Smaller ones, yes. But something this long, to tell the truth, no.

- Leave me the design and visit me in the coming days. It's too cold here.

A few months passed. Every now and then his secretary would announce that a man named Joseph Strauss had called, but those were very intense days for Amadeo and they never managed to meet. Amadeo almost forgot about that dishevelled inventor. In truth, some people told him about the bridge. People knew about this futuristic project because the ferries were uncomfortable and overcrowded, but nobody knew why it couldn't be done. In his frequent travels, Amadeo walked along the shoreline quite often and looked at the Golden Gate. But there was no trace of the bridge.

One day he was in the car with Cloe and they waited in line in front of the ferry dock for Marin Headlands.

Amadeo looked around with curiosity.

- Cloe, look how many people are waiting for the ferry.
- What are they waiting for to build the bridge?
- I don't know.

And, as if thinking out loud: - Of course if there was a bridge, people could live on the other side without making sea trips to go home. And maybe there wouldn't be all this traffic.

When he returned to the office, he thought about the bridge again and looked for those rolls of drawings that, to be honest, he had never looked at. They were all dusty. He spread them out on the conference room table. They were very interesting, actually. He called Strauss and had him come to the office.

- Forgive me for not calling you until today but, believe me, I have been very busy with extremely important Bank matters. How far along is the project?
- We're not that much further along than when we saw each other. I finally got the two pieces of land needed for the start and end of the bridge from military property. I also found companies that would produce the iron products and steel cables.
- And how come you haven't started building yet?
- Over a year ago, I arranged financing with a bond issue to be paid back with tolls. The bonds would be secured by the land and farms on both sides. This is what I got from the counties that are interested.
- I've heard about that. It's not just the two counties of the bridge, it seems like there is also Napa, Sonoma, and others.

\- Exactly. And Mendocino and Del Norte, as well.

\- So you are way ahead of the game. But I still don't understand why you don't start.

\- Because the bonds were supposed to be approved by county residents, but the signing has barely reached 25 percent.

He raised his head and looked intently at Amadeo.

\- Mr. Giannini, I have bet my life on this bridge. I have invested ten years of work in it and a considerable amount of money for me, believe me. But at this point the only thing I can do is to give up. I am totally discouraged. You are my only hope.

Amadeo looked back at him. Strauss was no longer the enthusiastic, visionary little man who bounced around in the cold looking out over the bay; now, he was a defeated man who had lost hope of realizing his dream. As he spoke to Amadeo, a flash of dignity lit up his eyes. Amadeo noticed it and became certain that this man, who seemed like a lunatic with his head in the clouds at their first meeting, was actually the right man.

\- Tell me one more thing, how long do you think this bridge will last?

\- How long will it last? Forever. If I make something, it is forever.

He was surprised by the question; he had never had the problem of even having to state how long it would last. In his heart he thought it was obvious. And the answer came out of him in a commanding, almost offended tone.

\- Are you certain?

\- I have no doubts! Believe me! My collaborators and I have studied it for a long time. With the maintenance I have indicated in the project, I really have no doubts!

Amadeo picked up a paper and began to write. Strauss watched him anxiously and did not understand.

\- Who is the issuer of the bonds?

- The Golden Gate Bridge and Highway District and it is formed…
- And how much more would you need?

Amadeo interrupted him. He was still writing.

- 32 million, unfortunately.

Amadeo finished writing, signed the paper, and handed it to him. Strauss took it and read it. His eyes welled up and he was overcome with emotion. On the paper with the Bank of Americaletterhead it read: "Please sign off on the bonds payable to the Golden Gate Bridge and Highway District in the amount of $35 million." And it was signed by Amadeo Peter Giannini.

- But this is more than I asked for!
- Of course, I wouldn't want you to run out of money at the end and not finish the bridge. Come to the Bank, ask for Pedrini, open an account in the name of the company where the money will be paid, and, when it will be finally finished, you pay us the tolls. Go ahead, get busy. Start right away. How long will it take?

Strauss was speechless. His hope was that Giannini would sign off on a portion of the bonds so he could use his fame to convince other investors. He never would have imagined such good fortune.

- I don't know how to thank you. You are a benefactor of this city. I will not let you down and I will even return the money I don't spend. When can I start? Today, we don't have to wait a minute.

For a moment it seemed as if he wanted to kiss him, but the austere figure of Amadeo dissuaded him.

Construction of the bridge began on January 5, 1933 and was completed in April 1937. A month later, President Roosevelt officially opened the bridge to traffic by pushing a button from his office at the White House.

The engineer Strauss kept his promises. The bridge was

built on schedule and cost one million under budget. The red color came from the fact that the only anti-rust paint in stock and in those quantities was that color. To make another one in a different color would have cost too much. As for durability…

9

Hollywood

While Mario intensely devoted himself to managing the Bank's expansive and technical aspects, his brother Attilio devoted himself to cinema-related business.

Attilio was in love with that world. In the ten years following the great crisis, what he did in Hollywood made him one of the main architects of its rebirth. During the war years and the years immediately after, business was cut in half and many film companies had to close. Paramount Pictures, among others, could not be saved despite having contracted actors such as Rodolfo Valentino and Gloria Swanson, and it was later taken over by a large distribution chain. Other companies that turned to Attilio, such as Metro-Goldwin-Mayer, RKO, United Artist, and Universal Pictures, were restructured and allowed to continue producing films.

If Attilio ever had any doubts, he would ask Amadeo because he was rarely wrong in his judgments and bets on the news. It was at Amadeo's suggestion, for example, that the bank financed the launch of 20thCentury Fox.

Attilio's closest clients and friends included major producers such as Samuel Goldwyn, for whom he financed the film *The Kid From Spain*. It was shot at the height of the Depression but was an enormous success at the box office.

Attilio actively collaborated with production companies such as Biograph, General Films, Vitagraph, and Lubin. He supported actors like Doug Fairbanks, Harold Lloyd, and, of course, Charlie Chaplin. Cecil B. DeMille was one of his best friends. Attilio had financed a number of films, including Cleopatra, which was a huge international success. Bank of America subsidized films such as *It Happened One Night* by Frank Capra, a personal friend of Amadeo's, for Columbia Pictures, King Kong for RKO, films for Metro-Goldwin-Mayer, and more than a hundred others.

Attilio once suggested that Amadeo involve his friend Cecile more, so DeMille became the Bank's executive advisor for film affairs.

But Attilio was more inclined to rely on people of certain prestige; he didn't have much trust in novelties. The real innovative mind remained Amadeo's, always knowing how to seize hidden opportunities.

One of the Bank's advisors, David O. Selznik, was very passionate about cinema and decided to set up his own production company, financed by the Bank itself. This caused a conflict between Amadeo and Attilio, who did not see this operation in a positive light. He spoke to Amadeo about it.

-    It doesn't seem right for the Bank to fund one of its advisors for the opening of a personal business. It doesn't seem like a good idea. We could be accused of internal favoritism.

-    I know, but we fund so many film producers that even if one of them has a preferential relationship with us I don't think it would make a difference. And in any case, Selznik has always had good ideas.

-    Not always. He's done some stupid things, too. I don't know if you've heard but he just spent $50,000, a huge amount, to buy the rights to a novel by an unknown writer named Margareth Mitchell.

-    He's already told me about it and I've already read the script, too.

Amadeo didn't want to be rude to his brother, but he knew his limits and sometimes decided to take the initiative himself when Attilio was uncertain. After going with Selznik to Culver City, where filming had begun, Amadeo realized that the film would never be finished without his financial support. He liked the story anyway and agreed to finance the film without listening to Attilio's criticism.

The production costs of the film became enormous, far over budget and more than what had ever been spent on a film at the time. However, *Gone with the Wind* became one of the masterpieces of world cinema and an extraordinary investment.

10
San Francisco

Giannini's success and the continued growth of his bank created great concern in the financial world. His process of expansion was continuous and the Bank's dominance in business was now feared by all. Every sector that Giannini focused on was usually already covered by small financial companies that specialized in that field, but when Bank of America decided to intervene, they were overwhelmed by its strength. There was no competition that could compete with that giant.

Roosevelt's respect and friendship did nothing to stop the growing hostility towards Giannini. Treasury Minister Morghenthau took on the finance world's concerns himself. A personal dislike for Amadeo also prompted him to express unflattering judgments to President Roosevelt himself, so much so that he was convinced to launch an antitrust campaign that seemed specifically designed to stop the Bank's expansion. This action was even entrusted to the Justice Department, which immediately began to hit the Bank with a series of charges based on the anti-monopoly program launched during the New Deal. Morghenthau's concern was based not only on the continued expansion of the Bank's branches, but especially on the way Amadeo ran the Bank, which was too liberal and unorthodox in Morghenthau's opinion. Other financial institutions were struggling because Bank of America had a policy of customer friendly, and thus very competitive, rates and was still distributing dividends to its shareholders despite the ongoing crisis. Bank of America almost always beat out the competition.

Amadeo had to request a meeting with President Roosevelt to ask him to ease the pressure, but he was unsuccessful. Morghenthau demanded that one of his most influential inspectors attend one of the Bank's board meetings. There, he made an explosive statement that their accounting records were falsified by more than $40 million, so the forecasted dividend distribution had to be cancelled immediately.

Amadeo flew into a rage. He was being accused of using dishonest and rash methods. These were the same arguments the East Coast bankers used to try to defeat him. And yet, he had managed to not only survive those attacks, but expand even further. However, this time the attacks did not come from private bankers, but from the highest offices of the federal government.

He decided to write a detailed report to the Federal Reserve Board.

> The real estate sector is the backbone of the country. It is the predominant part of the population's wealth, much more than any other asset. The federal and local governments get their largest share of taxes from this sector. Real estate ownership gives citizens their economic security. It is critical that the Bank's auditing standards take into account that our valuations of real estate are guided by considerations of this nature.

The long report was carefully evaluated at all levels of public administration, but the conflict did not subside. Amadeo was convinced that Morghenthau wanted to ruin him and did not accept the Ministry's impositions. He was so furious that he publicly and very harshly insulted Morghenthau. The dispute was so heated that only Roosevelt's intervention a few months later, a lot of diplomacy on Mario's part, and the new Treasury Inspector managed to bring back some calm. Amadeo had to comply with some important requests from the Ministry in exchange for a rather long adjustment period. But no apologies ever came from him.

The great satisfaction for Amadeo was that he could see that his son Mario had firmly taken the reins of the Bank. They had gone through a historic economic crisis that they overcame with good ideas and great skill. Their enemies were very fierce and caused them enormous problems that were difficult to solve. But in the end, Mario's good sense had proved more effective than Amadeo's wrath.

11
San Francisco
1936

Amadeo's illness had not subsided. In the moment of battle, the man's overwhelming personality had only dulled the symptoms, but little had changed. A sort of neuritis spread throughout his body, causing him severe pain. In the office, fortunately not too often, it could be so bad that he could not even sit at his desk. Walking also caused him sharp pains everywhere. For a long time he was on very strong medications that, as a side effect, intensely debilitated him. After the crisis it took a full day for him to recover, and he couldn't work during those days.

Cloe was feeling the weight of the years, of the many things she had done in life, and now also of the illnesses of her husband and son—illnesses with no end in sight and which often kept her up at night. When Amadeo told her that perhaps it was time for her son Mario to take over and retire from active work, she was somewhat afraid. Amadeo at home all day? It would have been a heavier burden than knowing he was in the office. But Amadeo reassured her.

-   Don't hope that I'll stay home. I'll still have a lot to do. However, I won't have to prepare for meetings or councils and I'll be free of all those formalities. I am now seventy years old and this disease debilitates me greatly. A little rest won't hurt.

-   Have you talked to Mario about this yet?

-   No, it's just been a thought I've had in mind for a few days. I wanted to hear your opinion.

Their daughter Claire came by, as she often did to visit her mom. Her sunny disposition and adventurous spirit justified the love that her parents hid from no one.

She was surprised to find her dad at home. - I didn't see you in the office. How come?

-   Nothing of concern. I thought maybe it would be time to give way to Mario and lessen my presence at the Bank. You are the second to know, even your brother doesn't know yet.

-   That sounds like a good idea. That way you'll have more time to take a few trips with Mom.

-   We'll see.

Claire followed his thoughts. - Mom has wanted to go back to Italy, you know.

-   In Italy? Right now? Are you sure? - Amadeo looked at Cloe.

-   Why do you say that?

-   Remember when I told you about Mussolini?

-   Sure, you spoke highly of him.

-   It was a few years ago, and I already had the impression that Mussolini was a fanatic. Now we know for sure. He turned into a dictator. He started a war, a disaster, in Abissinia with his crazed desire for his Empire. And the rest of Europe is not safe either. There is unreasonable enthusiasm, but in truth they are all preparing for war. Italy has become a dangerous country. I have a nagging feeling. I would say I'm almost certain that something bad is going to happen soon. The news from Germany is bad. My fear is that the situation will collapse at any moment.

Cloe looked at him, displeased. - What a horrible thing you're describing!

-    I don't want to scare anyone, but this is the news I have and it worries me greatly.

Mario was honored by his father's proposal. He was already vice president, so the step would not involve a significant increase in his workload. The state of his health was stable; his seizures were less frequent even though the actual illness was always present.

At the meeting, Bank of America's shareholders approved of his appointment as CEO as well as, by a unanimous vote, the appointment of Amadeo as President for life.

The newspapers put the succession between father and son on their front pages. Their reports included his words. "I want to pull back a bit and leave the helm of the Bank in younger hands". Some mocked the suspicious shift in power within the family in a company of that size. But, by now, Giannini's greatest enemies had lowered their weapons and did not pounce when they heard the news.

12
Hollywood
1939

Early on, Amadeo tried to enjoy his new status as non-operational president and considered himself "retired." In fact, he slowed down his visits to the offices to only when strictly necessary, or when his son requested his presence. Instead, he took advantage of his new "retired" status to indulge in his favorite pastimes, the countryside, and the outdoors. It was not uncommon to see him walking in the valley in San Jose with some of his friends who showed him the crops, or among the Napa Valley vineyards, sitting with the owner while sipping wine or, even better, grappa. Grappa was bad for him and he didn't abuse it but he always enjoyed a few little glasses when Cloe wasn't there.

Amadeo was invited more often to film premieres than to other social events. As a cinema lover, Cloe always pushed him to take advantage of those invitations while Amadeo tried to avoid them, preferring instead to go and see them without the social event. But sometimes he couldn't say no. They were also officially invited to the national unveiling of the latest Chrysler model, the New Yorker. The Detroit-based company chose Hollywood for the unveiling. It was a social occasion that Amadeo would have gladly avoided, but he was personally invited by the president of the company, his old friend, who also let him know there would be a surprise. He couldn't miss it.

That day, they arrived in front of the Chrysler showroom entrance and a large crowd was already forming in the parking lot in front of it. The entire building was festively decorated and there were flowers everywhere. A small stage covered with American flags and Chrysler flags awaited the guests while, in front, the shiny new model made a fine show on a low platform surrounded by vases of flowers.

After a few minutes of pleasantries, the president of the company, who had arrived expressly from Detroit, began to speak. He praised the car's mechanical qualities, its modernity, and its line. He then talked about the company, how many people they employed, how many cars they produced, and then he concluded.

-    Everything I have told you was able to happen because, five years ago, a person who knew better than anyone how to look to the future had the courage to help us with a loan that allowed us to invest in new machinery and design the new models that include this marvel. That is why the Chrysler board of directors decided to make a tribute to this person and I will have the honor and pleasure of presenting it to him this evening.

I ask you to give a warm round of applause for Amadeo Giannini, the president of Bank of America, who has allowed us to become a great automotive company.

Amadeo was not expecting it, as no one had warned him. The flashes of the cameras lit up before his eyes. He was truly surprised. He stood up from his seat in the front row and approached the microphone.

- Dear President, you have taken me by surprise. You didn't tell me that I would be not only a guest, but one of the main participants of the party. I would have prepared a speech. Luckily I didn't, so I'll be brief. I decided to finance your company because I have seen how you work and what you produce. And I could see that you care about blue-collar work, which you know I also care about, so my choice wasn't difficult. I'm surprised that others haven't come to the same conclusions as me. So, thank you for having that mindset.

He started to head off stage while a thunderous applause underscored his words.

- Wait a minute, you can't leave. There is still the gift I promised you.

And from a pants pocket, he pulled out car keys.

- Chrysler automobiles is pleased to offer you the gift of the first "New Yorker" model in the United States, with our warmest thanks.

He extended the keys towards Amadeo. Amadeo was stunned. The applause was never-ending.

The photographers gathered around the two of them to capture the passing of the keys and followed them as the president showed his guest the car. Amadeo standing in front of the car. Amadeo sitting behind the wheel. Amadeo with Cloe, who was made to stand up by the photographers. Amadeo shaking hands with the president. They wouldn't stop, and he was quite confused. In between the flashes, the suspicion crossed his mind that this was all just a way to get free publicity. They would be in all the newspapers the next day.

Amadeo resumed speaking at the microphone.

- Dear friend, I am speechless. You've given me a real surprise, thank you. This is an incredible gift and the car is beautiful. We have known each other for many years and you know that I have only done what I felt was right. I don't deserve awards of any kind. It's my job.

He went back to Cloe, followed by applause.

Gradually people began to leave. Even Cloe wanted to head back, but Amadeo still had to say a few words to his friend. He took him aside.

- My friend, I must confess that you surprised me. You've known me for so long. You know how I am, so you didn't inform me of anything because you knew I would refuse. You cornered me. What were you thinking? You know I don't like these things. Why are you giving me a gift like this? With all those photographers and the reporters who will publish that I accepted a gift from one of my clients. The Bank is publicly listed. You can't do these things. And beyond the rules, I'm the one who doesn't want this. I can barely accept a bottle of grappa as a gift, let alone a car. And besides, I don't even have a driver's license anymore. What do I need a car for? I already have one with a driver.

- I'm sorry you take it that way. We really believed in making a gesture of gratitude to you. Tell me what I can do. Believe me, I am truly sorry.

- For now I'll return your keys. Now take the value of this car and donate it to a charity of your choice. Tomorrow, along with the photographs of the two of us smiling, you will also have it reported that I donated the amount to charity. Please do it now, before nightfall.

13
Palo Alto
1939

The predictions of war in Europe had accelerated the production of war supplies. Heavy industries and naval shipyards were working at full speed to produce tanks, weapons, ships, and aircrafts. California was in full swing with its manufacturing industries and its oil sector, which had to supply the allies in Europe in addition to the domestic market. American ships cut through the ocean carrying all sorts of goods, medicines, food, and, obviously, weapons. Bank of America was, of course, at the forefront of financing companies engaged in the war effort.

The war in Europe was the dreaded outcome of a political situation that was no longer sustainable. The United States was heavily involved in wartime production. Bank of America's policy of financing small businesses allowed them to consolidate and grow significantly. Giannini created a new economic information office in Washington, the Bank of America Defense Information Office, which proposed new job opportunities for businesses and also offered them financing. This new office multiplied entrepreneurial activities throughout the United States and especially in California. In just six months, nearly 2,000 contracts were signed and businesses were lent more than $42 million.

Amadeo and Disney spent a lot of time together. Amadeo liked to see how an animated drawing was created and would often go to the Burbank studios to spend a few hours there.

On one of those visits he also met two young technicians who were working on synchronizing the sound with the images. After the huge success of Snow White, Disney was working on a film that was supposed to revive the public's interest in their favorite character, Mickey Mouse. Disney wanted to create a new innovation by combining classical music with animated figures. The film would be called *The Sorcerer's Apprentice* and the music was written by the German Paul Dukas, who was inspired by a ballad by Goethe.

But the real innovation that impressed Amadeo was that the two technicians he had met, Bill Hewlett and David Packard, were trying out a new sound system for the film. They called it an "audio oscillator" and it was an absolute novelty. Disney's new film would be the first animated film to feature stereophonic sound using this new technology.

Hewlett and Packard were two recent graduates who were full of ideas and working in Packard's garage in Palo Alto. Talking to them was electrifying.

A few years later, those two guys discovered that the system they developed and patented could also be used to connect new computers with electronic instruments. They were the first and only ones who could use that technology. Amadeo financed them from the early days, perhaps just because they worked together at Disney, or perhaps because he saw them as a source of ideas that would surely bring results.

HP, which had become an important company at this point, moved from Packard's garage to a more suitable area a little further away. In just a few years in that new warehouse in Palo Alto, they made the new computers and printers that turned HP into one of the giants of the nascent Silicon Valley.

14
San Francisco
1940

Amadeo, now free from the pressing commitments of the usual management of the Bank, devoted himself to its promotion and further expansion. He was never satisfied and would step in when the opportunity presented itself. He worked across the board not only for his Bank, but also for institutional businesses that promoted the industry. He financed hundreds of small companies to convert their production into new war products. This was the case for Technical Oil Tool Co., a company that produced tools for the oil industry. By using one of their inventions, they converted one of their factories to produce directional systems for bombs. The Grayson Heat Control Co. went from radiators to hydraulic controls for airplane wing flaps. Cole of California moved from producing swimwear to parachutes. A large part of these companies set up an industrial organization, greatly increasing both the volume of sales and the workforce.

Giannini was always at the forefront. He even financed Walt Disney for a series of educational and propaganda films. He never backed down when it came to large businesses like shipyards or weapons factories and contributed to large infrastructure projects as a co-financier with the federal government.

Some time ago he met Henry J. Kaiser, for whom he had financed an asphalt paving company in California. A son of German emigrants, Kaiser started as a laborer and now owned a road construction company. Like Amadeo, he was a dreamer who looked to the future with clarity and optimism. They were very similar and became very close friends. Amadeo helped him with more and more financing. He followed him as he created new businesses, from cement factories to large infrastructure up to the construction of the largest dam at the time, the Hoover Dam on the Colorado River. When Roosevelt became president, Amadeo still spent a great deal of time getting his friend Kaiser major financing for the major infrastructure projects that the president had in mind.

Kaiser and Giannini tried to see each other often. They were both fascinated by each other's ideas and, more often than not, they didn't need to ask for the other's opinion. They also had common tastes in food and wines. In fact, the two friends' favorite place was Sebastiani's winery. Amadeo introduced it to Kaiser and he fell in love with it. In that winery, they could discuss and drink well without their wives. The host's discreet presence mitigated the long business discussions or the rambling about wines.

Unfortunately, they had to move their meetings to Amadeo's house in San Mateo for some time because Cloe was beginning to feel the weight of her years and her heart was giving her problems.

- If you hadn't been a banker, you could have done any other profession and been just as successful.

Kaiser was fascinated by Amadeo and never stopped reminding him of it.

- I've been lucky. I took certain paths that turned out to be successful. But it was by chance.

- You never acknowledge your qualities. Every time I think about it, I'm amazed at how you figured out that the industry would only expand as small businesses grew. Large industries grow because small businesses grow.

- It didn't take much to figure out that if a shipyard builds a whole ship, they can't make more than that. But if they have others build the pieces and then assemble it, they can make five at once.

- Sure, but it took a banker to teach the industrialists how to work.

- The system is so simple that anyone could build a ship.

- Don't tempt me. You know I like to bet.

- Well, I'm betting for and not against.

- In that case, if it's the two of us together, we'll definitely win.

Henry J. Kaiser's life changed from that moment on. By now he was one of the country's leading builders, with commissions worth millions in the United States and other parts of the world. In years past, he built numerous dams, roads, highways, buildings, and bridges even in the Pacific Islands.

But from that point on he left everything to his collaborators and, with Amadeo's support and encouragement, built a ship-yard in San Francisco Bay. At Amadeo's suggestion, Admiral Emery S. Land, head of the United States Maritime Commission, commissioned 24 medium-sized ships for troop transport. The project was copied from a ten-thousand-ton English steamship and the 24 copies were built in record time. Later on, with the same efficiency, 2,500 new ships were built in just one year, and the troops and goods that they brought to Europe played an essential role in the successful end of the war.

At the end of the conflict, those ships were converted and adapted for cargo transport, taking the auspicious name of Liberty. They made the fortune of some European shipowners, the best known of whom was the Greek man Aristotle Onassis.

15

San Mateo
1941

The wartime economy had shaken up all the rules of how things were normally managed. The population of California had tripled, in some cities even quintupled, causing problems in daily life that seemed insurmountable. The new inhabitants didn't know where to stay; the housing projects were full, so they slept ten in a room or in garages or in tents or even under trees in parks. Everything became difficult, even food supply, waste management, and travel. Yet population growth seemed unstoppable, industries were working at breakneck speed, businesses were building, and commerce was flourishing. California had become a gold mine.

The banks, but especially Bank of America, were financing the construction of new housing as they had never done before. There were more than a million in the five years around 1940, but it was never enough.

One day, Mario came home quite worried.

-     For many months, I would say at least a year, we have had a problem that I can't seem to solve. Every Friday morning, administrative employees from companies that have to pay salaries come to the Bank to get the cash they need. This happens in all branches, without exception. In addition to the problem of finding cash that already takes up all of Thursday, the problem is that the branches become unmanageable on Friday mornings. We organized armored trucks escorted by the police to transport the cash, but we're talking about tons of coins and a huge risk of robbery. We've already had some. I've tried to apply to open new branches but, as you know, the Treasury does not want to grant them to us. They don't even understand what the problem is.

Amadeo listened and became curious. Frankly, the problem of cash had never occurred to him. - And what do you plan to do?

-     It would be enough to solve the payroll distribution for the military camps. There are more than 150,000 soldiers in California who add to the civilian population. If we could organize payroll within the camps, we'll have already solved much of the problem.

-     Even within the camps, it is the Treasury Department that authorizes the opening of a branch. That I remember well. However, if I'm not mistaken, the Banking Act of '35 provides for the opening of seasonal branches in tourist areas or areas of particularly unstable inflow. These openings are not subject to the Department's authorization, but only to the notifying to the offices in charge. Open as many branches as you can in all camps where you are required to be present. Then if the Department protests, we will defend ourselves. It will be interesting to see the Treasury confronting the military.

Over the next year Mario opened more than 50 temporary branches, even including two in the two Japanese internment camps. All these branches became very important and at the end of the conflict, the temporary seasonal branches were authorized to become permanent.

16

Age and the disorderly life Cloe lived following Amadeo had consumed her. The pains of the death of three newborn children and, much more recently, the heartbreaking death of Virgil had taken away her will to live. Virgil was the youngest son, the most enthusiastic, the most cheerful, and he filled her days with his jokes and funny stories. A commonplace domestic accident had killed him in a few days. From that moment on, she had lost the will to live. At home she gladly received her children and grandchildren, who often came to visit her. Mario came mainly for business matters with his father, but very often on weekends he came by with his wife Mercedes and their two children. Claire also came almost daily, and although she had been married for a long time, she had no children. But life in the house was no longer cheerful. The memory of Virgil loomed sadly and weighed on Cloe's health as well. The children playing in the garden no longer brought her joy; rather, sometimes they were too annoying and she asked Mercedes to make them stop.

At almost seventy years of age, Cloe was now an old, slightly heavy woman with sad eyes. She had been at her husband's side on all occasions. Amadeo never forgot to ask for her opinion, even on technically complex decisions. She lived through her husband's illness with authoritarian methods, imposing rules that did not defeat the illness but made it more bearable. And she had done the same with Mario, imposing a strict regime upon him that, with the help of his wife Mercedes, had saved his life.

But all these worries had consumed her. She was paying personally for the good she had done for her family and the charities to which she had steadfastly devoted herself. Now all that was over. No more travel, no more family celebrations, no more happiness and hope for the future. She felt her life was running out like the sand in an hourglass.

- I would like to be remembered as the wife of Amadeo and the mother of my children, not as the wife of the banker. I would also like to have a lot of flowers at my funeral - she said one day to her husband and son who were tending to her in bed. Amadeo was shocked. He didn't know where to hide. He didn't want to be seen crying, but he couldn't stop the tears either.

The doctor came and, after examining her, he wanted to speak with Amadeo and Mario.

- She is very tired. Her heart is irregular and her blood pressure is high. I must confess that I am not optimistic. The medicine I prescribed will do little good, unfortunately. Keep her resting and without too much excitement, if possible. I don't know what else to tell you. I'll be back tomorrow.

The winter rains gave no respite. The atmosphere was gloomy and it was also cold. The father and son sat outside in the shelter of the porch, unbothered by the temperature.

- What will we do?

Mario looked at his father. He saw an old man hunched over, wrinkles furrowing his face. His swollen, red eyes required no explanation.

Amadeo took a deep breath and, in a broken voice: - Nothing. We wait.

He could say no more. That hard and grumpy man, strong and generous, accustomed to battle, never giving up on any occasion, seemed defeated. Tears flowed silently down his face as he freed himself from the increasingly oppressive sadness that had accumulated each day since he received the phone call about Virgil's accident three years earlier. He hadn't cried then. But, with great effort, he had supported his Cloe by trying to give her strength. He hadn't succeeded. His son had

died and now his Cloe was dying too, perhaps also because
of that grief. What had he built in his life? Nothing. What he
cared about most was dying. He looked at Mario: - Nothing,
we can't do anything, only stay with her.

A few days before Christmas, while the whole town was
celebrating, Cloe had a heart attack and died.

17

Stunned, Amadeo stood in front of the bed. It was no longer the two of them. There was only Cloe, done up and well-
groomed, and he looked in disbelief at that skin color she had
never had. She was still, and did not smile at him. Her eyes
were closed forever. She couldn't be his Cloe. His Cloe had
never been like this. A sting of pain gripped his heart and
prevented him from breathing.

The people who were around him and saw him so stunned
did not even dare to approach. He didn't see them, he only
had eyes for her.

He left the room only when Mario and Claire came to get
him and brought him out with difficulty. The attendants were
coming to put the body in the coffin. The sight might have
been too much even for him.

The funeral was monumental. Hundreds of people followed
the body from the house to St. Matthew's Church, which was
a short distance away. Hundreds more waited in front of the
church. Hidden in the crowd were many of the Hollywood
actors who had known her. Volunteers from the charity that
Cloe was president of carried the coffin on their shoulders.
There were five trucks of flowers from all over the United
States. Those flowers she loved so much were placed along
the avenue and on the stairs leading to the church. The bells
tolled for the dead. Amadeo was surrounded by his children

Mario and Claire with their families, and the entire city of San Mateo was motionless. They were partaking in the mourning that was not only of the family but of everyone.

The coffin was placed in front of the altar and Amadeo followed it to the back of the church. He stopped in front and stood still with his legs apart and arms folded, almost in an act of defiance, and did not move until the blessing. Everyone present could see that tall, massive man who was loved by the people and feared by the bankers. Now he was hunched over, with his shoulders down and his gaze fixed.

At the end of the blessing, they heard him murmur: - Sweet Cloe, you were the best deal of my life. Thank you.

He kissed his fingers and placed his hand on the coffin.

It was Christmas Eve, 1941.

PART XV

1
San Mateo
1941

Although Cloe's health had been precarious for some time, Amadeo was shocked by her death. He stayed locked in his house and was not seen by anyone for several weeks. Only his surviving children, Mario and Claire, visited him to try to give him comfort. But Amadeo had become harsh and impenetrable and his temperament was terrible. It wasn't easy for anyone to be around him. Mario tried to distract him with the excuse of work, but there were more times he was called incompetent than there were times he received praise. His illness had also flared up again, perhaps due to the stress of the last few months. But now Cloe was no longer there to force him to take his medication. The children tried their best. Mario had poor results, Claire's were a little better. But it was always a battle.

In the midst of an economic boom at that time, California was faced with a new problem related to the war effort. Full employment and the call to arms of large numbers of young men had reduced the workforce in the bank branches. Replacing absences and hiring new staff became an issue.

- Why are you asking me? You're the one who has to solve these problems.
- I know, Dad. I just wanted to run my idea by you.
- Only if it's decisive. Otherwise, don't even talk to me about it.

Mario tried to keep going. - I hope.
- You hope or you're sure?
- These days no one is sure of anything anymore. But if you don't let me talk, I can't explain anything.
- Go ahead.
- Thirty percent of our employees have been drafted.

There are no men available to work in the Bank, so I thought about reserving these positions for women. We can probably only recruit them from the women workers who are interested in raising their job level. We would have to teach all these new recruits everything they need to work in the Bank.

-    Throughout the country?

-    Sure. Everywhere. I've been thinking about creating a banking school that I'd like to name after Mom, with four or five locations scattered across the United States where they teach office practices.

-    Good, so they learn and then go work at another bank.

-    That's a risk we have to take. We can try to engage them by paying for school. If they stay with us the school is free, if they leave then they pay for it. I don't see any other solution to fill the gaps we have.

Amadeo was silent. He was thinking and also silently holding back the anger that gripped his heart.

Mario continued, more to fill the silence than to state anything meaningful. - After all, we were the first to hire women and immigrants, so this would be nothing new for our clientele. And, if I had to be really honest, I think women in banking are better than men.

Amadeo looked at his son. He liked the idea, but didn't want to give him the satisfaction of approving it without discussion. But the idea was good. The idea of naming the school after Cloe was too.

-    Go ahead. Bye.

He stood up abruptly and shakily walked to his room. He didn't want him to see his shiny eyes.

The schools created and organized by Mario were a great success. Thousands of girls joined. More than half made it to the end of the courses, and of these almost all went to work for Bank of America. After two years, more than half of the Bank's clerical workforce was made up of women.

2
San Francisco
1941

Although he no longer had to deal with the day-to-day management of the Bank in theory, Amadeo had not changed his habits. He watched everything and inspected everything. In Cloe's absence, his way of life had become monastic. The only luxury he still allowed himself was to live in his beautiful house in San Mateo, but all superfluities were eliminated.

However, his mood remained grim. He was always unhappy with management. The Bank could only pay small dividends because, in his opinion, it spent too much money on "useless nonsense." He established rather strict rules on the expenses that employees could make. Savings were a must, especially during war time when all efforts, including economic ones, had to go into the war effort. During an intense meeting with Mario, he did not mince his words:

-    You need to stop authorizing unnecessary spending. Try to focus on profitability, which involves, for those who don't know, not throwing money away. It's hard enough to defend ourselves against problems we don't know about. At least try to deal with the ones you know well about.

Mario was embarrassed. He understood that his father's outburst was not due to the Bank's mismanagement, but to the emptiness he felt inside since his mother's death.

-    What are you referring to?

-    I saw in the expense report that Al Gock charged a car rental. Thirty-five dollars - Amadeo continued. In my opinion, these things are unacceptable.

-    Dad, it's $35! Do you really think it's necessary…

-    It's a matter of principle. If you miss these things, who knows what else goes unnoticed!

Mario realized it would be useless to discuss this further.

-    What should I do?

-    Let him know that I sold my car. I travel by train and I use the bus. And if I'm doing it as his president, I don't see why he can't do it since he's only vice president.

Mario had never seen his father so furious.

-    I certainly will.

3

San Francisco
1943

The secretary entered, barely knocking.

-    Mr. Mario, come quickly... your father.
-    My father? Is he sick?
-    No, no... on the contrary... come, please.

Mario rushed into the hallway. Amadeo's office was not far away. There were some speechless employees standing in front. From the door, which was open as always, you could hear the yelling:

-    Then let them arrest me too! What have those poor people done! Are you out of your mind?

Mario entered, frightened. Claire had just arrived and was looking at him, speechless. Amadeo was on his feet, wielding a newspaper and slamming it down on the desk as if he wanted-ed to destroy everything around him.

-    Dad, calm down. What happened?
-    Don't you read the papers? Do you think a civilized nation would behave like this?

Amadeo planted himself in front of his son.

-    Look what they're doing. Do you think being Italian is a crime? There are millions of us in the United States. They want to intern us all?

Mario immediately understood what his father meant. After Pearl Harbour and the subsequent entry of the United States into the war, all Germans, Japanese, and Italians had been placed on lists of "enemy aliens" and many of them had been arrested. That day, the New York Times had published a very severe article against Italians. It was prompted by the arrest of numerous Italians, who, according to the writer, were classified as "enemies" and potentially dangerous.

Mario tried to hold him back.

- What do we know about those who were arrested? Maybe they really are criminals. Let's calm down and think.

Amadeo looked at him in a rage, undecided on whether to attack him or listen to him.

He sat at his desk in silence.

- I am appalled. How is it possible that a thousand people were law-abiding until a few months ago and now they are all criminals? This is racial persecution, just like Hitler.

- That's not true. America has entered the war against Germany, which unfortunately is also an ally of Italy. But think about the fact that in California alone, there are more than a million Italians, and not all of them have been arrested. Who knows how many of us there are across the United States, and who knows how many are fascists. We can't rule out that there are spies or thugs or even just common criminals among them.

- I have to call the President.

- Wait, let me look for more detailed information. When we have it, you can call.

Several weeks went by and Amadeo became increasingly nervous. He no longer even hid the contempt he felt for Mussolini and fascism, and could not accept that there were still Italians in America who were staunch fascists. He thought of his countrymen and what advice his mother Virginia, or Lorenzo, or his dear Cloe would give him. What would they have said? What would they have done? Time was passing and he wasn't doing anything. He couldn't wait any longer. He called Mario on the phone.

- What were you able to find out?

- Not much, to tell the truth. Diplomats, embassy envoys, and some consuls have been expelled.
- I already knew that.
- There are about five hundred thousand Italians who are considered "enemy aliens" and, of these, about half have been interned.
- Where?
- That is what's hard to know. I couldn't figure out if they are scattered in the various camps or if they are all together. Even at the War Relocation Authority they don't know.
- Where are the camps?
- Texas, Tennessee, and Montana. Maybe also in Oklahoma.
- All very far away. Never mind. Send two of our people, Italian obviously, to confirm the location. And have them go there with clothes and medicine. Have them recount what happens. We'll see if we can get them released.
- If it's alright with you, I'd like to go. I'm afraid if I send two officials they won't even let them in.
- You're right. I'll call the White House to warn them.

4

A few days later, Mario and two officials left with two trucks full of clothes, medicine, and other useful things. The first stop was Texas, where they found a large community of Italians, many with wives and children in tow. Their stories were heartbreaking. They had been taken from their homes, which were searched, turned upside down, and then sealed with wooden boards. They confiscated their cameras and even their radios, especially shortwave ones. They lost their jobs and the children could not go to school. Fortunately, the treatment in the camp was decent, so they didn't suffer from hunger or any particular disease. But the situation was still terrible.

When Mario returned from his first trip, he recounted the details to Amadeo, who was appalled.

-   Who gave these directives? - he asked.
-   It appears that the FBI made the lists and did the searches, too.
-   Hoover!
-   Yes, J. Edgar Hoover. And he puts a lot of effort into it.
-   I've never liked him. He has too much thirst for power, and he has no heart. Now where are you going?
-   To Tennessee. I leave in two days.
-   You'll find the same things.
-   I think so, too.

Mario visited all of the confinement camps and Amadeo got in touch with the section of the FBI that dealt with interned people. It was a huge job that occupied the father and son for almost six months. There were countless verbal altercations between Amadeo and Hoover and long phone calls with President Roosevelt, but in the end their intervention was crucial to the release of about half of the interned Italians.

5

San Francisco
1945

In April 1945, the days were frantic. News of the war in Italy and Europe was increasingly tragic. Italy's declaration of war on Germany had unleashed a bloody civil war with retreating Germans on one side, supported by a small minority of Italians loyal to fascism. On the other side, groups organized in armed resistance were formed by civilians and soldiers who had escaped Nazi deportation and were supported by the United States and England.

Amadeo was reading the latest news in the newspaper when one of his employees, who was quite distressed, came in.

-    Mr. Giannini, turn on the radio now. It seems that there is important news from Italy.

Claire and Mario also arrived. The radio had just interrupted the program to broadcast Sandro Pertini's proclamation, which announced a general strike and called the entire population to revolt against Nazi-Fascism.

Amadeo commented on the news right after.

-    If they don't arrest Mussolini, it will trigger a civil war even worse than the one that already exists. There are still too many fascists around Italy.

-    The population is tired. They can't take any more war, death, and destruction. They will rebel. - Mario was hopeful.

-    Groups of still well-armed Germans are resisting and will not leave without a fight. I don't think the partisans alone can stop them. - Amadeo was more pessimistic.

Three days later, the news came that Mussolini, who was on the run, had been arrested and shot. In addition, after Milan and Turin, the cities of Genoa, Bologna, and Venice had also been liberated. The radio transmitted the audio of the joyful citizens who poured into the squares and streets to celebrate as American and British vehicles packed with soldiers and partisans entered the cities.

Amadeo was happy and moved. He looked out the window and could hear singing from below. There were many Italians marching in the streets waving the Italian flag.

Amadeo called loudly to his secretary. - Linda! Take the Italian flag right now and put it in the window. How many do we have? Put up them all, and put the American flag there, too. Call the branches as well and instruct everyone to do the same. Today must be a big celebration in our Bank. Today is a great day. The war in Italy is over!

He hugged his children, then closed the office door, sat down at his desk, tried to calm himself, and finally let out his emotions.

6

The news of the past few weeks had given him plenty to worry about, but now was the time to act by doing things that even Cloe would approve of.

He called Claire and Mario. - I wanted to tell you that I have decided to go to Italy. We are needed over there.

Mario tried to stop him. - Dad, look at the state you're in. Let me go there.

- I've decided, I'm going. And I'll only take Russel Smith. You two can stay here.

Mario didn't reply. It had been impossible to have discussions with his father for some time now. He had become even more grumpy than before. Even Claire understood that the arrangement of this trip was final and made without their consideration.

Mario then discussed it with Smith, whom he himself had appointed to head the Bank's international activities.

- Your father is stubborn, I know. But he has very clear ideas, and nothing gets past him. The fall of fascism allows us to go and discuss the Bank of America and Italy's release from sequestration so that we can refinance it.

- But why does he have to go there? You or I would have been enough. It's a difficult and tiring trip, and in his condition…

- A few days ago, he told me the story of the name of the Bank. His mother suggested it to him, if I'm not mistaken.

- Yes, it was my grandmother, just before she died.

- That's why he wants to go to Italy. He wants to put things back in place. The memories nag at him. And you'll see, I'm going just to keep him company.

As expected, the trip was very strenuous. The flight on the DC4 felt never ending and the plane teetered at every gust of wind. It was noisy and cold, too. They went from New York to London, then from London to Rome. They stayed overnight in London so they could finally sleep peacefully without the roar of the engines. The next morning they sat in a restaurant waiting for the next flight. Amadeo was still sullen and had a strong argumentative streak:

-    You haven't asked me anything about this trip.

Smith was prepared for Amadeo's short temper.

-    I knew you would talk to me about it. I didn't want to force you.

-    Talking during the trip is quite tiring. I prefer to mind my own business.

-    I understand. If you want to tell me now that we're settled in…

-    Yes, indeed. I heard that some members of the U.S. government are thinking about giving aid to Europe for reconstruction.

-    I've heard that, too. Many are afraid that Russia will step in and bring a good portion of the states under its influence.

-    We have to get there first. Before the government has agreed upon, established, and allocated the funds, Russia will have already covered the whole continent with money. Let's be ready. You will see that the Italian government will have no problem with releasing our bank from sequestration. Then we'll just have to refinance it so that lines of credit can be opened to industries and agriculture. Let's also find a quick way to facilitate the export of goods to America. You take care of it, but let's make it quick.

-    I'm ready. In a week, I can send as much money as you want.

As they approached Rome, Amadeo looked out from the plane at the ruins of the war that had just ended. He was reminded of Mussolini, who, in the early days, had seemed like a great statesman to him and instead had turned out to be an exalted lunatic. He saw the devastated villages, the rubble everywhere, and the countryside scarred by bombs. That sight made his journey even sadder.

- Smith! Look down here. So much destruction! What a tragedy! "War is a lesson of history that people never quite learn." Benito Mussolini wrote that. But even he didn't learn it. What a fool, what madness!

The roar of the engines almost overpowered his words, but Smith had noticed his shiny eyes. Once again, he had no difficulty in understanding how much humanity was hidden in that tough and determined body.

7
Rome
1945

As expected, the Ministry of Post-War Reconstruction confirmed to him the prompt release of the Bank of America and Italy from sequestration. They met with the Bank's executives, most of whom were from Rome except for a couple who had moved in together from Naples a few years earlier. Amadeo wanted to know about the condition of his beloved Italy after the armistice. What he heard did not please him. A barely-hidden underlying bitterness came through from the words of his Italian collaborators. The Neapolitans were particularly silent. Amadeo knew that American and British bombers had ravaged their city in the past year, and he didn't know how to ask for news without inciting their resentment. He asked about their families, fortunately all of whom had moved to Rome before the disaster. But one of them, in Neapolitan dialect and with a broken, emotional voice, mustered the courage to say:

- They bombed the Santa Chiara monastery.

It wasn't the dead, it wasn't the destruction, the houses, the factories, the people. No, it was the Santa Chiara monastery, the most beloved symbol of Naples' antiquity that still pulsed powerfully in their hearts. A chill descended in the room. Everyone understood that, for the Neapolitans, that was the most serious affront that the Allies had committed against their city. No one spoke for a few minutes, then Amadeo got up and approached the two of them. There were no words to say—just a hug, a gesture of emotional closeness, like an apology for the atrocities committed, albeit in order to free Italy, by fellow Americans. Amadeo felt spurred to do what he was about to do.

Fortunately, after a brief inspection, they discovered that the Bank was in good condition. Amadeo and Smith, along with those executives, planned a series of essential interventions for Italy. Among other things, they decided to finance large companies. FIAT was one of the major beneficiaries, as well as other powerful businesses to facilitate the importing of raw materials from the United States to allow these companies to restart.

They worked intensely for a month. Amadeo did not spare himself; he visited the businesses and the countryside, making promises and, as always, keeping his word. A year before the Marshall Plan became operational, Bank of America had already distributed over 37 million dollars in aid, most of which went directly to the Italian population and industries.

At that same time, Secretary of State George Marshall confirmed that the United States would help the nations that had suffered most from the war. "Our intention is to fight hunger, poverty, despair, and chaos. We want to restore jobs and the economy in a free society that no longer has political and social emergencies," he declared before Congress. A year later, more than 5 billion dollars were made available for Europe, which soon became 12 billion. The plan was very generous: only a fifth of these sums had to be repaid, and the rest was considered a gift from their American friends.

Bank of America participated with a considerable sum of about 400 million dollars, which was diverted almost entirely to Italy. The director of the Marshall Plan's "Food and Agriculture" department, Harry McClelland, was also one of the vice presidents of the Bank of America. On Amadeo's instructions, he designed and financed the agricultural reconstruction from north to south. It was so successful that, a few years later, a plaque was hung up on the facade of an irrigation pumping station in the middle of the Po Delta that said: "The project to restore this valley was begun by Duke Ferdinand in 1596 and finished by McClelland in 1950."

8
San Francisco
1945

Amadeo got up from his desk. It was almost dinner time and a deep sadness had fallen upon him. He wasn't hungry but he didn't feel like being in the office anymore either. His desk was filled with new projects and follow-up reports. When he looked at those papers, the lines blurred together. He was tired, tired of this life that no longer satisfied him.

He walked down the street and slowly made his way to the streetcar stop. He passed by the florist: how many times he bought a flower for Cloe! Now he could take it to her grave, but without the joy of meeting her smile.

Out of an almost self-destructive instinct, he decided to enter the shop.

- Good evening, Agnese. Agnese? Is anyone there?

The small store, brimming with flowers, was deserted. He could hear some noise from the back, though.

- Agnese? It's Giannini.

A disheveled middle-aged lady came in, wiping her eyes with her apron.

- Good evening, Mr. Giannini. Sorry, I was in the back... Nice to see you...

- Agnese, you're crying! What happened?

- It's nothing, Mr. Giannini. I'll be fine, this time too.
- Stop it. Tell me why you're crying.

Agnes resumed sobbing. She could not speak. - It's just that... the owner of the store came... he says that... the rent... isn't enough for him anymore, that he has to raise it.

- And you're not able to pay for it?
- You see what kind of life I have here... from morning to night, every day... I can't afford any help... Since Piero died, I've slept in the store more nights than I have at home.
- So if he raises your rent, you can't pay anymore and he sends you away.
- That's what will happen, he's already told me. But without a store I'll starve. I have no one left.

Agnes had slumped down onto a bench.

- Please stop crying. I haven't been here in a long time. You make me even more sad than I already am.
- I'm sorry, you caught me at the wrong time. Sorry to greet you like this. I'm glad you came again. How can I help you?
- Remember when I used to come and get a flower for Cloe?
- How could I forget? If you only knew how much I cried when I heard.
- I miss her terribly, but maybe a flower would give me some peace of mind.
- Of course, I understand. What flower would you like?
- What would you give me?
- Depending on the season, I would give you a gardenia now. This red one is beautiful and Mrs. Cloe would love it.
- Thank you, it's beautiful. Who is the owner of the store?
- The Chinese people from the dry-cleaners.
- They have six or seven dry-cleaners. I'll see what I can do. Here.
- Excuse me, but I don't have change for fifty dollars. You only owe me fifty cents. Actually, no, I'll give you the flower in memory of Mrs. Cloe.

She returned the bill to him.

\- You didn't understand. This flower gives me great joy and I want you to take this money in memory of my Cloe. In fact, prepare me one for tomorrow and for all the days I'll be here. Give me this joy. Please.

Agnese looked at him. She had always appreciated that grumpy big man, who you could tell actually had a heart of gold. She had always loved that middle-aged couple who often came to buy flowers and have a chat. Now, however, she was looking at her savior. She didn't know what to say or how to say it. She walked over to him and hugged him. She was tiny and he was big and tall. She held him without speaking but wet his jacket with a few tears.

Amadeo turned to leave with his gardenia in hand.

\- See you tomorrow, Agnese. And don't cry anymore.

His soul felt lighter. This act, which would help a poor woman he had known for many years and who had loved Cloe, had gratified him. He felt ready for new ideas, for more challenges.

9

He ignored the streetcar stop and decided to keep walking, especially to get over his emotions. Where were the notes he wrote down and put in his pocket? He thought about giving them to Mario to discuss. But then, between one thing and another, he left them in his jacket.

It had all started when the bank handed him his bank statement and he didn't like it. A few years earlier, he told an astounded *San Francisco Examiner* reporter, "Why accumulate so much money if you're going to leave it to others after you?" He smiled at the memory, especially the reporter who had begun to stutter. But he hadn't changed his mind. He had too much money. And there were many people, like Agnes, who didn't have any money at all.

As he strolled along, he tried to clear his head but needed help. Some advice from his great friend and advisor, Marriner Eccles, would be crucial for him.

He called him very early the next morning and summoned him to his office

As they drank their coffee, prepared in the Italian style, he explained that he wanted to leave a sign of his earthly adventure—something related to the Bank but that was also a reminder of his family who fought for a more humane society with more social justice.

- I get what you're trying to do. But if you're putting up the money, mixing private money with Bank money is not an option.
- And if I create a foundation?
- If you create a foundation, the money you put in will never come back to you, and neither will the money from the Bank. Otherwise, I'd say it's fine.
- Perfect, that's what I wanted.
- What would you like this foundation to do?
- I would like to give the Bank's employees some benefits that they couldn't get anywhere else. Some sort of bonus that would put them on a better social footing. We have had in-house schools for years that allow employees to learn new things. But it is a Bank school that is useful, but limited. So I would like to give them the opportunity to let their own children study. Education is the only way to elevate their social status and the children are the future of my employees. I was thinking of some sort of substantial scholarship for all those deserving in their field. Another thing that matters to me is that my employees and their families have the ability to get treatment and have access to the best medical care. I would love to be able to provide some sort of insurance against illnesses, which often ruins a family because they spend everything they have on treatment. I would love for it to become

normal for my employees to think that they are not part of a detached institution but part of a big family that cares about its children.

    - I understand. I'm going to try to make a proposal in line with what you're saying. How much money are you talking about?

    - I would personally put in five hundred thousand dollars, and I would have the Bank put in just as much.

    - That seems like a lot of money to give to charity.

    - It's not charity, it's an investment in the social growth of my employees. An investment, not free giveaways. My kids have everything they want. This money is leftover, so I might as well make it available to those in need.

    Thus the "Bank of America-Giannini Foundation" was born. Its purpose was to help Bank employees' families with medical care and education of their children. A substantial portion of the funds were also allocated to medical research.

10
San Mateo
1949

Amadeo opened his eyes. It was dark and late at night. Only a vague glow came from the garden. The house was completely silent. A sudden dull pain had woken him up. It was like a dagger stuck in his heart, causing a growing twinge that squeezed his chest and took his breath away. He was sweating. He tried to call for help, but his voice wouldn't come out. He didn't even have the strength to get up.

    There was a sudden flash in his eyes and another sharp pain in his chest shocked him. He clung to the sheets, but quickly calmed down. The pain was now passing.

    It came clearer. The glimmer became a bright light.

    His father, Luigi, came out of the light on a cart. He was getting closer.

He called him: - Dad!

He smiled at him. He saw that his face was filled with blood.

- Dad, what's wrong?

His mother, Virginia, was behind him, looking so young and beautiful.

- Mom! Mom! - he called. Virginia smiled and did not notice Luigi's blood.

- Mom! Mom! Look at Dad - he said to her, worried.

Cloe was coming now, too. She was holding Mario, their first son.

- Look at him Amadeo. Look how beautiful he is. What do you want us to name him? - she asked him.

- Cloe! Watch out! - he shouted at her. There was rubble and smoke from the fires all around. But Cloe walked towards him without fear. Amadeo looked at her with love. He reached out and embraced her.

11

When the doctor arrived, the whole family was already there. Mario and Claire were called by the faithful maid Carmen who had gone to wake him up. For two weeks, they followed him from one hospital and another. He seemed to be doing better for a few days, so they had not expected this sudden end.

The doctor could do nothing else but verify Amadeo's death.

- A sudden heart attack. He died almost without noticing it, you see? He clung to the sheets, but they were barely crumpled. It was a matter of seconds. He died peacefully, it looks like he was smiling.

Amadeo was lying in bed. His face had now lost its color, but that shadow of a smile remained on his face.

It was June 3, 1949.

12

An annoying drizzle dripped from a gray, damp tarp onto the many thousands of people attending the funeral. Many remarked that this made it seem like the entire city of San Francisco was crying over the death of its oldest, most beloved son. Many friends were among that grieving crowd, but many more were those who had received some good from Giannini without knowing him. Some had only seen him from a distance, or had only heard of him. But Giannini had come into their daily lives to bring prosperity. Thousands came to thank him, grieving, in silence, in the rain. He was convinced that he had built a Bank, but instead he had created a legend whose fame would surpass even that of his own self.

At St. Mary's Cathedral, Archbishop John J. Mitty delivered an unforgettable funeral oration that moved everyone. He concluded with these words:

-   We now mourn our son Amadeo, a pride of this city and of the entire nation. I want to remember his words, the last ones he addressed to his managers during his farewell as president of the Bank: "... and if I ever hear that any of you try do business with big men while forgetting about the humble people, if I ever hear that, know that I will come back here and slap you with these hands of mine" This was our great son, Amadeo!

First one, then five, then a hundred, then a thousand, then all the thousands in the crowd applauded. It had never happened before and many were surprised, but that was the last tribute, spontaneous and full of gratitude, of the city.

Afterword

Amadeo Peter Giannini left behind a Bank with 517 branches around the world and over $6 billion in assets upon his death. Bank of America was the largest bank in the world. Giannini's personal liquid assets at his death were just under $590,000 and, according to his wishes, the sum was donated in its entirety to the University of California.

Upon his death, his daughter Claire took his place on the Bank's board of directors. She later had a remarkable professional career and became the only honorary member of the American Bankers Association and the American Institute of Banking. In 1977, President Nixon asked her to become Governor of the Federal Reserve, but since she was asked to leave her duties at Bank of America in return, she refused.

Claire Hoffman Giannini annually spent vacations in Italy, staying in Tuscany and Liguria, for as long as she was able to travel.

In 1985, she resigned as an honorary member of Bank of America's board of directors in protest of the betrayal of the ethical and moral values under which her father had created the Bank.

Chronology

Modern California was born in January 1850, and the population grew from 1,000 to 20,000 in the ten years following the gold rush.

After the Unification of Italy in 1861, the first mass emigration of Italians began. Before the end of the century, more than 9 million people left northern Italy for other European countries and the United States.

1869: The First Transcontinental Railroad is opened.

1869: Luigi Giannini and Virginia De Martini got married. A few days later, they departed for New York.

1870: Amadeo Peter Giannini was born on May 6 in San José, California.

1877: His father Luigi was murdered by a farmhand.

1878: His mother Virginia married her second husband, Lorenzo Scatena.

1882: The Scatena/Giannini family moved to San Francisco.

1884/1902: Amadeo Giannini worked with his stepfather at Lorenzo Scatena & Co. Amadeo's business acumen helped the company to grow from $10,000 to $100,000 in revenue in just 3 years.

1892: Amadeo Giannini married Clorinda Flores Cuneo.

1893: John Fugazi founded the Columbus Savings & Loan bank in North Beach. Joseph Cuneo, Clorinda's father, joined as an important shareholder.

In 1900, the population of California was about 1.5 million.

1902: Joseph Cuneo, who became the largest shareholder in Columbus Savings & Loan, dies.

1902: Amadeo is appointed manager of Columbus Savings & Loan. He resigned 2 years later.

1904: Giannini founded the Bank of Italy on October 17.

1906: On April 18, the earthquake destroyed San Francisco, the largest city on the West Coast.

1906: Six days after the earthquake, Giannini reinstated the Bank of Italy's operations on the dock of San Francisco's harbor.

1909: Giannini financed the opening of San Francisco's first movie theater.

1909: The Bank of Italy opens its first branch in San José.

1909: Oil was discovered in California.

1912: Amadeo and Cloe returned to Favale di Malvaro on vacation.

1913: The Bank of Italy opened a branch in Los Angeles.

1913: The Lincoln Highway opened, connecting New York and San Francisco.

1915, 1918: World War I broke out in Europe.

1918: The Bank of Italy was California's largest bank by number of branches and had $100 million in financial resources.

1919: In July, the Bank of Italy becomes a member of the Federal Reserve.

1919: Giannini founded the Bancitaly Corporation, a financial company for the purchase and sale of bank shares and holdings.

1919: Bancitaly opened Banca dell'Italia Meridionale in Italy (the Bank of Southern Italy), which later became Banca d'America e d'Italia (Bank of America and Italy).

1919: Giannini acquires the East River National Bank in New York.

In 1919, the government passed the Volstead Act, more commonly known as Prohibition.

1920: Lawrence Mario Giannini began working at the Bank of Italy.

1920: Amadeo's mother, Virginia, died.

1920: Giannini financed Charlie Chaplin's "The Kid."

1924: A.P. Giannini resigned as president of the Bank of Italy but remained a member of the Executive Committee.

1927: The U.S. Senate passed the McFadden Act that allowed for branch expansion.

1927: Giannini brought all 276 branches and banks in 199 locations under the Bank of Italy National Trust & Saving Association.

1927: The Bank of Italy was authorized to issue legal tender bills throughout the United States.

1928: Giannini allocated $1.5 million in dividends owed to him to the University of California.

1928: Giannini met Walt Disney and financed the film "Snow White and the Seven Dwarfs."

1928: He founded the Transamerica Corporation, which conferred the shares of all the banks.

1928: Giannini went back to Italy and met Mussolini.

1929: Wall Street crashed.

1930: Lorenzo Scatena, Amadeo's stepfather, died.

1930: The Bank of Italy and the Bank of America California merged into the Bank of America National Trust & Saving Association.

1932: In a memorable shareholder meeting, Giannini led the Associated Transamerica Stockholders in defeating their adversary Elisha Walker, who represented the bankers of the East.

1932: Giannini financed the construction of the Golden Gate Bridge.

1932: The U.S. Senate passed the Emergency Banking Act that gave the president total power over the banks.

1935: The U.S. Senate passed the Banking Act, which transferred the power to appoint the President and Secretary of the Treasury from the district banks to the Federal Reserve Board.

1936: His son Lawrence Mario succeeds his father as president of Bank of America.

1937: Walt Disney's animated film "Snow White and the Seven Dwarfs" was released.

1939: Novels about the Great Depression in the United States with strong criticism of Bank of America were published, including "The Grapes of Wrath", John Steinbeck's masterpiece, and "Factories in the Field" by Carey McWilliams.

1939: The movies "Gone with the Wind" and William Wyler's "Wuthering Heights" were released.

1939: World War II broke out.

1941: Amadeo's wife, Cloe, died.

1943: Giannini instructs his son to protect Italian emigrants locked up in internment camps.

1944: Amadeo's brother Attilio dies.

1945: In May, Giannini resigned as Honorary Chairman and announced that Bank of America National Trust & Saving Association had become the largest bank in the world.

1945: Bank of America provided financing for the Marshall Plan.

1949: Amadeo Peter Giannini died on June 3. It is estimated that his personal fortune amounted to $489,278.

My Sincere Gratitude

My first thought goes to the wonderful Giuliano Montaldo who, after "forcing" me to write a book on Giannini, helped me tremendously in the making of this novel. He gave me suggestions on many topics, but mainly on Hollywood history. My teacher was one that any writer would want to have, even one who is not a beginner like yours truly. I hope I have learned enough and transferred it to this work of mine.

My second thought goes to my wife, Angela, for her knowledgeable reading and corrections, even when I disagreed.

For the English version of my book, I would like to express my gratitude to Francesca Casazza and The Italian Cultural Society of Washington D.C. who promoted the presentation in the USA and contributed to sponsoring the translation.

I am also grateful to Donatella Melucci, professor in the Department of Italian at Georgetown University, Washington D.C., and her precious former students, Martina Benedetti Marshall and Danielle Guida, who provided an excellent translation.

Milton Keynes UK
Ingram Content Group UK Ltd.
UKHW031336180324
439705UK00011B/1333